This proposal is anything
but modest...

In his sights . . .

"I'm not hungry," he interrupted her. He came around the desk, his empty glass in his hand.

"Whisky is best sipped on a *full* stomach," Aileen advised, her words fading away as she realized he was moving toward *her*.

He had loosened the knot of his neck cloth. She realized she had never seen him looking anything but impeccable. She understood the desire to always be perfect. When she'd been going through the humiliation of her divorce, she'd always taken extra time with her appearance, not wanting anyone to find a flaw about her if it had been within her control. He had to feel that way as well. Perhaps he, too, knew that people whisper, that they judge, that some condemn.

And no matter how well he dressed, he'd never be accepted. Not completely.

Oh, yes, she knew he understood that as well.

He stopped with not even a foot of space between them.

He was tall, foreboding . . . mesmerizing.

"Kiss me," he ordered.

By Cathy Maxwell

The Brides of Wishmore

THE BRIDE SAYS NO

The Chattan Curse

THE DEVIL'S HEART
THE SCOTTISH WITCH
LYON'S BRIDE

THE SEDUCTION OF SCANDAL
HIS CHRISTMAS PLEASURE • THE MARRIAGE RING
THE EARL CLAIMS HIS WIFE
A SEDUCTION AT CHRISTMAS
IN THE HIGHLANDER'S BED • BEDDING THE HEIRESS
IN THE BED OF A DUKE • THE PRICE OF INDISCRETION
TEMPTATION OF A PROPER GOVERNESS
THE SEDUCTION OF AN ENGLISH LADY
ADVENTURES OF A SCOTTISH HEIRESS
THE LADY IS TEMPTED • THE WEDDING WAGER
THE MARRIAGE CONTRACT
A SCANDALOUS MARRIAGE • MARRIED IN HASTE
BECAUSE OF YOU • WHEN DREAMS COME TRUE
FALLING IN LOVE AGAIN • YOU AND NO OTHER
TREASURED VOWS • ALL THINGS BEAUTIFUL

Coming Soon

THE BRIDE SAYS MAYBE

CATHY MAXWELL

The Bride Says No

THE BRIDES OF WISHMORE

AVON

An Imprint of HarperCollinsPublishers

AVON BOOKS
An Imprint of HarperCollins*Publishers*
10 East 53rd Street
New York, New York 10022-5299

Copyright © 2014 by Catherine Maxwell, Inc.
ISBN 978-0-06-221925-1
www.avonromance.com

First Avon Books mass market printing: February 2014

Avon Trademark Reg. U.S. Pat. Off. and in Other Countries, Marca Registrada, Hecho en U.S.A.
HarperCollins® is a registered trademark of HarperCollins Publishers.

Printed in the U.S.A.

10 9 8 7 6 5 4 3 2 1

For my friend Deborah Barnhart
What a joy it is to be in the company of writers.

The
Bride Says No

Prologue

Annefield
The Tay Valley
Scotland
February 8, 1807

Why are you leaving me?"

Startled by both the question and the pain in her sister's voice, Lady Aileen Davidson turned from her bedroom mirror, where she'd been striving to set her velvet-lined bonnet at just the right, jaunty angle.

Her twelve-year-old sister, Tara, stood inside the door, her shoulders tense, her arms crossed tightly against her chest as if she needed to hold herself together. Her nose was red and her expression pinched, a sign that she had been crying.

Those words, that question had been torn from her.

Aileen already wore her coat and gloves. She was ready to go, to make the most of this opportunity to finally launch herself into the world.

Beyond the bedroom door came the sound of footsteps running down the hall. Echoes of the butler's irritation that his orders weren't being following quickly enough drifted up the staircase while Mrs. Watson, the housekeeper, expressed concerns that Aileen's trunk wasn't lashed tightly enough to the roof of the waiting coach.

But in this moment, in this space, came silence.

For the first time since their father had reappeared into their lives unannounced and declared that the time had come for his oldest daughter to be presented to society, Aileen considered what her leaving would mean to Tara . . . and her heart divided with the desire, the *need*, to seek the world beyond Annefield and her love for this half sister whom she had nurtured and cherished since the day Tara was born.

There was seven years difference in age between them. Tara was a wee thing with thin arms and legs and a mop of impossibly thick red-gold hair that could never be tamed. Her almond-shaped blue eyes seemed to take up her whole face and offered a hint of the blossoming beauty she would someday become.

In contrast, and in homage to their different mothers, Aileen's hair was the color of the darkest honey and her eyes light gray. Her looks were pleasant but unremarkable when compared to Tara's vivid coloring.

What was important was what they did share: Davidson pride and a strong sense of independence. Aileen understood all too well what asking such a question cost Tara.

"I am not leaving forever," Aileen said quietly.

"*Yes, you are*," Tara returned, the words tumbling out of her. "Mrs. Watson says you will take in no time. An Englishman will snap you up and I'll never see you again—just like we never see Father. You will live with *them*"—her emphasis on the word an indication she meant the English as a whole—"in London. You'll forget me."

"Little bug, I could never forget you," Aileen protested, coming over to the door. She put her arms around her sister. "I *won't* forget you."

Tara resisted Aileen's promise, keeping her arms crossed. "But things will change," she whispered into Aileen's shoulder.

Aileen would not deny the truth of Tara's prediction, or her own anticipation in the future. "Yes, things will change, but they must. It is the way of the world."

"*No*," Tara protested, pushing away. "It doesn't have to be."

Conscious that they stood in the doorway where anyone could hear them, Aileen pulled her sister into the room and closed the door. Facing Tara, she admitted, "I want to leave."

"*Why?*"

"Because I want to marry."

Tara made the dismissive sound of an annoyed child. "Why is it so important to marry?"

"Because it is what we do," Aileen answered. "What we were born to do. Marriage is our duty and what we owe to our ancestors and our family name."

"I do not believe that sounds pleasant at all," Tara stated baldly.

Her frankness startled a laugh out of Aileen.

Tara frowned. "I am not being amusing. Father has been married several times and he does not seem happy. Nor does he want to marry again. He told me so."

"When was that?" Aileen asked in surprise. Tara and the earl kept a bit of distance between them. Aileen understood why. Their father was not the doting sort. Aileen remembered a parent's love. Her mother had died of smallpox when Aileen had been old enough to have a memory of her. But Tara's mother had died in childbirth, so Aileen's care and concern was all she knew. The earl had walked out of his wee babe's life the day after the funeral, only to visit sporadically over the years.

"The last time he came home," Tara said. "When he brought the horses."

That had been over two years ago. The earl had won some money and, feeling flush, had invested in turning Annefield's run-down stables into a breeding farm. His gambler's instinct, which had failed him numerous times, had thought it a gentleman's way of bringing in money, and perhaps it would someday.

Aileen had been hopeful that the endeavor would encourage him to stay home, but London's lure was strong. The earl preferred English society to Scottish country life, a source of some bitterness amongst his neighbors and in his family.

"You know Father does as he pleases," she murmured to Tara.

"I do. What makes you believe he will pay any more attention to you in London than he does here?" Tara said, proving once again that, in spite of her age, she had a keen ability to see to the heart of matters.

"He will ignore me unless it suits his purpose," Aileen answered. "Fortunately, Aunt Lucille will be my sponsor."

Tara pulled a face. "I can't abide her."

"She does smell of camphor, but she knows the right people." Lucille, the dowager duchess of Benningham, was Aileen's mother's aunt. She did not approve of the Scottish or her niece's marriage to the profligate earl of Tay. However, she had informed the earl that the least she owed her niece's memory was to see to the proper presentation of her one and only child. The dowager was a haughty, rigid woman who refused to acknowledge Tara existed. Aileen had protected Tara from the slights in letters and gifts as best she could. However, the one time Lucille and her sister had met, the dowager had been so rude that Tara had never forgotten.

"I can't imagine her with any friends," Tara muttered. "And she would never open her door to *me*."

"You won't ever have to worry about her," Aileen replied. "When your time comes to be presented, my husband and I will see you are presented, and *I* shall be your sponsor." *My husband.* The words filled Aileen with anticipation.

"I don't want to be presented. I don't want to leave Annefield."

"Someday you will," Aileen predicted gently. "The day will come when you begin to wonder if there isn't something more than what you have in the valley."

More. The word haunted Aileen, contributing to a restless energy that had dogged her days, and nights, for the past several months.

"Can't you marry someone here? Someone like the Reverend Kinnion?"

"He is a very nice gentleman," Aileen hedged.

"And he admires you. He is always disappointed when he calls and I must tell him you are indisposed. You never spend time with him, and he adores you, Leenie," Tara said, using the pet name she'd developed in her earliest childhood, when saying "Aileen" had been too difficult. "Everyone remarks upon it. He stares at you during his sermons as if speaking only to you." Tara aped Reverend Kinnion's most earnest proselytizing manner, widening her eyes and fixing them on Aileen with intensity.

Aileen laughed because the mimicry was so accurate. "And life would be easier if I returned his admiration," she admitted, "but that is not the case." She reached over and tucked a stray lock of hair behind Tara's ear, suddenly overwhelmed with her love and affection for this sister. "Furthermore, if something happens to the earl, we shall need a home. Reverend Kinnion does not earn the sort of living necessary to care for two earl's daughters. I can only find a man with the means to support us in London."

"Uncle Richard will not turn us out," Tara said with a shrug, referring to the uncle who was their father's heir, "although I shall have to tolerate cousin Sabrina's constant disapproval. I might prefer living in the woods."

"It will not come to that. Not if all goes according to what I pray will happen."

"Which is?"

For a second, Aileen hesitated. She'd not spoken aloud of her hopes, of her dream. But this was her sister, the one person who would understand. She lowered her voice and confided, "I want to marry for love."

"Love?" Tara repeated the word as if it had been foreign to her thinking . . . and perhaps it was. Love, *marital love*, was not a quality either of them had witnessed in their lives. The earl married for money. He'd married each of their mothers for that reason.

No wonder marriage didn't sound attractive to Tara.

"Yes, love . . . like what Cleopatra felt for Antony," Aileen confirmed, referring to Shakespeare's play. To entertain themselves, especially in winter, the sisters had often read Shakespeare's works aloud and had even tried some of their own theatrics with Ingold, Mrs. Watson, and the other servants as an audience. "A *consuming* love. A *desire* above all others."

"Cleopatra does not come to a good end," Tara pointed out. She should know. She was the one who'd enjoyed acting out Cleopatra's death by asp bite.

"I shall fare better," Aileen promised.

"Nor did Juliet."

"I will avoid warring families."

"And I know you believe Katharina was happy with Petruchio, but I can't agree," Tara continued. "He was so overbearing. I would prefer Reverend Kinnion to him."

This was a long-standing argument between them, tied in with Tara's championing the humble minister. Aileen made an impatient sound. "I believe Kate *found* happiness. The text does not say she was unhappy. Indeed, we are to believe her content."

Tara cocked her head as if seeing Aileen's situation in a new light. "Would you want to be merely content?"

"You can be such a challenge. I didn't say I wanted to be 'merely content.' I said I want to fall in *love*, embracing the full meaning of that word."

"And what sort of man will you love?"

"I don't know yet," Aileen said happily. "That is the adventure of it. I know he won't be like Father. I don't want a gambler or someone selfish."

Tara nodded her head in agreement.

"But I know he will love me as completely and passionately as I love him."

"Will he be handsome?" Tara would put forth such a question. The shiniest bauble always caught her eye.

"Handsome to me. He will also be noble and brave, and very well respected." Aileen had thought long and hard about this man of her dreams. She knew what she wanted.

"How will you be able to tell amongst the men you meet if you have found the right one or not?"

"Oh, I'll recognize him," Aileen answered. "A

voice in my head will say, *He's the one*, and he shall be."

"The *one*," Tara repeated, as if beginning to understand.

"And then I'll bring my husband to Annefield and we shall take care of you," Aileen continued with a touch of pride. "There is so much to life we are missing, Tara. But now the door is opening. For both of us."

"But I shall miss you," Tara said, the sadness returning.

"You needn't fear not seeing me. I'll return soon. You will see. All will be well. We are sisters. Our bond is forged in blood."

Before Tara could reply, a footstep sounded at the door, followed by a hurried knock. "Lady Aileen," Mrs. Watson said through the door, "Lord Tay says if I don't bring you down immediately, he shall leave without you."

"I will be right there," Aileen said. She looked to Tara. "I will return. Soon," she promised.

Tara nodded. Tears were welling in her eyes again, but the fear was gone. "Go, Leenie. I'll think about you every day. I know you will find love."

"And someday you will as well," Aileen said.

Tara shook her head, but Aileen wasn't going to

let her dodge her future. "It may seem overwhelming now, but one day, you will want to do what I'm doing. Even if it means leaving people you care about." She hugged her sister close. "Please look after Folly for me."

"I'll ride that silly mare every day."

"Thank you. And, Tara, we shall see each other soon." With those words, Aileen gave her a squeeze, then released her hold and rushed from the room. She knew too well the earl didn't make idle threats. He would leave without her.

Moments later, with the crack of a driver's whip and the turn of the coach's wheels, Aileen was on her way. Tara stood on Annefield's step, waving as hard as she could. The tears were gone.

Aileen would sometimes remember this moment of departure as the happiest of her life. She'd been full of anticipation. Her intentions were good, her expectations great.

Only later would she realize how naive she'd been that day. How simple.

She had thought all would be wonderful.

Instead, she lost it all.

Chapter One

Annefield
August 26, 1816

I once believed time was linear, that one event followed another. One action; one consequence. However, now, I sometimes, no, almost always have the sense that everything, all that I know, believe and experience happens in a great swoop of chaotic activity like the tumbling of dice in a cup.

For example, I am here at Annefield, but all too often, my thoughts return to London, to moments best forgotten and, hopefully, forgiven, if it is at all possible.

I can literally see myself sitting in this chair at my desk in the library, marking my journal, but I also sense myself stepping out of the coach for the first time onto

Mayfair's hallowed streets or attending the Countess of Churnley's ball and being introduced to Geoffrey Hamilton. Dancing with him and feeling my father's greedy eyes upon us. Ah, yes, it is the past because I realize the portent of such moments now.

When they happened, I was blessedly oblivious.

I experience other occasions as well. They come to me in dreams, in my imaginings, in any unguarded thoughts. I see my mistakes and am powerless to call them back, and yet the question of why I should destroy myself remains. I cannot explain my own actions, because I do not fully understand them.

No, that is a lie. I know too well why I made the decisions I have. I've faced my demons. I let them believe I betrayed my vows because I needed to survive. Peter saved my life, for his attention to me spurred Geoff to divorce.

Such maudlin thoughts! Encouraged, no doubt, by the knowledge that Tara marries in three days' time. I shall not be there. My appearance at the wedding breakfast would be decidedly uncomfortable. A divorced woman is not included in polite society, not to say that any society in London is polite.

In truth, it is not terrible to live beyond their approval. I am content in a fashion. I accept.

I wish Tara well. I hope she is happy. I worry as a sister who knows too well the danger of expectations.

*And I pray that at some time in my life, I shall find
peace in all that has happened and that I can stop dodg-
ing the shadows of my past. Or, at the least, time returns to its proper form when there is the here and now
and nothing matters beyond this very moment.*

Aileen jabbed the pen back into its place on the
inkstand and stared at the words she'd written.

She sounded like a lunatic. If anyone read her
journal, they would believe her ready to be locked
up, and sometimes she agreed.

Oh, yes, too often she feared she was losing her
mind.

She closed the journal and shoved it into the
desk drawer. She kept this drawer locked. It con-
tained Annefield's ledger of household accounts
and the precious diary she'd started writing upon
her return almost three years ago. She'd arrived
and, in the same day, Tara had been swept away
by their father to try her own hand at the London
Marriage Mart. He'd undoubtedly wished to keep
his youngest away from Aileen's poisonous presence, or at least that was the impression he'd given.

For Aileen, however, life wasn't terrible in the
valley. There were those who ostracized her, but
the majority accepted her. London was a good

distance away, and what did loyal Scots care for English opinion?

However, the Scots did take pride in Tara's spectacular success on the Marriage Mart. She was about to wed Blake Stephens, the catch of the season and the duke of Penevey's illegitimate son. They called him the Bastard, a simple, direct title—although everyone knew that the powerful duke favored this son over his legitimate ones, presumably because the Bastard was rich. Stephens was said to be very clever when it came to investments and had become extremely popular in the way only wealthy, handsome men could be.

"I pray she is happy," Aileen murmured, closing her eyes. "Please, God, save her from the hell I endured."

Images rose in Aileen's mind: Geoff's shouts, the burst of pain, the anger of society, the moment when another man's touch gave her hope—

She opened her eyes with a start. Even her pulse had picked up its pace. She stared at the room's comfortable furniture, torn between fear and desire. She need no longer be afraid. What had happened had been a long time ago.

But what of her deepest yearnings and the craving for affection that were part of every woman's soul? Those she fought by grounding herself in Annefield's blessed peace and the daily list of duties that kept her occupied.

And self-pity, her constant companion if she allowed it to linger, could only be staved off by a bit of exercise.

Aileen rose from her chair and left the room, but her thoughts as she walked away were on Tara. Good, sweet Tara.

Out of all that had happened over the last nine years, losing her half sister's trust and affection had hurt Aileen the most because she knew her own culpability. She'd gone to London in search of love while turning her back on the one person who had loved her most of all. Why, she hadn't even written Tara over all those years of separation. In the beginning, she'd been too preoccupied with her own life and then, later, too ashamed.

Aileen fetched her gloves and a wide-brimmed straw hat from her room and went downstairs into the front hall.

"Going for your walk, my lady?" Ingold asked. The butler was a huge, hulking man with a thatch of blondish gray hair on his head and a cold manner when he wished it.

"I believe I shall," she answered.

And after I take my walk, then what? My life is empty.

The cynicism of the thought threw her out the door. She needed to stop this nonsense. It was what it was. A Davidson never complained. That was one thing her father had taught his daughters—

Her thoughts were interrupted by the sight of a lad wearing a misshapen hat pulled low over his eyes boldly striding across the front lawn straight for the front door.

As she pulled on her gloves, Aileen frowned. Something about this boy caught her attention. He seemed familiar . . . but she couldn't place how, since she was certain she didn't recognize him.

His clothes were a size too large and had seen better days. The shirt was filthy, and the jacket had tears at the sleeve seams. The boots were so tall they were well over the lad's knees, but the leather was thin and worn in such a way that the height didn't hamper his movement.

The lad carried a huge portmanteau that appeared half his size. *That* was made out of good, expensive leather and was out of character with the way the boy dressed.

Perhaps a neighbor was having him deliver something to Annefield?

Aileen knew her neighbors and their servants. This boy was not one of them.

And if he was and she was wrong, the lad should have better sense than to approach the front door. Annefield was one of the premier estates in the Tay Valley, and servants used the side entrance.

Catching sight of Aileen watching him, the boy stopped at the edge of the front drive. He dropped the portmanteau on the ground with the finality of someone who had reached the end of a long journey and could not take a step more. A smile split his face, a smile that made Aileen's heart stop in its familiarity—

No, it couldn't be.

"Hello, Leenie," the boy said. He spread his arms. "I'm home."

Aileen stared hard, her mind rejecting what her eyes were seeing.

The lad realized her confusion and laughed as he came toward her. "I imagine I've surprised you. It has been almost three years. The bag is full of dresses. Who would have thought they could weigh so much? I almost tossed the whole lot a time or two before I reached Annefield. But I would have been sorry, as well you know."

He was no lad. *He was her sister.*

Dressed as a boy.

In *smelly* clothes. The wind carried a whiff of their odor right to Aileen. And she was more confused than before.

Lady Tara Davidson, feted as the "Helen of London" because of the number of hearts she had broken, would not be strolling around the Scottish countryside carrying her own luggage and wearing clothes bearing someone else's body odor. From everything Aileen had heard about her, Tara would just not countenance such a thing.

And then Tara solved the matter once and for all by pulling the hat off her head. Her hair had been braided and coiled around her head, creating the odd shape. Now her braid fell past her shoulder in one long, thick rope of honey red hair.

Aileen almost collapsed in shock.

Tara had the grace to blush even as she moved forward to embrace her older sister, but Aileen held her off with a raised hand.

"I believe you are to marry come Saturday?" Aileen said. "In London?"

The smile vanished from Tara's face. "I don't believe I shall be there."

"Does the bridegroom know?" Aileen feared the answer.

Tara's vivid blue eyes shifted to the row of firs

bordering Annefield's lawn. A rook flew away and her gaze followed it a moment, the line between her brows deepening before she faced Aileen and said, "He should have an idea by now."

"You *jilted* him? And the earl?" Aileen asked, referring to their father. "Did you tell him?"

Tara's jaw hardened. "What do you think? Would you have told him?"

"Oh. Dear." Aileen found it hard to breathe. "Please, Tara, don't tell me you have run away."

"Very well, I won't."

Aileen didn't know how to respond.

At her shocked silence, Tara said, "I don't know why you seem so put out. After all, *you* weren't invited to attend."

"That has nothing to do with the matter," Aileen said. "You are about to jilt the son of one of the most powerful dukes in England—"

"His *illegitimate* son," Tara emphasized. "There is a difference."

"Not much since Penevey has recognized him."

Tara made an impatient sound. "Recognize him? Yes, he did—as his *bastard*. And all the *chats* of society may flatter me to my face, but I know what they say behind my back. I'm Scottish, a gambling fortune hunter's daughter. They are happy for this marriage because it saves their precious sons from me and their whey-faced daughters from Mr. Stephens. Not that I care. Not anymore." She started to move into the house, but Aileen blocked her path.

"There will be the devil to pay for this, Tara— and don't think that because you are *here* you will escape it."

Tara's shoulders straightened. A flash of fire came to her eyes, but in the next second, huge, luminous tears filled them. Aileen was caught off guard by the sudden change. "I thought if *anyone* should understand, *you* would," Tara said. "I can see I was wrong—"

The front door behind Aileen opened. Ingold said, "Lady Aileen, is there a difficulty? Is this lad giving you—"

His voice broke off and his eyes widened as he had a good look at exactly whom Aileen had been speaking with. "Lady Tara?" he said in wonder. Tara had always been his favorite. Aileen was respected, but Tara had always been favored by all the servants at Annefield.

Tara's tears disappeared. "Yes, it is I, Ingold. I'm home. Home at last." She bounded forward, moving past Aileen. "I need a bath. These clothes smell terrible. Tell Mrs. Watson to have one prepared for me. Oh, and the bag on the lawn is full of dresses. They must be aired and pressed. I'm heading for the kitchen, I'm famished."

She would have disappeared into the house except for Ingold filling the doorway. "Is the earl here as well?" the butler asked anxiously, looking around as if he expected their father with his coach and team to be hiding in the shrubbery by the side of the house. "And Mr. Stephens?"

Tara hummed noncommittally before saying with great authority, "No, they are not here. They won't be. I came alone."

That news surprised Ingold enough for her to slip by him, but Aileen was not about to let her off that easily. She set out after her sister, pushing her own way past the butler.

Tara was already down the hall. She seemed to quicken her step as she sensed Aileen behind her. Bullying and ordering her way might do the trick with the servants, but it would not work with her older sister. Still, Aileen didn't catch up with Tara until she was down the back stairs and into the kitchen.

"*Fresh* bread," Tara said with delight as she reached for one of the loaves Cook had cooling on the wooden table in the center of the room. Without ceremony, she pulled it apart and stuffed it into her mouth.

Cook and the scullery maid had turned at the entrance of a stranger. Cook raised the wooden spoon she had been using to stir the pot over the fire, ready to defend her loaves of bread, when she recognized Tara. Her manner changed in an instant. "My lady? Is that you? Oh, blessed beings, it is. You have been gone too long from us."

Her mouth full of bread, Tara smiled, as beatific as an angel. "This is delicious, Cook," she said around chews. "Better than any I've ever tasted, even in London."

Cook preened. "You know my mother taught me how to bake that bread. Our family secret. Will carry it to my grave—"

"*Excuse* us," Aileen ordered, grabbing Tara's arm and swinging her sister out the door toward the steps.

Tara grunted her farewell to Cook, since her mouth was full.

Aileen propelled Tara halfway up the stairs and stopped, so incensed with her sister that she could not go a step further. "*What do you think you are doing?*" she demanded.

"Eating," Tara said, and that flippant reply set Aileen's temper off.

"Listen, missy, enough of this. Why are you here? Why aren't you in London preparing for your wedding? How did you even travel here?"

Tara swallowed and drew a deep, satisfied breath before saying, "I'm here because I live here, and I rode the mail coach. That is how I traveled."

"Dressed in men's clothing?" Aileen was incredulous when she imagined the dangers.

"I didn't want anyone to recognize me," Tara said as if it was obvious. "And I must say, there is much freedom in being a man. But you are right. I need to remove these clothes." She would have started up the stairs, but Aileen grabbed the hem of Tara's jacket.

"Why?" she demanded of her younger sister. "And don't accuse me of wrongdoing for asking questions. I'm not someone you can twist around your finger."

For a second, Tara's expression let her know she resented the challenge, but then the defensiveness left her. She leaned a shoulder against one wall, her hip resting on the bannister. With sober eyes, she said, "Because I started thinking."

"About what?" Aileen pressed.

"About happiness."

"Go on."

Tara made a frustrated sound and then said, "Oh, be honest, Leenie, don't you wish you'd questioned yourself more *before* you married Geoff?"

At the mention of her divorced husband, Aileen took a step away. "I couldn't have known what a terrible man he was before we wed. I *didn't* know. But if I had, if I'd realized how cruel he was, yes, I would not have married him. Are you saying Mr. Stephens is as harsh?"

A frown formed between Tara's eyes. She picked at the bread, dropping crumbs to the floor. "He isn't completely like Geoff. I mean, I don't think he would hurt me."

Aileen didn't realize she had been holding her breath, waiting for her sister's answer, until she released it. Tara was a canny one. She knew exactly which approach to take to gain sympathy. Of course, Aileen would not wish for her sister the hell that her marriage had been, but now she wondered with concern about when her charming little sister had become so manipulative. Of course time and distance had played their tricks. The two of them, who had once been so close, were now practically strangers.

Still, Aileen wanted to believe Tara had good

reason to be here. "Tell me. Explain to me. You want me on your side, and I understand that what is done is done. You realize you are ruined, don't you? Jilting the groom is the worst sort of offense, even if no one had liked him, which I understand is not the case with Mr. Stephens. He is respected. There is no way you can return to London."

Tara flicked a few more crumbs to the floor, the corners of her mouth tightening.

Aileen placed her hands on her sister's shoulders and leaned forward so that Tara had no choice but to face her. "You are fine with becoming an outcast?"

"*You've* managed."

"Yes, I have. But it isn't easy being the black sheep of the family."

"I'm sorry," Tara whispered, sounding as if she truly meant the words. "I wish the whole matter, the divorce, Geoff, all of it, hadn't been so terrible on you."

"The terrible part was being his wife," Aileen said. "I can live with the rest as long as I have my freedom. And," she added, "life is more pleasant here in the valley than it was in London. Our cousin Sabrina offered staunch support, and few are willing to cross her."

"That is good to know," Tara said. "I worried."

Aileen didn't know if she believed her.

In Tara's defense, her wisest course had been to distance herself as far as she could from Aileen. The scandal wasn't just that Geoff had divorced her, an act that required a vote of Parliament. No, the worst part had been the Criminal Conversation trial—also called the Crim Con—that had preceded the divorce, during which he'd publically branded Aileen as an adulteress for her affair with Captain Peter Pollard, one of Geoff's fellow military officers.

And now, in one of life's unexpected twists, here was Tara, running to the haven of Annefield just as Aileen once had.

"Why, Tara? What drove you here?"

For a long moment, Tara studied the remains of the bread in her hands, then she said, "The closer the time came for my wedding, the harder I found it to breathe."

"Do you not like Mr. Stephens?" Aileen asked.

There was a beat of silence. Then Tara answered, "He is pleasant."

"That is not the strongest recommendation for a groom," Aileen said. "But it is not a bad quality in a husband." She knew. Geoff had not been pleasant.

"I needed to come home."

"You could have come home after the wedding."

"It wouldn't be the same."

"Tara, tell me your story," Aileen said in a voice only an older sister could use. "You could have cried off. There would have been talk, but if you truly had no desire to wed, it is what should have been done. Instead, you have humiliated Mr. Stephens, and men don't respond well to that."

Tara's mouth took on a mutinous set. She was hiding something, keeping her true motives to herself and evading Aileen's questions.

"Did you even bother to leave a note for the earl?" Aileen asked. "Does he know where you have gone?"

Before Tara could answer, there was a footstep on the stair below them. Two lads from the stable were starting up the stairs with buckets of hot water, probably for Tara's bath.

The women stepped aside and let the boys pass. If Tara felt any discomfiture at being seen by the servants in male attire, she was too stubborn to admit it.

But the stable lads were embarrassed. Bright color flooded their faces, and Aileen could just imagine what they were thinking . . . and she wondered if Tara remembered, after the sophistication of London, how provincial life and morals were in the valley. If she didn't, she would quickly receive a dose of reality.

Alone again, Tara said to Aileen, "No, I didn't leave a note. I didn't want Father to stop me. Mr. Stephens is paying a fortune to marry me."

Aileen sighed. Geoff had done the same. The earl knew how to auction off his daughters.

"So you ran away from the marriage to humiliate the earl?" Aileen asked, begging to understand.

"I don't wish to humiliate anyone. And don't give a thought to Mr. Stephens. He didn't want to marry me any more than I wanted to marry him." Tara unceremoniously shoved the bread in her pocket and yanked off her jacket. She started up the stairs.

"Then why did he ask you?" Aileen said, following.

"For the same reason they all do. They know they must marry. It is expected. And I—" Tara stopped, as if troubled by a thought. "And I am—or *was*—the prize. When one man wants a woman, they all want her. It is much like the bidding on Father's horses. One buyer has a notion that he must possess one of our nags, and then they all want the exact same horse—even though Father has several in the stable just like it or even better. It is the way men think," she decided, moving up the stairs again, saying as she went, "Mr. Stephens's brother was one of my suitors. The marquis has such an affected manner I would never have married him." She shook her head. "He always smelled of the worst cologne. He also gambled, and lost consistently."

"Like the earl."

"Exactly," Tara agreed. "Except he had access to Penevey's resources. Father favored the marquis until, all of a sudden, Mr. Stephens swooped in and offered more. You know how it is. Geoff's father paid handsomely to marry him to you."

He had.

"Besides," Tara continued, "Mr. Stephens was a prize himself. So many women had set their caps for him that I was flattered he would pursue me. And he did chase me, Leenie. He was persistent."

"So you *wanted* to marry him?"

"I told myself I did. But in truth, Father pressured me for the match, and it did appeal to my vanity."

Tara had not stopped at the ground floor but continued up the narrow winding back staircase to the family quarters. She opened the door and walked down the wide hall.

"Then what changed?" Aileen asked.

Facing her, Tara's expression grew pensive. "Do you remember the conversation we had the day you left for London?"

Aileen shook her head.

"You spoke about love?" Tara reminded her softly. "You said you would only marry for love."

A hard weight settled in Aileen's chest. "I remember the conversation. I was naive." *A silly Highland lass without much understanding of the world.* "Please don't tell me you shredded your reputation for my ridiculous notions."

"It didn't sound ridiculous to me at the time. And it doesn't sound ridiculous now."

"But it is. Tara, love is a myth, an illusion . . . a fantasy. Men and women are too selfish for such an emotion to exist between them for any length of time."

"You sound so jaded."

The accusation stung. "Not jaded, *experienced.* I've seen both sides. I had a marriage in which the earl passed me on to the highest bidder. And I tossed it all away because I thought I was in love."

"Weren't you?"

"With Peter Pollard?" Aileen shook her head. "I don't know anymore. Certainly I had intense feelings for him, or could that have been a reaction to

Geoff's cruelty? In the end, it doesn't matter." She soothed a hand over her sister's shoulder. "What is important is that for women of our station in life, there are expectations. I was foolish to believe I could do otherwise."

"But what if I want more?"

Tara's question hung in the air between them a moment before Aileen informed her sadly, "There is nothing more. You should use my life as a cautionary tale."

A flash of rebellion came to Tara's eye. "I am not you—" she started, but she broke off as the door to her bedroom opened. The two lads with the bathwater came out with empty buckets, followed Mrs. Watson. She was a petite, thin woman with steel gray hair and a kind nature. She appeared a bit flushed, and Aileen could only imagine the running around she'd been doing to hastily prepare for Tara's arrival.

"Lady Tara, welcome home," she said, bowing her head in welcome.

"Even dressed as I am?" Tara asked.

"We will accept you any way we can receive you, my lady," Mrs. Watson answered. "And clothes can be changed . . . which I suggest you see to now," she added briskly.

Tara looked to Aileen. "This is why I had to return. It's been too long since anyone just accepted me for being me. And it is good to be surrounded by Scottish voices, and Scottish attitudes." She smiled. "Excuse me, Aileen. I am now under instruction to change from these clothes. I'm thankful the lad I purchased them from didn't have fleas."

"I didn't have time to assign a maid, my lady," Mrs. Watson said. "May I be of assistance?"

"Thank you, Mrs. Watson, that will be all," Tara answered. "I know how to undress myself, and I shall appreciate a moment alone."

"Very well, my lady."

Tara walked into her room and turned, holding the door and preventing Aileen from chasing after her. "We'll discuss this later, sister," she said. "I'm tired to the point of fatigue." She shut the door, practically in Aileen's face.

"It is good to have her home," Mrs. Watson said. "So very good."

"Aye, it is," Aileen murmured absently, wondering why Tara had *really* bolted days before her wedding.

Her sister was not being honest. She told some of the truth, but not all.

Geoff had been a mere baronet's son. His had been a difficult nature, and Aileen knew all too well why his father had been willing to pay to see him married. However, Mr. Stephens was allied with a powerful and undoubtedly proud duke. In spite of the unconventional circumstances of his birth, he had a good reputation. Aileen prayed her sister knew what she was doing.

She also hoped Tara understood *why* she was doing it.

Aileen knew all too well that the "whys" were always more important than any other questions.

*I*n the safe haven of the room of her childhood, a room of soft blue, rose and greens, Tara finally drew her first relieved breath.

She had done it.

She had escaped London, escaped a future mapped out for her, escaped a genteel life of affluence, security, prestige and honor. She'd run away from it all.

Tara walked over to the window. Her room overlooked the back of the house. Aileen was a gardener, and Tara could see the work of her sister's hand on the flowerbeds and an herb garden that had not been there before. The world was peaceful here, not hectic and uncaring like London. Tara hadn't realized how much she'd missed the valley.

Her eye went to the stables a short distance from the house. A line of beeches formed a boundary between the garden and the important business of breeding the racehorses for which Annefield was becoming renowned. Who would have thought their father's whim would turn out so handsomely? Then again, the success of the breeding program was not by his hard work. That was owed to another—and she wondered if *he* was there.

Through the trees, she glimpsed a handsome, big-boned bay tethered to the hitching post. Her heart sprang to life.

Ruary Jamerson was here. His presence at this very moment of her homecoming had to be a divine sign.

Aileen might not believe in love, but Tara did.

She turned and took two steps, ready to run down to the stables, but then paused.

What was she going to say? What *should* she say?

She'd been so intent on coming back to him that she hadn't given a thought of how she would explain herself. It had been three years since they'd had that last argument. Three years since she'd spurned his suit and walked away.

But Ruary had never left her thoughts. He was the man by which she had judged all others. She'd even dreamed of him. Indeed, the closer the time had drawn toward her wedding, the more frequent and vivid her dreams had become, until she'd faced the truth a week ago: she loved Ruary Jamerson, and she *always* would. She just hadn't realized it until that moment and with a wedding to another man staring her in the face.

She caught a glimpse of herself in the looking glass above her dressing table. She'd changed over the years. Her looks had matured, sharpened. Gone was the softness of youth. She was a woman now, one who finally knew her own mind.

And one who was dressed in a lad's garb and smelled foul of her own odor and sweat.

Tara began ripping off her clothes and within seconds was scrubbing herself in the tub. The fine-milled soap smelled of lavender, and she lathered herself twice to be certain the stench was gone.

Mrs. Watson had already hung a few of the dresses from Tara's portmanteau in the room's wardrobe, and she'd placed shoes and smallclothes in the drawers. Tara grabbed the first garment available, a creamy gauze trimmed in her favorite Belgian lace. Was it too fancy for Annefield? She didn't care. She couldn't waste a second longer before confessing her love to Ruary and begging his forgiveness.

Within minutes she was out the door.

Chapter Two

The chestnut challenged him on this clear summer day. The horse's nostrils flared and he kept his head high, pulling on the lead line, but Ruary Jamerson was patient. He'd not met a horse yet he could not conquer. His pride demanded it. And this stallion was a beauty. With his spirited nature, he would win races from here to Newmarket, which would please the earl of Tay and burnish Ruary's growing reputation as a top-notch trainer.

Stone and timber stalls lined the yard in a horseshoe shape. Ruary believed horses learned more by watching each other than they did from any man. The lads laughed at him, but his methods worked. Annefield had produced two renowned racehorses, and this chestnut could be the third. Already there was a list of buyers interested in him.

The fourth wall held a wide entryway lined with storage and grain rooms. Vehicles, plows, rakes and the like, along with cows, chickens and pigs, were kept in the other barn off and away from the horses.

Annefield was a large estate, but it was no longer Ruary's only stable. He now trained horses throughout this area of Scotland and had received offers from as far away as the Netherlands. Not that he would ever leave the Tay Valley. This was his home.

Keeping a critical eye on the bay, Ruary said to the stable lads watching him work, "I see no lameness." He held up the lead, a signal for the colt to slow down. "Exercise him on the morrow. Our regular schedule, but start him easy. Build him up to gallop the last three-eighths and we'll go from there."

"Aye, Mr. Jamerson," Angus, the head groom, said. "Will you be here for the morning ride?"

"I'm not planning to be," Ruary answered. "Breccan Campbell wants me to look over some stock. I'll come later." He started gathering the colt's line. The horse followed, his head low, submissive. Ruary patted his neck. "We did well, Angus."

"I didn't agree with you when you said you wanted to breed his dam to Emperor. Thought the stud too hot, but he must know how to run, because this one does."

"I wouldn't place money against him."

"Neither would I, Mr. Jamerson. Neither would I."

Mr. Jamerson. The respect in the groom's voice filled Ruary with pride. He'd worked hard to reach this point, and it had not been easy.

He'd been an orphan, a Romany by-blow no one had wanted. His mother had been blonde and fair, a kitchen maid whose good looks had caught her the wrong sort of attention. His father had been swarthy and dark. Together, they had created a son who had his mother's blue eyes and father's black hair. He stood six feet tall, and he had square shoulders and a horseman's grace. The ladies had always been wild for him.

But his turbulent childhood had kept him humble. He would have come to a bad end if his path hadn't crossed Old Dickie's. A groom much like Angus, Old Dickie had been wise in the ways of horses and men. He'd spotted something in

Ruary that had been different from most others, and he'd given a lost boy food and a future.

Of course, Ruary had once come close to losing it all. He'd been foolish enough to fall in love with the wrong woman. Lady Tara Davidson had been too far above his touch, he understood that now; however, at the time, he'd wanted her. He'd loved her.

And he had thought she'd loved him.

Love. It could blind a man to what was important.

If three years ago he'd tossed all aside for Tara, then they would not call him *Mr.* Jamerson with so much respect. That didn't mean his heart hadn't been broken, but he had survived—and he was a wiser man for it. Life was good now.

He handed the lead line to Angus. "The lads are doing well with the colt." He looked to a group of stable boys. "Who rides him?"

The smallest, a towheaded boy of perhaps nine years of age—the same age Ruary had been when he'd started riding horses—said, "I do, sir."

"Keep your hand light when you work him. He's a sensitive animal and we want to keep him that way," Ruary said.

"Aye, sir. And he does like to go."

The pride in the boy's voice made Ruary smile. "Keep that in him."

"I will, sir."

Ruary said, "I'll see you on the morrow, Angus, later in the day." He started walking toward the entryway.

Tack boxes lined the entryway's walls that faced the windowless grain room. This was where Ruary mixed the special feed from the recipe he had developed himself. He thought to check the oat supply, but before he could go inside, a woman walked into the entryway, a woman he had thought never to see again.

Lady Tara Davidson.

Her unannounced appearance caught him off guard almost as much as her beauty did.

Had he truly believed he had overcome his emotions for her?

In this moment, seeing her with the sun behind her, highlighting her glorious red-gold hair curling down around her shoulders, Ruary's heart slammed against his chest with a force that robbed him of breath and stopped him in his tracks.

She was more lovely than ever. Achingly so. The years in London had added maturity to her face that enhanced her beauty.

Her lips parted as if his presence had surprised her as well, and then she smiled, her eyes glad, welcoming—and Ruary felt as if all the solid ground beneath his feet had suddenly given way.

*T*ara had come in search of Ruary, but she hadn't expected to almost walk into his arms.

For a second, all she could do was stare.

He had changed . . . but in the right way, a good way. He seemed taller, stronger, more commanding.

This is what she'd missed in the men in London. Yes, with his sharp blue eyes and dark looks, he was handsomer than the majority of them. But, save for Blake Stephens, they had lacked Ruary's masculinity.

Of course, Blake did not care about her. Not truly. She knew that.

But this man, *her* Ruary, had once offered his heart and soul to her. And she had not valued them. She had not realized how precious a gift his love had been.

Ruary broke the silence first, his gaze shifting away from her. "Lady Tara, how good to see you." His words sounded rote, wooden, as if he groped for them.

"It is good to see you as well," she returned, equally formal in spite of the wild pounding of her heart. She had traveled a long way for him and had imagined him throwing himself at her feet in gratitude. It was a ludicrous picture. She knew that. But she had not expected this sudden awkwardness.

Ruary stepped to the side. "If you will excuse me, my lady?" He didn't wait for her response but began to pass her.

She could not let him go. Not until she'd said her piece. She had given up so much, traveled so far. She reached for his arm, took hold of it. He stopped. Surprised. They now stood inches from each other.

"I need to speak to you," she whispered.

He frowned at the ground. "That is not necessary—"

"*It is.*"

Ruary didn't respond. He didn't move. He seemed to study the rusted hinge on the nearest wooden tack box, yet she knew he was as aware of her hand on him as she was. This connection was a force stronger than any she had ever known.

"I've surprised you," she said. "I know my appearance is a shock."

"This is your home." There was a beat of silence, then he said, "I understand you are to marry."

Of course he'd heard about her upcoming marriage. That was the reason for his restraint.

Tara could have laughed for joy, but then she heard voices in the stable yard. They were not alone and she needed to speak to him, to pour out her heart. She pulled him into the shadowy haven of the grain room. They used to meet here. It had been one of their hiding places.

He came. He followed.

He did care.

"I *was* to marry," she admitted, keeping her voice low, not wanting them to be overheard and disturbed. "In three days' time—but then I found I couldn't go through with it. I bolted."

She had his complete attention now. "Bolted? Tara, what are you saying?"

"You called me by my given name," she said with a touch of wonder.

Ruary reacted as if she'd struck him. "I'm sorry, I meant, my lady—"

She stopped his apology by throwing her arms around him, an impetuous move that brought her right where she wanted to be. She held tight. He smelled of fresh air, shaving soap and leather. She had missed the scent of him. "*You* are not out of line. You never could be. It's just that I'd feared never hearing my name upon your lips again. It sounds like music to me. How could I have been so foolish those years ago as to leave you?"

Ruary responded with a moment of stunned silence. He stood very still, as if he was not ready to return the embrace. "What do you mean?"

"I couldn't go through with the marriage. I realized it was you I wanted. *You*, Ruary. I can't live without *you*."

She expected a response. For three years, the finest men in London had begged her to say such words to them.

Ruary's mouth opened, but he could not speak.

"I have shocked you," Tara said, wanting him to know she understood and excused his uneasiness. "Our parting was difficult. I've thought of it often."

She didn't wait for his answer but charged ahead, "I was cruel to you when I left. Do you remember begging me to choose you instead of going to London? I could not hear of it because . . . I was afraid. There. That is the truth. Father would have been angry. Yes, he would. I also feared that if I didn't go to London, if I didn't see all the world had to offer, then *I* would have regrets. I would always wonder, *What if?*"

"Tara, you have nothing to explain—"

"*But I do.* I hurt you when I chose to leave. I know I did."

Ruary took her arms and slowly, gently pushed her a step away. Dear God, she had so missed his touch. And there was such a look of concern in his eyes. He loved her. She knew he did. In spite of the years apart, the connection between them was as strong as ever.

"Tara—" he started, his expression serious, but he had no chance to continue because, from out in the entryway, a woman's musical voice interrupted the moment.

"Hello, Angus, have you seen Mr. Jamerson?"

Ruary released Tara's arms as if he'd been scalded. He turned to the door, blocking Tara's view.

Angus answered the woman, "Aye, Miss Sawyer. I saw him earlier, but I thought he'd left." Their voices were so close they had to be practically standing by the grain room door.

"Marcus is still here," Miss Sawyer answered, referring to Ruary's horse.

Sawyer. Tara knew the name.

Ruary started for the door. Tara reached out, wanting to grab his jacket and hold him back, but before she could, he said, "I'm here, Jane."

Jane Sawyer. Of course, Tara knew her. Jane was the smithy's daughter. They were of the same age and had attended kirk services and valley assemblies together. The Scots were more egalitarian than the English. When there was a dance, everyone was invited, although all knew their proper place.

"Right *where*?" Miss Sawyer asked, her frustration evident in her tone.

Ruary stepped out into the entry. "In the grain room." The doorway framed the two of them for Tara's vision. "I had to check the supplies."

Jane Sawyer had grown up in the last three years. Tara remembered her as being hopelessly bookish. She was now less dowdy, although her plain blue day dress was practical and obviously locally styled. She'd coaxed her dark hair into curls beneath a straw hat trimmed in yellow ribbon.

She *was* pretty . . . in a provincial way, if one liked cherry cheeks.

"What brings you here?" Ruary was saying.

"I thought to surprise you," Miss Sawyer said happily. Her tone warmed as she said, "You have been so busy of late, and I have missed seeing you."

A sudden, primitive, protective urge rushed through Tara. Miss Sawyer wanted Ruary. It might not have been clear to him, but Tara recognized a rival when she saw one.

And she was not going to let another woman moon over the man she loved. She had gone through too much to return to Annefield.

Tara marched to the grain room door and stepped out into the light, right between the two of them.

At her appearance, a dull red came to Ruary's face. Miss Sawyer blinked in incomprehension at Tara's sudden appearance. But she was not a stupid woman. Her gaze went from Tara to Ruary and then to the darkness of the grain room.

Angus was off to the side, shuffling gear around in a tack box. He straightened. "Why, Lady Tara, we did not know you'd returned from England. There has been no announcement."

"I arrived in the past hour, Angus," she said in her best lady-of-the-manor voice. "It is good to see you again."

He pulled his forelock. "We are happy you are home, my lady. Very happy, yes, we are. Do you plan to ride?"

"Perhaps. I was hoping Mr. Jamerson could help choose a mount for me." As Tara spoke, she took a step closer to Ruary, staking her claim. "How are you, Miss Sawyer? It has been some time since we last met."

But the potency of the moment broke as Ruary

moved to deliberately take a place beside Miss Sawyer. He took her gloved hand. "My lady," Ruary said, his voice formal, official, "I hope you will wish us happy."

"Happy?" Tara echoed, careful to keep her tone neutral.

"Yes, Miss Sawyer has honored me by agreeing to become my wife. The banns have already been announced once."

Chapter Three

$\mathscr{T}$ara didn't want to believe she had heard Ruary correctly.

He was hers.

He *loved* her.

Hadn't she just felt something between them? The spark of connection? A pull of desire?

He had to have felt the same surge of emotions. *He must have.*

But he had promised himself to another woman . . . ?

Tara didn't let any of her confusion show on her face even as her heart seemed to writhe with shock.

"Why, congratulations," she heard herself say,

her voice bright, brittle. "Is the wedding to be soon?"

"Yes, my lady," Miss Sawyer said, smiling her happiness. "As soon as the last of the banns are announced. That day can't come soon enough. I'm excited to start our life together."

Tara nodded even as a new, immediate understanding struck her, one that Aileen had tried to impress upon her: *she was ruined.*

She had delivered the worst insult a woman could give a man—she'd left him practically at the altar . . . and her reason for such outrageous behavior, the man she had sacrificed everything for, was going to marry another.

"My lady," Ruary said, "are you all right?"

She frowned at him. No, she wasn't all right. She'd never be all right again.

"She doesn't look good," Miss Sawyer murmured. "She has gone pale."

"Here, have her sit on this tack box before she goes off into a swoon," Angus ordered.

But Tara wasn't about to stay here. She needed time alone, time to think. "I must go to the house," Tara said decisively. "I must leave."

Leave to go where? She couldn't return to London, not in time for her wedding.

Angus urged her to "Please, sit," but her feet had started moving outside. She raised a hand to her head as if expecting to be feverish and was surprised to discover she was cold. Very cold. She began walking with great determination to the house. She had to reach its safe haven. She could think there.

Miss Sawyer might find her sudden departure odd, but Tara didn't care. Ruary would tell her what had happened and then the chit could be pleased that he had chosen her over Tara. Then she would brag that she had bested the earl of Tay's daughter, who had once been the reigning beauty of the valley and who had set hearts afire in London.

But the worst was that Tara had been certain Ruary had been waiting for her. She'd gambled on his love . . . and lost.

Aileen was right about love.

Footsteps sounded behind her.

"Tara," Ruary said, his voice low. "Wait."

She shook her head, denying him, not even glancing in his direction, but his legs were longer. He moved past her to block her path.

"I'm worried," he said. "So is Jane. Are you ill?"

So is Jane.

Those words swirled in the air around her. No man had ever placed another woman before her.

She found strength in anger. "I thought you *cared*."

He glanced toward the stables as if to be certain they could not be overheard. Then he said quietly, "I loved you."

"No, you didn't. You didn't hesitate to *replace* me." She used the words like whiplashes. "Although you could have done better."

The corners of Ruary's mouth tightened. "This is not about Jane. And I didn't 'replace' you, my lady. You walked away. You left me as if I was a lapdog to be tossed aside because you were bored. I mourned for you. I grieved. It took me *years* to heal my heart. And now you have returned expecting me to *still be* the lovesick fool I once was?" His outrage seemed to overwhelm him. He gathered himself to say, "I believed you when you said you returned my love. You crushed my soul when you left, but my life has gone on. I've built a reputation for myself. My name means something in the valley, and I will not toss it aside by reneging on my promise to a good and *faithful* woman just because you've decided to crook your finger in my direction."

He turned on his heel and walked away without waiting for her response.

Tara felt paralyzed. Ruary had never spoken to her with such vehemence before.

No one had.

Ever.

She was the darling, the cossetted, the favorite—and Ruary was telling her there were limits?

Limits she might have overstepped.

Tara glanced over her shoulder, catching sight of Ruary rejoining Miss Sawyer. Tara could imagine her asking, "Is she all right?"—the universal question women always asked when they wished to pretend concern.

Tara's stomach cramped. She suddenly felt light-headed and not quite herself. She took a few steps toward the haven of the beech trees, where she would be out of sight from the stables. Once there, she leaned a hand against a beech trunk and became ill.

She hadn't much food inside her. Her meals on the road had been little more than stale bread and cheese. The travel had not been pleasant. She had been squeezed into small spaces by pushy, common people who'd seen her as a boy. She'd suffered, suffered terribly . . . just to reach Ruary—

Her stomach tightened again. She started to bend over, then stopped when she heard Aileen's voice.

"Now will you be honest with me?"

Aileen had gone to Tara's bedroom with a tray prepared by Cook and had been surprised to find her sister gone. Her filthy boy's clothing had been tossed on the floor. Puzzled, Aileen had glanced out the window and noticed her sister running from the stables with the horse master in hot pursuit.

Sensing that something had been amiss, Aileen had dashed to her sister's aid. She had to catch her breath now.

Tara raised the back of her hand to her lips as if she could hide that she'd been indisposed. "I don't know what you mean."

Aileen made an impatient sound. "Do you believe I am truly that ignorant to what goes on at Annefield? I'd heard of your infatuation with Jamerson."

"You don't know a thing about it," Tara challenged.

"I know he would not be Father's choice for a

husband for you . . . especially if it meant jilting a very wealthy man like Mr. Stephens."

Tara crumpled. "I have done a terrible thing. I have destroyed myself and all because I love Ruary. I love him, Aileen, truly I do—but he is going to marry another."

The pain in Tara's voice touched Aileen to the core. She went to her sister and put her arms around her. She'd known Mr. Jamerson was going to marry the blacksmith's daughter, but that information had held little meaning to her until this moment.

Silent tears rolled down Tara's cheeks. She pressed her lips together as if she was trying to hold them off, reminding Aileen of Tara at the age of four and needing her older sister's hugs of reassurance.

"I love him," Tara repeated. "And I've lost him. I should never have left him. But I didn't know three years ago that there was no other man like him."

"It will be all right," Aileen soothed.

"No, it *won't*," Tara answered. "Nothing will ever be right again. You didn't see him, Aileen. Ruary hates me."

"He does not—"

"*He does*. He said I hurt him when I left. I've hurt many men's feelings . . . but I always thought

Ruary would be there no matter what. If you love someone, shouldn't you want to forgive her? Isn't that part of love?"

"Darling, life goes on."

"Mine won't. Mine will never be the same again."

"Tara, you are being overly dramatic—" Aileen started, wanting to calm her sister down.

"How would you have me be? I should have realized sooner what he meant to me. If I had returned even a week ago, the banns would not have been read and there could have been hope for us."

"Or perhaps not," Aileen answered. "Mr. Jamerson must have strong feelings for Miss Sawyer. He is not the sort of person to enter marriage lightly. Furthermore, let us be pragmatic. You and Mr. Jamerson are from two different classes. Father would never have agreed to such a match."

"I did not come here with Father's permission," Tara shot back. "And people respect Ruary."

"They do, provided he stays in his proper place. Father's response would be swift. If he knew that you jilted Mr. Stephens for Mr. Jamerson, he would give the horse master the sack. Then where would the two of you be?"

"I wouldn't have cared as long as I was with him."

"Now that is nonsense—"

"Only because you haven't ever known love. Real, true love."

Aileen took a step back. "I don't know what to reply. You are right, of course. And perhaps I am thankful, because 'real, true love' has led you to make the most serious mistake of your life."

"All the more reason that I must believe," Tara replied, her voice small. "I've no other option."

Her soft confession tugged at Aileen's heart. She forced a smile. "It is not so terrible to live beyond the pale of society."

Tara nodded solemnly. "I shall miss London."

"You would have given it up if you married Mr. Jamerson," Aileen reminded her. "And who knows? You might have tired of him. Or you would have discovered he wasn't the man you believed he was."

"Please, Aileen, you have made your point. You believe, like so many others, that I am a spoiled, pampered brat who can't make up her own mind—"

"That is not what I said—"

"My only hope is that I don't become as cynical as you have."

The truth of Tara's accusation cut Aileen to the quick. "Cynical? I prefer defining myself as cautious and rational. You might be wise to develop those traits yourself, sister."

"I shall keep that in mind," Tara retorted as she began walking toward the house.

Aileen felt her temper sizzle. "Don't walk off from me as if you are dismissing a servant."

"I need something to eat besides bread," Tara said querulously.

Aileen huffed her frustration. So this was how it was going to be. Perhaps she shouldn't be so glad to have her sister home. And she wasn't about to let Tara behave in a miserable manner and expect everyone to fret over her. Aileen had a life of her own to live, and she would let her sister know.

But just as she started to charge after Tara, her sister came to a sudden halt as if frozen in place. She stared at the house, her jaw dropping. She turned to Aileen and squeaked out, *"Father."*

"What?"

Tara pointed toward the front drive, where the earl of Tay's coach and a team of travel-weary horses stood. It had arrived while they'd been arguing. Servants carried in luggage.

"He should still be in London," Tara said. "I left a note that I was with friends. He shouldn't have discovered I'd run away so quickly or even believed I'd come here."

"Apparently he is more clever than you gave him credit for," Aileen observed dryly.

"Could he be here for another reason?"

"No, I believe searching for a runaway daughter would be his only reason for driving to Scotland three days before your wedding."

"I don't want him to see me," Tara said as she started back for the stables. Aileen hooked her hand around Tara's arm and turned her around.

"You will have to face him sooner or later. Be bold," Aileen said. "He may bluster and rage, but there is little else he can do at this late date."

"He can force me to marriage."

"No, he can't. There is no way the two of you could travel fast enough to arrive in time for your wedding breakfast." The ceremony would have been an intimate, family affair, but the wedding breakfast served afterward had been rumored to be one of the choice invitations of the summer. Aileen had heard that even the Prince Regent was returning to town for the event. "When you decide to create an uproar, you do a very fine job of it."

"You may keep your opinions to yourself," Tara snapped, but she began moving toward the house. She had gone a few steps, Aileen at her heels—after all, she wasn't about to miss the dustup between the earl and Tara—when a man walked out of the house.

He was tall and broad-shouldered, with the sun shining off a head full of dark hair that would make any Corinthian proud. He moved with intent of purpose.

Aileen did not recognize him—but Tara did. She skidded to a halt, her eyes widening in shock.

The man didn't see them. He reached inside the coach for something he'd apparently left behind, made a comment to one of the footmen, and walked back into the house.

"Who is he?" Aileen asked.

A short, hysterical laugh escaped Tara, a sound of impending doom. "Who is he?" she repeated. "He's my intended. Mr. Blake Stephens."

Chapter Four

"Are you certain?" Aileen insisted. Why would Mr. Stephens make an appearance anywhere close to Annefield?

"Of course I'm certain," was the terse reply. Tara whirled to face Aileen. "I can't see him. I won't know what to say. Or are you going to prod me into being *bold* and confront a man who might very well wring my neck?"

Aileen stood a moment in indecision. When she woke this morning, nothing could have prepared her for the unusual circumstances of this day.

Yesterday her life had been predictable and, yes, boring.

Today she was being called upon to rescue a

sister whose friendship, in spite of their bickering, she had missed very much.

"I don't even know why Blake is here," Tara was complaining. "He should be furious with me."

"He should," Aileen thoughtfully agreed. "And perhaps he has come so that the earl can bully you into marriage, but I won't let that happen." She began walking toward the house, every step filling her with new purpose.

"Aileen, what are you about to do?" Tara called.

"Defend you," Aileen answered.

"Defend me?" came the incredulous response.

Aileen turned. Her sister hadn't taken a step to follow but stood alone, looking lost and fearful.

"Aye, defend you," Aileen said. "I am even going to *relish* the battle." A bitterness she'd kept tamped down so deep inside her that she'd almost forgotten it swelled forth. "The earl knew Geoff was not a suitable husband for any woman. *He knew,* Tara, and still he pushed me into marriage to Geoff because he wanted the money. He *sold* me, and he sold you. And then, when I went to him battered and beaten, an arm broken and bruises all over my body, the earl told me it was my problem, not his."

Tara's eyes widened. "I didn't know Geoff had done that to you."

"That and more," Aileen admitted bitterly. "But he couldn't break my spirit. After all, I am a Davidson, and I give thanks every day that I am free of the monster I married. It was a blessing to hear the French shot him."

"You don't truly mean that," Tara protested.

"I do," Aileen assured her. "No other woman will go through what I did. Furthermore, I am not about to let the earl bully you into a match you do not want. A woman should be able to choose her husband, or *un*-choose him if she so desires."

"What are you going to do?" Tara asked, uncertain.

"I'm going to tell the earl that you shall marry for love and no other reason. Yes, *that* is what I will say." Aileen started for the house.

"But you don't believe in love," Tara reminded her.

Aileen paused in her charge. "I do for my sister. You have the right to want what you want. Are you coming? Or shall I plead your case alone?"

Tara looked to the house in indecision. "Father will be angry. He won't understand."

"Aye, but he will manage." White-hot anger surged through Aileen. "In fact those are the very words he said years ago when I went to him over Geoff's bouts of temper. He told me 'to manage.' I shall enjoy returning the advice when he realizes that his youngest daughter will not be cowed as I was. He can no longer sell us to the highest bidder, and he will have to 'manage' to find funds from some other source. Or he can give up gaming," she said brightly. "There is a brilliant idea!" She leveled her gaze on Tara. "So are you joining me?"

Her sister drew breath and released it before saying, "I still don't want to see Mr. Stephens."

"You must. The man has obviously traveled here to see you, and the truth is, you do owe him an apology."

"What will I say?"

"You will say that you regret you have changed your mind and you cannot marry him."

"Do I mention Ruary?"

"I wouldn't, but you should inform Mr. Stephens," Aileen continued, warming to the idea, "that you have decided you will only marry for love. That will reinforce *my* position with our mutual sire." Oh, yes, she could not wait to deliver this blow to the earl. His creditors were probably breathing down his neck. They usually were. But the day had come for his daughters to say, *Enough*.

"We shall then see what this Mr. Stephens is made of," Aileen observed. "If he deeply cares for you, then he will protest his loving concern—"

Tara snorted her doubts.

"If he doesn't, then he should see that the two of you are not a match," Aileen finished. "After all, marriage is not easy. A woman loses so much. She must be clear-eyed."

"Yes, clear-eyed," Tara echoed. "And that is what I am. I love Ruary. I will not settle for anyone else. I'd rather be alone."

Aileen doubted her sister's resolve. Living alone was not easy. However, now was not the time to quibble. "Good. Then let us go tell *Father*." Since that day almost six years ago when a frightened Aileen had run to her parent for help and had been rebuffed, she'd not used that term of affection. And there was no respect in her voice when she used it now.

She started for the house. This time, Tara hurried to fall in step beside her. They walked together as sisters should. In spite of the distance of age and the passing of time, the bond between them was strong. Together they could battle dragons.

They entered the house.

"Where is the earl?" Aileen asked Ingold, who had been in a conversation with Mrs. Watson while servants dashed around to respond to their master's sudden arrival.

"His lordship is in the library with his *guest*."

Ingold emphasized the last word as if to warn the sisters what they would face. He was no fool. Aileen was certain he'd known from the moment Tara had arrived dressed as a lad that something was up.

"Thank you," Aileen murmured and set off for the library, located down the hall across from the family sitting room.

Tara's step started to slow, but Aileen took her hand. "You have done nothing wrong," she whispered.

"Just jilted my intended and masqueraded as a boy all over the countryside," Tara answered.

"Masquerading is not murder. Jilting is not mayhem," Aileen replied, wanting to put the issue in perspective. "A woman has a right to change her mind."

"Not if she is one of Father's daughters."

"Then we are starting a new tradition," Aileen answered. "Besides, if anyone should understand the capricious nature of women, it is a man who has had two wives and is renowned for the pursuit of women in all shapes and sizes." She rapped smartly on the library door.

"*Come in,*" was their father's gruff response.

Aileen had forgotten the sound of his voice. She'd put it out of her mind. Since Tara made no move to open the door, Aileen reached past her and turned the handle. She gave the door a small push and it slowly swung open.

Annefield's library was Aileen's favorite room, and she was accustomed to using it as her own. An ornately carved walnut desk dating back to the Reformation sat in front of the window so its occupant could take advantage of the light. Her great-grandfather Darius Davidson had been a great collector of books, and the shelves lining one whole wall were filled with tomes on botany, history and ancient classics.

Aileen had seen to the arrangement of furniture before the marble hearth—large, upholstered chairs with goose down pillows. Her own mother had picked them out. The best was a red and gold brocade with a deep seat and cushioned arms. Aileen had spent many an evening before a fire enjoying a good book in that chair, her feet resting upon a wooden footstool.

She'd added a table in the center of the grouping so she always had a place to set a tray or a glass of sherry, and she'd instructed the servants to always keep a vase of fresh flowers from the summer garden on the table. She liked this feminine touch to such a masculine room.

Mr. Stephens sat in Aileen's favorite chair.

From afar he had appeared tall.

Now he seemed almost gigantic; not only did his figure fill the chair but his presence commanded the entire room as well.

He did not rise for them, as would have been proper. Instead, he seemed to settle deeper into the chair, his long legs, encased in well-cut breeches and highly polished boots, stretched out in front of him. He held an empty glass in the hand of the arm resting over the side of the chair, and his hard jaw spoke louder than words that he wished to be anywhere but where he was right here, in this moment.

He was also one of the most intriguingly handsome men Aileen had ever laid eyes on.

She had assumed Blake Stephens would be good looking. His reputation as a marriage catch and Tara's interest in him had preordained that would be true.

But what Aileen had not anticipated, what she was not prepared for, was *her* reaction to Mr. Stephens.

She lived in a country known for brawny, masculine men. She'd come to expect broad shoulders and well-formed legs. They were everywhere.

What she hadn't expected was for Mr. Stephens to have these qualities *and more*. His face was interesting. His nose was slightly crooked, as if it had been broken, and there were laugh lines at the corners of his eyes and cynical ones around his mouth.

He also didn't strike Aileen as the sort who could be forced into anything he didn't want to do. He appeared full of pride, with an almost defiant sense of his own self-worth, and he seemed far from heartbroken.

Oh, no, he had the air of a tiger, an angry one.

Now she understood Tara's reluctance to confront him.

The earl stood by the liquor cabinet—of course.

He had apparently just finished a dram and was ready to pour himself another from one of the five decanters kept there along with glassware, always ready and waiting for the moment that he should deign to make an appearance at Annefield.

The earl of Tay had once cut an imposing figure. He was a rapier-thin man. From him, Aileen had received her height, and Tara could claim his coloring. His once flaming red hair had long ago vanished. It now resembled the color of a mouse pelt, and he combed it forward to hide his receding hairline.

He'd aged since Aileen had seen him last. His paunch was more pronounced, the lines of his face more self-satisfied. And yet, there was still an air of masculine vigor around him.

Tara had not moved since the door opened. Aileen gave her a wee nudge in the back. Her sister took a step forward.

Aileen nudged again.

Another step, and then another. They were fully in the room. Tara in front and Aileen standing staunchly behind her, ready, and so willing, to leap forward and protect her.

"So, you've decided to present yourself," their father said in his booming voice, ignoring Aileen and directing his sneering comment to Tara. He had a mild accent, an Anglicized one. Aileen had once tried to tone hers down as well. Now she happily embraced it, proud of its soft, musical lilt.

Tara stood silent, her expression tight. Aileen wished her sister was bolder, but she could forgive her. It was hard to face their father when he was angry. Displeasure always made him unpredictable.

Aileen felt herself bristle. She was ready for battle, but before she could speak, Tara turned to her intended.

"Hello, Mr. Stephens." She sounded very young, defenseless.

He didn't speak. If he had truly been a tiger, his tail would have twitched his response—and Aileen decided she did not like him.

In fact, this whole interview was a bad idea. Tara wasn't ready for confrontation yet, so Aileen took her arm. "Mr. Stephens is apparently suffering from a lack of manners. Come, Tara. Let us not linger here."

Mr. Stephens did not like that, not one bit. Outrage lit his eyes, and Aileen couldn't help but smile. If she'd learned one thing while she'd been married, it was how to tweak a man's nose.

But Tara shook her arm off. She took a step forward. "I owe you an apology, sir." Her voice trembled slightly, but it was filled with determination. "I'm sorry that I treated you with such disregard."

Mr. Stephens did not move. He sat still, too still. Aileen wanted him to say something, to respond to her sister's very pretty apology in the way a gentleman should, but that undercurrent of anger was all around him.

Their father spoke. "You did make a muddle of this wedding, Tara. And a sorry one it is. However, *I* have saved the day."

Tara turned to him. "Saved the day?"

The earl capped the whisky decanter and raised

his glass as if celebrating his cleverness. "There *will* be a wedding. I learned of your leaving in time to send word that the breakfast would be cancelled since you decided you wished a Highland wedding surrounded by family." He didn't wait for a response but plunged ahead, announcing, "And so we shall have the wedding here in Kenmore." He referred to the village a short distance away. "We will be right and proper, with the banns and all."

Tara frowned, as if she wasn't certain she understood. "We are still to marry?"

Their father walked up to her and placed his hand on her shoulder. "Aye. Stephens has agreed." His voice lowered as he said, "You are very lucky, daughter. Your rash actions have made matters very difficult. We are fortunate for Stephens's good humor. Another man would have shamed you, but he is forgiving."

Aileen slid a suspicious look at Mr. Stephens. His shoulders had stiffened with the earl's announcement. She wondered what the true reason was for his agreeing to this marriage.

"Consequently," the earl was saying with his air of pompous importance, "in London, they aren't discussing your reckless behavior and your ruin but how charming it is that a bride wishes to properly celebrate the sacrament of marriage. Of course, *I* went to considerable trouble to make these changes. You understand how difficult it was?"

Tara nodded.

Mr. Stephens studied the cold hearth. Aileen could not divine what he was thinking, but he did not act like a man anxious to marry.

And here it was—the hypocrisy. The same nonsense that had led to her disastrous marriage to Geoff and all the other foolish decisions she'd made after that event.

Someone had to speak the truth. Aileen appointed herself. *"This is rubbish."*

The earl pivoted on his heel, scowling his first acknowledgement of her presence since she'd entered the room. "Your opinion is not necessary."

"But Tara's is," Aileen coolly shot back, "and she does not want to marry Mr. Stephens. Look at what she has done to escape him, and then you *bring* him *to* her? Perhaps instead of plotting a way to save your face in society, you should be asking yourself why your daughter ran from her own wedding, especially at considerable danger to herself."

Mr. Stephens snapped his head round to glare at Aileen. *Brown*, she registered. His eyes were brown, and they burned with outrage.

Well, she, too, was angry. "You don't know what cruelties men are capable of," she informed the earl. "You have no idea what hell it is to live in a *loveless* marriage."

"Cruelties? Loveless?" the earl repeated. "A man can't be cruel to his wife. She's his. He owns her. And people of our class don't give a care about love. We marry for alliances." He took a sip of his whisky, saying, "It is the way things are done."

Aileen was tempted to hoot like a dairymaid over that comment. "The way things are done? Perhaps in the days when we warred against the Campbells and other clans, but those times are past. And there was never a need for an alliance with the English. We detested them. Oh, I beg pardon. Since you spend *all* of your time in London, you have probably forgotten your Scottish pride."

The whisky glass literally shook in the earl's hand. Aileen doubted if anyone had ever spoken to him in such a high-handed manner before, and she was proud of herself even as she prepared for the bite of his tongue.

However, his response was to give her his back. He focused on Tara, his voice fatherly, cajoling. "What if Mr. Stephens had bolted? And left *you* to stand humiliated in London?"

Tara bowed her head.

"Not a pleasant thought, is it?" the earl said. "But Stephens is here because I have explained to him that sometimes young women are not aware of what is in their best interest."

"Oh, you are clever," Aileen said. "You know exactly how to play on a daughter's guilt. For the first time I realize how neatly you manipulated me into marrying Geoff. How you said the right words to make me do your bidding."

The earl practically roared his rage. He whirled to face Aileen. "This is not about you and Geoff. I'm telling the girl she must do what she promised—"

"What *you* promised—" Aileen charged, taking a step toward him. "You are selling her into marriage. She'll not see a penny of the bride's price Mr. Stephens is paying—"

"This is not your concern."

"Of course it is. She is my sister."

The earl moved forward. "And my daughter to do with as I please."

Aileen doubled her fists. She wanted to punch

him. "She has her own mind. Her own will. You do not own her—"

"*I gave her life—*"

"I will marry Mr. Stephens." Tara's quiet words had the power to slice through the argument, severing it.

Both Aileen and her father turned in surprise.

Mr. Stephens didn't move. He didn't so much as blink an eye.

Aileen found her voice first. "No, you mustn't marry him." *What of love?* Aileen wanted to ask. *What of all you have done for another man?*

But before Aileen could give voice to her questions, Tara moved to stand before Mr. Stephens. "I have been dishonorable, sir." Her voice was stronger than it had been before, and it was now filled with resolve. "It is as my father said. The idea of marriage and all that it entailed is . . . *was*"—she paused as if overcome with maidenly modesty—"overwhelming. I should have discussed my fears with my father. But now that I am with my sister, they are in the past. And I am deeply grateful that you, Mr. Stephens, are willing to marry me. The idea of a Highland wedding pleases me very much." She released her breath and waited, as if she expected a response.

Mr. Stephens watched her with his dark eyes and said nothing. No hint of what he was thinking could be seen in even the tiniest detail of his expression.

Right then, Aileen understood why Tara should reject him. A man who kept such close counsel would drive her mad.

It seemed to annoy Tara as well. Her chin came up. "Well, Blake? Have you nothing to say? I've apologized. I was wrong. Foolish, even. But I wish to make amends."

"Yes, she does," the earl chimed, coming to his youngest's side. "She's a bit feather-brained, Stephens. You know how women are. But she is a tidy bit, no?"

Aileen felt her stomach lurch. "Why don't you show him Tara's teeth while you are auctioning her off?" she dared to say. "And don't forget her bloodlines. They always help sell a mare."

The earl raised his glass as if he would throw it at Aileen. "Do you *wish* her ruined? Are you so miserable that you relish company?"

His accusation stung. Was she meddling more than she should? And what were her honest motives?

Guilt, fear, and, yes, a touch of jealousy shot through Aileen. She did want what was best for

Tara, but the fact that Aileen could see the many pitfalls ahead did not give her the right to interfere. The only person who could stop this farce at this point was the silent, brooding Mr. Stephens.

The earl, too, wished to know what his guest thought. "Come, Stephens. Speak up. My daughter is *the* catch of the season. You are already the envy of every man in London. Don't make a muck of it."

Those last words seemed to rouse Mr. Stephens from his sullen contemplation.

"I came here to marry." His voice was deep, a touch raspy, distinctive. "Let us be done with the bloody business."

"That's charming," Aileen couldn't keep from saying, earning a growled warning from her parent.

But Tara was grateful. "Thank you, sir. We shall do well together. I promise we shall." The color had returned to her cheeks, and her smile was blinding.

The earl set down his glass and clapped his hands together, his good humor restored. "Splendid, splendid. Come, Tara, my girl. We need to tell Ingold and Mrs. Watson to expect guests for the wedding breakfast. Prinny won't be here. It will be a smaller affair than we would have had in London, but there are a hundred details you will need to see to for this to be right. Mind you, Penevey will attend. He assured me he would himself if I could make this marriage happen."

"The duke knows what happened?" Tara asked, concerned, as the earl took her arm and steered her to the door.

"How do you believe I convinced Stephens to come with me?" the earl answered as he walked her out of the library . . . leaving Aileen alone in the room with the tiger.

Chapter Five

Blake Stephens, the oldest of the duke of Penevey's four sons, albeit his only illegitimate one, seethed with fury.

His pride had made him a fool. A trapped one.

The moment Lady Tara had accepted his marriage offer, he'd known he'd made a mistake.

He didn't want to be married. He liked being a bachelor. He wallowed in his freedom. He had his mates, a group of the finest sportsmen in London, he had more money than he could imagine spending, and he'd had what mattered to him most—his father's respect, or so he had thought.

Penevey had wanted Blake to marry the Davidson chit. He'd advised Blake that it was time for him to be respectably settled and the marriage would be a good one for any children that might come of it.

Children had been the right argument for Blake. He planned to have them someday, and he didn't want them to suffer from the shame of his dubious parentage or the vicious teasing he had received in school. It had not been easy being Penevey's bastard. Blake had earned the respect of his peers, but he'd had to constantly prove himself. They had tested him hard. Meanwhile, his younger half brother Arthur, the duke's *legitimate* heir, was accepted everywhere in spite of being a horse's ass.

Too late did Blake learn that Penevey had pushed him to marry Lady Tara Davidson not for Blake's well-being but to keep Arthur away from her. Arthur had tumbled head over heels in love with the lovely Tara, and, yes, Blake had received great satisfaction when Tara had chosen him over Arthur . . . but that was before he'd realized Penevey had paid the earl of Tay to accept Blake's suit. Penevey had played upon Blake's jealousy of his half brother to remove the threat of Tara from his heir. He had not wanted Arthur associated with a Scottish nobody, no matter how beautiful.

But his bastard was a different story. . . .

And then Tara had decamped.

If London knew she had jilted him, Blake would be a laughingstock. He did not like gossip, especially directed at him. He'd fought hard for everything he had, and on a whim, Lady Tara had been willing to humiliate him. He was already furious that Penevey knew she'd run and had given him strict orders to make it right. Penevey did not want to take the risk that Arthur would be the one to chase after her. No, she was only good enough for his bastard.

Bitterness set heavy in Blake's gut.

And it did not help that Tara Davidson had just left the room without so much as a backward glance at him. She really did believe that a few pretty tears and a pretense of contriteness was all that was necessary as an apology.

She was going to make his life hell.

And he was stuck.

At least her sister had enough sense to know he was angry. She eyed him warily.

He eyed *her* with interest.

Blake had not met the notorious Lady Aileen before. He'd heard about her. The Crim Con case investigating her adultery had been the talk of London during a slow and lazy summer. Her husband, Captain Geoffrey Hamilton, had not held back in painting his wife as some lascivious Jezebel. Peter Pollard, her lover and one of Hamilton's fellow officers, had not made any appearance to defend either himself or her. Since Hamilton's father had held a Ministry position and Geoff was considered a war hero, the divorce had been speedily approved. It had not helped her reputation that within six months of the divorce, both men had died in battle.

Now, face-to-face with the woman who had launched a thousand wagging tongues, Blake could see what Hamilton and Pollard had admired. Before, he'd been hard-pressed to understand why such a profligate womanizer as Hamilton would begrudge his lady *one* lover, but here was a woman any man would jealously guard.

To the conventional, she wouldn't be deemed half as pretty as Tara. Although her hair was thick and shining, it was brown with just a touch of gold but not striking enough to raise comment. Her mouth was too wide, too generous for beauty. Her eyes were not as blue as her celebrated sister's, and she would have been dismissed as too tall by the people who chronicle such things. Height didn't bother Blake, provided the curves were there. He was a tall man, and he liked a woman willing to look him in the eye.

Of course that didn't have anything to do with one's height as much as it did one's intellect, and Lady Aileen struck him as possessing a keen mind, a trait Blake valued. He also liked the energy that swirled around her.

Of course, she'd just energetically used her intelligence to argue for her sister to unceremoniously reject him. That was a strike against her.

Of course, she, too, had been left behind.

She stared at the empty doorway as if puzzled at how quickly the tables had turned on her. Her shoulders lowered, giving her the air of being graceful in defeat—until she swung her attention to him and the lines of her mouth tightened.

For a long second they took each other's measure, then she said with a tartness her lilting accent could not sweeten, "Well, are you happy? You will have a wife. It's not right, you know. One shouldn't be 'forced' to marry."

"I knew your husband."

His intent was to surprise her, and he succeeded. Her manner changed. She reacted as if the air had been sucked out of the room.

"Relax," he said. "If I'd been married to Geoff

Hamilton, I would have done anything I could to free myself of him." He rose from the chair, his empty glass still in his hand. For a second he had to stretch his muscles. "That was a punishing coach ride. I don't like being tucked into small spaces."

"Especially with a man like my father."

Blake shot her a glance. The earl of Tay was known for his rambling monologues and prodigious drinking. What most people didn't know, and Blake now did, was that the earl had a whole array of disgusting personal habits, from flatulence to picking at body parts. Blake never wanted to be that close to the man ever again.

"It was not a pleasant trip," he commented.

"But you achieved what you wished. You have a bride."

That was, unfortunately, true. . . .

"How did you know my husband?" Lady Aileen asked, her manner defensive.

"I was in school with him. We did not like each other. He was a scoundrel, a liar and a cheat."

"He was." The words hung in the air between them.

Usually, women were eager to babble their business. He'd thought them all magpies. But Lady Aileen was tense, her lips pressed in such a way that he knew she was determined to say no more. She expected him to think the worst of her. After having been the target of gossips for most of his life, Blake understood.

He changed the subject. "So you believe in love," he said, walking over to the liquor cabinet to place his empty glass upon it.

"Certainly," she replied a touch too briskly. "Don't you?"

"Oh, certainly," he answered, echoing her breezy tone and letting her know he saw through her. "After all, I am here, aren't I?"

"Very well . . . I *don't* believe in love." She raised her arms as if asking him what he wanted to do about it. "But my sister does, and I'm certain you have little feeling for her."

"Why would you say that?" Blake asked, curious to know her impression of him.

"It was very obvious," she said. "You barely looked at her a moment ago, and you don't act like a wounded swain. When you didn't rise when my sister and I entered the room, I thought it was poor manners born out of a sense of arrogance. And I'm not going to say you aren't arrogant—but . . . ," she said thoughtfully, "I don't think you are afraid to let her jilt you."

"Afraid? No, but my pride is all I have that is

truly my own. I have no desire to be known as the man Tara Davidson refused to marry, not without a hand in my own destiny."

"Oh, you will have a hand in your destiny, sir. You'll have a miserable hand, one that will make you rue the day you agreed to this marriage."

He already did wish he wasn't promised to marry, but no good would come from admitting it to the sister.

"I also know that Tara will make you a beautiful and dutiful wife. You will be the envy of your peers, and your children will be precious replicas of the two of you—"

"You sound resentful," he observed.

"*Although,*" she continued, ignoring his statement but exerting the authority of her opinion, "the two of you will live separate lives. That is completely to be expected, since it is so *common.* But it makes me sad to contemplate the possibility. While I am not acquainted with you, I do know there is more to my sister than meets the eye. She deserves better than a cold marriage."

Her blunt assessment stung. "Says the woman who is divorced."

Her chin lifted a notch. "Yes, I am divorced and at peace with it. Trust me, I am not comparing my marriage to yours."

"That is comforting," he murmured.

"Because if I did," she went on, her smile growing steely, "I would have a pistol in my hand and not allow you a step closer to Tara."

"I shall consider that a warning," he answered.

"It's a promise. But if I were you, I would be afraid to give up my life to another. 'Till death do we part' can be a very long time."

"Not if we have separate lives," he reminded her.

She gave him an assessing look. "Is that what you really want? A life spent avoiding your wife, of pretending all is good?"

"So I take it that you plan on marrying again?" he challenged, baiting her, wanting to know what she would do.

A sad smile crossed her face. "You said you knew my husband. Perhaps you did not know him as well as you thought or you wouldn't have asked such a question." She walked to the door. "We eat early in the country, Mr. Stephens. Dinner will be in two hours. I pray you make yourself comfortable. If you need anything, you have only to ask a servant." On those words, she left the room.

And with her went that strong sense of presence, of vitality.

Aileen Davidson Hamilton was a force of nature. And perhaps one of the most interesting women he'd ever met. She didn't hesitate to speak her mind. Nor was she coy or flirtatious in the way one would imagine a woman rumored to be promiscuous would be. He found her directness and her loyalty refreshing.

He walked to the door. The hallway was already empty. She'd disappeared somewhere in the house. He leaned against the door frame and wondered what he would do, what he *could* do, to honorably escape a marriage to Tara.

Because she was right—he would not be able to stand the married life she had described.

His mother had been the most manipulative woman he'd ever known. And his early years of being raised in her room at Madame Lavatt's whorehouse had taught him that any woman could give a kiss as quickly as a slap. They were mercurial, difficult, grasping and greedy.

They were also a necessary evil for any sexually vigorous man, and Blake was that . . . although he was wise in his choice of partners. Discreet. He valued quality over quantity.

He also knew himself well.

If Tara had not been *the* loveliest woman in

London, if everyone had not wanted her, especially Arthur, he wouldn't have courted her no matter how hard Penevey had pressed. There had been a challenge in winning the woman they had all wanted. However, when he'd paid calls on Tara, there had been times when fifteen minutes had seemed like fifteen hours. She bored him.

But he had a feeling he would find Lady Aileen anything but boring.

It was said that a wise man stayed away from a clever woman. Blake had always wondered what the saying meant. He'd known women who were witty and humorous . . . but he'd never met one he'd consider "clever" in a dangerous sense.

He believed he'd just met one.

I had not heard that Lady Tara was planning to return to Annefield," Jane Sawyer said.

She and Ruary were riding on the tree-lined road to Aberfeldy. At least once a week, she managed to steal away from her father's watchful eye and catch Ruary at whatever stable he was working at that day. She valued these rides. She liked being near him, and not just because she adored looking at him. He was a handsome man. But there was also something about his presence that filled a need deep within her. Something she'd not felt with any other man before.

If that wasn't love, then she didn't know what was.

But this was the first time she'd been with him and sensed that his thoughts were far away from her . . . and perhaps on Tara Davidson?

Ruary gave a small start at her mention of Lady Tara. A dull red rose up his neck. "I don't believe anyone was expecting her."

"Isn't she supposed to be married sometime soon?" Jane knew the answer. The whole countryside knew. It was all anyone could talk of since they'd first heard the news a month ago.

"I don't know what she is supposed to be doing or not doing," Ruary answered, a note of annoyance in his voice. "I work for the earl of Tay. I don't keep track of his daughters."

He kicked his horse into a trot. The action itself was a signal that in his mind the discussion was over, and that was very unlike him. Ruary was known for his patience. Even the annoyance in his voice was not his usual manner.

Jane had to wonder why.

Ruary trotted a good ways up the road before he realized she was not beside him. She was surprised at the distance he'd traveled; in the past, he would have noticed her absence immediately. She halted her horse.

He reined in his horse and frowned before walking back to her. "Is there a problem?"

For a long moment, she studied this man she loved so dearly. Her heart always gave a little skipping beat whenever she saw him, just as it had that first time they'd met when he'd come to talk to her father about training the very mare she was riding.

That he had chosen her for his wife filled her with pride . . . and also a sense that perhaps he wasn't aware of how plain and ordinary she was. On market day, women would stop and stare when they saw him, and there would be admiring whispers and giggling, even when Jane was standing right there by his side. It was very clear they didn't think Jane was worthy of such a fine-looking man, a fear she equally harbored.

"Jane, I'm already late for Laird Breccan. I told him I would see him before afternoon."

"I know."

Something in those two simple words seemed to give him pause. "Are you all right? You are very quiet."

Jane started to speak, then realized she didn't

know what she wanted to say. The words roiling in her mind came from her worst fears, her doubts.

And when she did answer him, she was startled to hear herself say, "I love you."

She had not said these words to him. She'd felt he should speak them first. Even when he had asked for her hand, he had not mentioned love. Instead, he'd said he'd come to "greatly admire" her.

Then there was the day he said she gave him peace . . . but, of course, that was before Lady Tara had returned.

Her declaration hovered in the air between them.

He spoke. "I appreciate you as well, Jane. That is why we are going to marry."

Had such a statement been enough before?

It was not now.

"Did you not hear me, Ruary? I didn't say I 'appreciate' you. I said, I *love* you. I can't wait to be your wife."

"Jane, I can't wait to marry you either," he answered, but something was missing in his tone.

Something had *always* been missing, and she'd not noticed its lack until this moment.

"Lady Tara isn't going to marry, is she?" Jane guessed.

Ruary had the good grace to appear startled. "I don't know, Jane. I don't know."

His repetition of the phrase gave him away.

He *did* know.

And she realized she had a choice to make. She could pretend as if all was well.

Or she could confront the niggling doubts that had started to assail her the moment Lady Tara had come out of the dark grain room, where she'd obviously been with Ruary.

"I don't mean to annoy you," she said.

"You *aren't* annoying me. I just—" he started and then stopped. Releasing a breath of feigned exasperation, he said, "I sense you are accusing me of something, and I don't know of what."

"I'm not accusing you of anything." She had trouble meeting his eye. "It's just that you have become my life," she said, studying the well-worn leather of her gloves holding the reins. "I care so deeply for you that I can sense your moods, and I believe there is something *strained* between us right now."

"What is strained is your sudden, odd behavior. Are you unhappy? Is that what you are trying to say?"

"No, of course not," Jane answered, caught by

how quickly the focus of this conversation had turned to her. "I want *you* to be happy—"

"I am happy. *I am.*"

There was that repetition again, and that is when Jane *knew* that his feelings toward her were changing. Her mother had told her that when a woman loves a man, she can sense what he cannot say.

Ruary and Lady Tara, together, was not innocent.

"Are you satisfied?" he asked her, leaning over to lift her chin so that she had to look at him.

A deep weight pressed against her chest, making breathing difficult. "I just want you to be certain," she murmured.

"The time for being certain was before I went to your father. The banns have been announced once, and they will be announced again this Sunday. You will be my wife, Jane—" He broke off, studied her a second and then said, "Unless *you* have doubts?"

"I have no doubts at all," she rushed to tell him, and she prayed that was true.

"Good," he said, and, for a moment, she expected him to kiss her. She wanted him to.

Ruary rarely gave into passion. He respected her that way. He was always circumspect, and this was public road.

Still, she hoped, and was once again disappointed when he dropped his hand and leaned back in his saddle. "Perhaps I shall see you on the morrow?"

"Of course," Jane answered, picking up her reins and trying to not let her discontent show.

He gifted her with a smile that melted her heart, then rode away with a wave of his hand. Jane watched him before turning in the direction of her home.

And knew all her suspicions were correct.

Chapter Six

Aileen was now more convinced than ever that Tara would be making the gravest mistake of her life if she married Mr. Stephens.

He didn't care for Tara, just as Geoff had not cared for her. If it was within her power to stop this marriage, she would.

And how dare he challenge her? He thought he was so quick, but she saw through him. He didn't value Tara, not in the way she should be cherished.

Right now, Tara was emotional, afraid. This talk about love had confused her. That is why she needed Aileen's support. The brain was a far better barometer of the future than something as fickle as a heart.

Filled with a new determination, Aileen set off to find Tara. She assumed her sister was with their father. However, an inquiry of Ingold revealed the earl was in the kitchen. He did not know where Lady Tara was.

Assuming Tara had to be with the earl, Aileen marched down the stairs to the kitchen. Fortunately, she had the good sense to wait on the stairs a moment before charging into the room. Listening carefully, she realized that the earl was in the process of eating Cook's pork pies by the handful and washing them down with copious amounts of cider. Cook was giggling with glee over his effusive praise of her "good Scottish cooking" while she assured him they were all pleased to have him home.

"So much for planning a wedding," Aileen muttered under her breath, quietly backing up the stairs. She continued her search.

But Tara was nowhere to be found. Aileen even walked to the stables.

And Aileen began to worry.

Her sister was not acting herself—first running away, then changing her mind this way and that about the marriage. Who knew what she was about now?

Eventually, Aileen looked where she should

have started—Tara's bedroom. Her sister was there. Through the closed door, Aileen heard her crying, low, muffled sobs, as if her heart was breaking.

Aileen knocked.

The crying stopped.

"Tara, please, we must talk."

There was no answer.

Aileen leaned toward the door. "Please, Tara, let me in. I can help." She *wanted* to help.

She waited, expecting the door to open.

It didn't, nor did Tara say a word . . . and Aileen felt slighted. Her goal wasn't to make Tara feel worse. They were sisters, and she had Tara's best interests in her heart—

A door *did* open, but not the one she had anticipated.

No, the door that opened was to Mr. Stephens's room only two doors down the hall, and the man himself poked his head out. He had removed his coat and waist coat, and his neck cloth was undone.

Aileen was a bit startled to see him that way, as well as embarrassed to think he might have overheard her pleading.

"Is something the matter?" he asked.

"No, nothing," Aileen said, a trifle too quickly. "I have a message for my sister."

"Warning her away from me?" he suggested.

"Of course not," she lied.

At that moment, Tara blew her nose in the most unbecoming manner. Not even Annefield's strong doors or thick walls could hide the sound. She'd never been an attractive crier. Even when she was a child, the whole household always knew when she was distressed. She chased her nose blowing with hiccupping sobs.

Mr. Stephens's brows rose to his hairline even as he tried to stifle a laugh.

A dimple. He had a deep one in his left cheek. Its appearance surprised Aileen, because, well, she didn't want to notice charming little quirks about him. She wanted him gone, out of their lives.

And he knew it, just as he believed there was nothing she could do about his presence. He nodded toward Tara's door. "Is she reacting to your warning? Or had you warned her yet?"

Hundreds of years of Scottish pride surged through Aileen's soul. "Are you mocking us, Mr. Stephens?"

He shook his head at the stiffness in her tone, as

if he found it amusing. "Why would I ever think of mocking you, Lady Aileen?"

"For the same reason you feel it is safe to challenge me, but I warn you, sir. I will not be patronized."

"I shall remember that fact, my lady," he promised, turning as the door leading to the back stairway opened. A man of slight build and a meticulous air entered the hall. Several garments were draped over his arm, and there was no doubting he was Mr. Stephens's valet. He glanced at her, then went about his business, entering the room.

"Until dinner, Lady Aileen," Mr. Stephens said. He followed his man, shutting the door behind him.

"He didn't offer a bow or a nod of his head or an 'I beg your pardon,'" Aileen muttered to herself. "The man is as high-handed as a duke . . . or a bastard."

Her conclusion was punctuated by another bout of Tara's heartbroken snuffles.

"You will make yourself sick if you keep this up," Aileen warned her through the door.

The answer was more boo-hooing, and Aileen felt drained.

Even if she could gain admittance, Tara was

in no condition to listen to her. Indeed, Tara was probably done for the night. She would take a tray in her room, and Aileen would be forced to suffer through an evening with her obnoxious sire and a houseguest too full of himself.

For a second, she debated asking for a dinner tray herself, but she knew that Mr. Stephens would believe she was avoiding him. He seemed to take a mildly perverse pleasure in goading her. So far, she had held her own, but she'd only known him less than two hours. Undoubtedly he would grow more insufferable with longer acquaintance. Men with an overabundance of confidence usually did . . . but her pride would not let her cry quarter.

She went to her room.

It had been ages since Aileen had "dressed" for dinner. With just herself in the house, she'd had little use for formalities. She wondered where Ellen, the upstairs maid, was. The girl usually checked with Aileen each evening before she left. Tonight was the first time Aileen could truly use help.

She went to her wardrobe and chose a gown of pale peach muslin she hadn't worn since the days of her marriage. The gown was trimmed in a dark green ribbon that contrasted nicely with the dress and her coloring. It took a few more minutes to find the finely woven stockings she used to wear in London.

In London. Those days seemed so long ago. She had told herself that she had not missed the city, and she hadn't . . . until now. Yes, her heart was in Scotland, but she also relished life in town. She'd forgotten how much.

Aileen set to dressing, taking more care than was her custom. There was a certain reverence in dressing properly. But she was also honest enough to admit she did not want Mr. Stephens to consider her dowdy. After all, family pride was at stake.

She was dressed and massaging lotion into hands roughened by gardening when a knock sounded on the door.

"Come in," Aileen called, hoping it would be Tara.

Instead, Ellen entered.

"I'm sorry I'm so late, my lady," the maid said. She was of Aileen's age, with pale blonde hair she kept neatly hidden in a mobcap.

"That is fine. There have been so many unexpected changes today."

"Very true, my lady. Is there anything you need of me?"

"Please help me with my hair," Aileen instructed, sitting down before the mirror at her dressing table. "It's been so long since I've done anything but knot it at the nape of my neck, I've forgotten where to put the pins or even if I own them."

"You own them, my lady," Ellen assured her. She took a box of hair fripperies from a draw in the dressing table and set to work. However, after a few minutes of Ellen combing and tugging at her hair, Aileen began to lose patience.

"Don't fuss overmuch," Aileen told Ellen. "It is almost the dinner hour, and I need to see to the details. Plus, I should check on my sister before I go downstairs."

Ellen paused, holding a twisted strand of Aileen's hair in her hand. "Lady Tara has already gone downstairs for dinner. I came to you as soon as I'd finished with her."

"She's gone down to dinner?" Aileen repeated dumbly.

"Aye, my lady. She had me help her dress."

"But . . . she was very upset," Aileen protested, trying to reason the matter out. "She was overwrought."

Ellen thought a moment and said, "She appeared well to me. Well, her eyes were a bit swollen, but you know how it is when you are young.

What would linger on our faces disappears from theirs. She told me she wished to please her intended. She wanted to make him feel as if he was marrying the loveliest girl in the valley, and she was a fetching sight when I finished with her, although that isn't difficult to achieve when one has Lady Tara's looks."

"No, it isn't," Aileen said, distracted. Her sister was surprising her. She was far more resilient than Aileen credited her for. She also acted as if what Aileen thought was of no consequence— well, unless she was in trouble.

And she was already downstairs.

For some reason that Aileen could not quite define, that last thought annoyed her most.

"Thank you, Ellen. I've decided I don't want much done with my hair after all."

"Let me gather it up on top of your head and give it a bit of style the way Lady Tara instructed me," Ellen said eagerly. "She said the fashion is all the rage in London."

"And I especially don't wish that," Aileen answered, waving the maid away and twisting her hair herself into a quick knot at the nape of her neck. She stuck three pins in it and announced, "It shall be fine." She was uncertain if she was speaking to the maid or to buoy her own spirits.

She rose from the table, forced a smile for Ellen's benefit, and left the room.

There was no mistaking the matter, Aileen thought as she went downstairs: Tara was avoiding her—and it hurt. They were sisters, yet how well did they truly know each other anymore? The bond was there, but was it strong or a mere thread of memories past?

As Aileen reached the bottom step, she once again had that sense that life was happening somewhere else, to someone else. There had been a time when she'd come down these steps and her family had been waiting for her.

Now they were gathered in the front receiving room, and by the conversation about pork pies and racehorses, no one had noticed she was missing.

Aileen walked to the doorway.

This room was usually the first to greet visitors to Annefield. It was decorated in cream and greens. Portraits of Davidson ancestors looked down from their places on the wall. A pianoforte took up one corner of the room, and the seating was designed for comfort, but with a stately elegance.

The earl, dressed as if for dining at his London club, was pouring a glass of whisky at the table set up for such things. Because of the cool night air, a small fire burned in the hearth. Mr. Stephens, his attire more fitting for a country evening, with tall boots and an excellently tailored green wool coat, stood in front of it. At his elbow was Tara.

She looked especially lovely this evening in a gown of blue gauze the delicate color of a robin's egg, and a finely woven shawl over her shoulder. She'd had her shining curls styled high on her head so that they fell artlessly down to her shoulders. She looked young, fresh and vibrant.

And there wasn't one sign of her earlier tears in the way she smiled adoringly up at her betrothed.

Aileen suddenly felt very provincial. Dowdy, even . . . and wished she had let Ellen play with her hair.

Tara saw her first. "Here's my sister. I am so glad you are here, Aileen. I'm famished, and Cook has promised to serve venison. That's your favorite dish, isn't it, Mr. Stephens? I requested it for that reason."

There was a breathlessness to her voice, a forced eagerness. It was the sound of a woman pleasing a man, and it tugged at Aileen's heart. Women should not feel as if they had to pretend. That was one of the lessons she'd learned from the horror of her marriage.

No pretense, not for her, not anymore.

A step behind her warned her that Ingold approached. She turned as he formally announced, "The dinner is served."

This simple formality annoyed Aileen. Even when *she* had guests, Ingold did not "announce" dinner. They were simple Scottish folk, and Mr. Stephens was a bastard. He might act like the duke himself, but he wasn't. He did not need dinner "announced."

She took charge of the room. If they were going to be staid, then she would be the staidest. "Shall we proceed to the dining room?" she drawled out in London formality.

Tara slid her arm into the crook of Mr. Stephens's. "This way, sir," she said, her voice cajoling, tempting. "You will escort me, won't you?"

Aileen wanted to roll her eyes. Of course he would. There were only four of them in the room.

What happened to women when they were around men? Why did they think men couldn't see through such pandering? And why wasn't that true? She'd played the game herself, and she'd not met one man who hadn't wished to be flattered—

"Daughter?" the earl said, interrupting her ranting thoughts.

Aileen tore her attention from the ninnyhammer her sister had become to see her father offering his arm. "Since we are being formal?" he said. He had added his own fawning drawl, aping the tone she had used.

She placed her hand on his arm. "She shouldn't work so hard to try and impress him."

"Hard?" her father echoed.

"Yes, having Ingold announce dinner and the like."

"I'm the one who insisted upon that. You've been languishing in Scotland for so long, you've forgotten fine manners. Or what is expected of a lady dressing for dinner. Your hair is a mess."

She wanted to retort that his breath smelled of pork pies. "I didn't have a choice about 'languishing in Scotland,' Father," she said tightly. "You banished me here, remember?"

"I sent you *home*."

She shrugged away his denial and released his arm to walk into the dining room on her own.

The dining room walls were a soft gold so that the carved marble fireplace stood out. The smell of well-prepared food scented the air. The table had belonged to Aileen's mother. The dishes and silverware had been part of the dowry she'd brought to her marriage to the earl of Tay.

When Aileen was first married, she had been resentful that her father would not let her have these things. Now she was thankful. Geoff would have kept them in the divorce.

The leaves had been left out of the table so that it seated four cozily. The earl took his place and instructed Mr. Stephens to sit opposite him. Ingold saw to the earl's chair while Simon, who served as stable lad, kitchen boy, or footman as the occasion warranted, pulled out Aileen's chair. Mr. Stephens gallantly seated Tara himself.

Tara dominated the conversation during dinner. She flirted outrageously, or so it seemed to Aileen. Granted they hadn't spent any time together for three years, but this false laugh, this coy tilt of the head, this silly banter could not be Tara.

And Aileen wanted to say as much. She tried to keep her attention on her food, to ignore what was happening. *It was not her business*—even if it did fill her with foreboding. She'd been this foolish once. She'd gone after Geoff. She'd wanted him desperately, and when he'd asked for her hand, she'd been as proud as any hunter who had bagged a rabbit.

Of course that was before she'd learned Geoff's parents and her father had arranged the whole matter. All she'd had to do was act insipid and obey instructions like a lamb to the slaughter.

For his part, the earl kept signaling for his wineglass to be refilled. The candlelight reflected on the sheen of his face. There was pallor to him, and, for the first time since his arrival, Aileen noticed he was looking a bit unkempt. He had not changed his neck cloth, and it was stained from the pork pies, or perhaps some other eating adventure.

Meanwhile, Mr. Stephens was the epitome of the discreet guest. He answered Tara when necessary, referred a few remarks toward Aileen, and deferred to the earl in the most flattering way possible.

Aileen found him completely intolerable.

The meal finally ended with the earl suggesting, "Why don't my daughters retire to the sitting room while Stephens and I enjoy our port?"

"Excellent idea," Aileen said, jumping to her feet, anxious to end this interminable meal.

Her sister held her seat. "Can't we stay?"

Through groggy eyes, the earl looked at her as if she was daft for making the suggestion.

"Very well," Tara said with a little pout of her lips. "Don't linger long." She placed her folded napkin beside her plate and gracefully rose.

"We'll be in the sitting room with sweetmeats to settle our dinner." There was a definite purr to her tone on the word *"sweetmeats."* "Hurry to join us."

"I shall," Mr. Stephens answered, an equal warmth in his voice, and Aileen squelched a strong desire to scream.

Instead, she led the way out of the room. At last she had her chance to speak to Tara. Simon closed the dining room doors behind them.

However, before they reached the privacy of the sitting room, Tara confronted her. *"Don't* lecture," she said, a warning finger raised at Aileen. "Don't say one word."

Startled by the attack, Aileen said, "What makes you believe I wish to lecture you?"

Tara made an impatient sound and walked into the sitting room, where candles and a lamp had already been lit for them. The furniture was more worn and designed for comfort, for a family to gather and relax. In one corner was a small table with two chairs and a chess game already in play.

"Your thoughts can be plainly read on your face," Tara said. "You are so grim, so stiff-necked."

"I have good posture," Aileen said, guilty as charged.

Her sister waved her words away. "I know you feel this marriage is wrong—"

"You love another man, enough to run away from this one—"

"*Would you keep your voice down?*" Tara demanded in a furious whisper. "And my feelings for Ruary no longer matter, because he is marrying someone else. I've accepted I must face a different future. It's been hard—"

"You have been sobbing your eyes out—"

"And I will again. I know it is my fault I lost him. I should mourn. What I don't understand is *your* change of heart. When I first arrived, you were scandalized I'd run away."

"That is because I did not know the full story."

Tara made an impatient sound. "It is not your life, Aileen. It is mine."

"And you seem intent on making a muddle of it."

Tara opened her mouth to retort, but a footstep in the hall warned them that someone was coming. A moment later, Mrs. Watson entered the room carrying a tray with cake, nuts, cheese and sherry.

If she'd heard any of the argument between the sisters, she didn't let on, but then the housekeeper was a sly one. She knew secrets about the family that Aileen could only imagine.

"Will there be anything else?" Mrs. Watson asked.

"That is all," Aileen and Tara both started to answer and then exchanged glances. Here, too, was another battle brewing between them, one for authority of the house.

Mrs. Watson gave a small curtsey and left.

There was a moment of silence, then Tara said, "I'm accustomed to being the hostess for Father. That is the way it was in London."

"Well, I plan the menus here," Aileen answered, needing to exert her authority.

Tara sat on the settee and poured sherry. "I shall remember that the next time I make a request for a *guest*," she murmured, using Mr. Stephens as her excuse to tromp on Aileen's role at Annefield.

"Perhaps we should discuss the matter with Father?" Aileen dared her, albeit certain the earl would rule in favor of Tara.

Tara flounced back against the settee, holding her sherry. "No, Aileen, don't. And I don't want bad blood between us. I won't be here that long. Mr. Stephens will take me back to London as soon as we are married." She pushed a loose curl back in place. "I can't wait."

And she would leave, very soon, Aileen realized. Life would always take them in opposite directions. She sat in the chair opposite Tara. "I don't mean to lecture."

Tara frowned at some point in the far corner.

"I just fear for you," Aileen confessed.

"You needn't. Blake is not Geoff."

"I know that . . . but marriage is hard."

"For some," Tara said, bringing her full attention back to Aileen. She ran her free hand over the textured brocade of the settee cushion. "I know what is expected of me. You needn't worry."

"But I shall."

"Only because you choose to do so. Aileen, we are sisters, but you are not responsible for me. Not any longer. You haven't been for years."

"There is still a connection between us. There always will be."

Before Tara could comment, a sound of shuffling feet and the grunts and groaning of their father came from the hall. He sounded like a bawling calf.

Both women hurried to the door in time to see the earl being carried by Ingold and Simon up the stairs. Mr. Stephens stood by the dining room door. He was wiping his hands with a napkin, as if he had helped with the earl.

Aileen looked to him in askance. "The port did him in," Mr. Stephens said diplomatically to her unspoken question.

Bodily suspended between Ingold and Simon, the earl roused himself enough to slur, "Aileen, I've decided we are going to treat Stephens to a hunt. I need it organized."

"Pheasant? Deer?" she asked, needing direction.

"*Fox*," her sire said grandly. "Stephens likes being out with the horses. And what better way for us to introduce him to the locals than a hunt. Plan it all, plan it all. Highland wedding and all," he babbled before being carried to the top of the stairs and around the corner.

"Pheasant and deer would be fine," Mr. Stephens said quietly. "Anything, truly."

"Good," Aileen answered, more concerned for her parent than hunting.

"He had a seizure," Mr. Stephens explained. "It was momentary, but not a good thing to happen."

"Seizure?" Tara asked.

"Yes, he started shaking and then seemed to lose consciousness for the briefest moment."

Aileen nodded numbly. The eating, the gambling, the drinking . . . the earl's behavior was not wise. She told herself her alarm wasn't because she cared for the earl. She wanted to think her motive selfish; after all, if something happened to him, what would happen to her?

His heir was her uncle, her cousin Sabrina's father. As kind as Sabrina was, he was the opposite. Since the scandal of the divorce, he was one of those in the valley who refused to speak to her.

Then again, the way her father was going, there would be nothing left of the estate to inherit.

Mr. Stephens walked past her into the sitting room. Tara stood to one side of the door, her head bowed and her thoughts her own.

"Thank you for seeing to Father's welfare," Aileen said.

"Not a problem." Mr. Stephens had wandered over to the chessboard. He studied the board a moment, then asked, "Whose game is this?"

But before Aileen could answer, Tara roused herself from her contemplation to say, "I believe I am for my bed as well. It has been an exhausting day." Without so much as a by-your-leave to Aileen or Mr. Stephens, *the man she vowed she wanted*, she muttered, "Good night," and was gone.

And Aileen was left with their guest.

"I imagine with your travel from London you are fatigued as well," she said.

He looked up from the chessboard with a distracted air. "Ah, yes, well, of course . . . except this game is almost a draw. At least it was until I threatened the queen."

"You moved a piece?" Aileen's attention had been on Tara's leaving and not on him.

"It seemed sensible."

Aileen felt annoyed. "That is not your game, and moving a player without permission is rude."

"Ah, rude," he repeated offhandedly. "You have accused me of that already once today. Or has it been twice?"

"I've not spoken those words," Aileen countered.

"You don't need to, my lady. Every thought that crosses your mind can be read plainly on your face, especially when you are annoyed."

"I have not been annoyed," she retorted, disconcerted by the accuracy of his accusations.

"Irritated then," he amended, his attention already returning to the study of her chess game, his hand moving toward a piece.

Seeing what he intended, Aileen rushed forward. "If you take the queen, you place the black king in jeopardy."

"Your game?"

"Yes, on both sides."

"You are playing yourself," he said with a touch of respect. "No wonder the board appeared evenly matched. Well, it isn't any longer. If I follow your thinking, I move this bishop—"

"Unnecessarily risking him," she pointed out.

"He is worth the risk," Mr. Stephens said and moved the black player.

"And I take him with a lowly pawn," she answered in triumph, claiming his piece.

"He's not a loss. I'm not fond of church members," he said as he moved his rook.

She smiled, she had anticipated this move—

No, she hadn't.

Aileen stared at the board, frowning. She started to move a piece and couldn't.

"Check . . . and mate," Mr. Stephens said in a low, satisfied voice.

Aileen frowned. "I've studied this board for hours. That move was not there." He had to have moved some of the pieces when she hadn't noticed.

Then again, all looked as she had left it.

"Playing one's self is never a challenge," he observed.

"And you know this because . . ."

"It makes sense. But also," he continued, resetting the board, "I've done it often enough." He looked up at her, and she realized that in her surprise over losing the game so easily, she had moved close to him. *Too* close.

Almost without conscious thought, his gaze drifted over her, to her shoulders, her breasts, her mouth . . . and there it lingered.

A bolt of lightning could not have been more devastating to her.

She'd struggled so hard to tame yearning needs—and yet here they were, hungry from a long famine of denial and responding to just the hint of desire from him.

There was a darkness in his brown eyes, a mystery that appealed to something deep inside her. Something best kept buried.

She knew what she wanted, and she knew he was open to her as well. The pull of attraction had been swirling around them from the moment they'd met—*but this man belonged to her sister.*

The thought brought her to sanity.

She practically fell back, as if needing to physically pull herself away from him.

Mr. Stephens gave a start and reacted as if he was startled by his response as well. Or, at least, that is what she wanted to believe, and she knew she shouldn't. Men were wolves. She must never forget that.

"You are to marry my sister, sir," she whispered. "Do not insult me."

He shook his head as if her charge offended,

yet he did not refute it. "I don't plan seduction. I assure you, Lady Aileen, that was a momentary lapse on my part. I'm as taken aback as you are."

She denied his words in her own mind. How many men had assumed she would be easy prey? Many had tested her. Of course, that was because they'd all believed the evidence that had been presented at the Crim Con trial. It had never crossed anyone's mind, including her friends' and confidantes', to doubt that which had been presented in court or the adultery to which she'd been pronounced guilty.

Then again, they could never have imagined how far a woman would go to escape a marriage that had become prison.

Aileen backed away from him. He watched her, a question in his eye, but he did not follow. He did not command . . . and, to her incredulity, she was not afraid of him.

At the door, she said, "Good night, Mr. Stephens." She spoke as a formality, a civility.

Instead of answering in kind, he responded, "I will tell you something, and you will not thank me for it."

Aileen didn't know what to do with such a claim. She had one step out the door. She was ready to leave. "Then don't tell me," she replied, proud of herself.

"Very well—"

She raised a hand. "Tell me." She couldn't help herself. Curiosity was one of her sins. Besides, he'd expected her to ask.

He smiled. He'd anticipated her reaction, but his gaze was serious as he said, "You are not responsible for the world."

He was wrong. "I know that."

"No, you don't—yet. Your sister will do as she wishes. Your father will be who he is. The only person you *must* please is yourself."

"And what of the bonds of family, Mr. Stephens? Of clansmen?"

"By all means, continue to worry about everyone else," he said, raising his hands as if to show he played no tricks. "You obviously have complete power over each and every one of them."

Of course, he knew she didn't. Tara had become a willful minx, and the earl was as he'd always been—careless.

"But I must try," she found herself saying. "Without family, what are we?"

"A bastard," he commented, the word heavy with self-irony.

Aileen could feel the frown on her forehead. He didn't understand. He was male, and he couldn't begin to comprehend the weight resting on her shoulders.

But for a mere second, a part of her wanted to embrace his advice, to allow Tara the freedom to ruin her life if she chose or to even allow herself to forgive the earl for all the things he wasn't and never could be.

However, if she did that, if she released the tension that had become her constant companion for so long and tossed aside the regrets etched on her soul, who would she be then? A person could not escape her past . . . although Penevey's bastard had. She'd known the duke had rescued him from the streets. However, the man who stood in front of her was accepted in most of London's drawing rooms.

"We can't all be like you," she replied, sounding petulant to her own ears, although that was all she could offer. She left the room and half expected him to pursue.

Perhaps she *wanted* him to pursue.

But he didn't.

No footstep fell in the hallway behind her. And once she reached the sanctuary of her bedroom, she did not have a sense that he was lying in wait, breathing against the door, ready to attack.

Ellen did not wait up to undress her. Aileen never expected her maid to do that, especially in the country. As she unlaced her dress, she caught a glimpse of herself in the candlelight reflecting off her looking glass. Her color was high, her eyes large, wondering.

Mr. Stephens's advice echoed in her ears. Or was it her own far too passionate nature pushing her toward him and disaster, and consequently giving his opinion more importance than it warranted?

She'd learned the hard way not to trust herself.

Aileen climbed into her bed and pulled the covers over her head. A few moments later, she surprised herself by falling into a deep, dreamless sleep, the deepest she'd had since those days when she had been an innocent girl who had still believed in love.

*B*lake held the white queen up to the light.

What the bloody hell was the matter with him?

He could be as great a rascal as any other man, but he had some sense of honor and a code of conduct. He didn't like affairs. They involved too many loose ends, and he was not a rash man. He prided himself on always being in control.

There had been a time in his life when he'd been treated as if he'd been of no consequence. Even now, there were times when he was dismissed as a by-blow, an afterthought. It rankled that the duke's acknowledgement of his parentage opened doors that Blake felt should have been available to him on his own merit. He was Penevey's oldest, damn it all.

And a bit of his need to prove himself had been behind his pursuit of Lady Tara.

But it was her sister that captured his imagination . . . in a way no other woman had before.

And he'd just met her.

Blake carefully returned to what he had started, setting up the chessboard, but with one difference. He placed the white queen in the middle of the game.

In the square confronting hers, he positioned the black king.

For a second, he debated moving the two pieces, then he decided to let them stay.

He would not act upon his attraction to Aileen Hamilton. He would marry her sister because that was what was *expected* of him. He'd fought to be considered a gentleman. A man's reputation was the most fragile thing he owned.

And no woman should matter that much.

Especially one he'd just met.

Blake went to bed then. What else was there to do here in the wilderness of Scotland?

He expected to fall asleep. He was tired from travel and the weary contemplation of his future. He would have a beautiful wife, and his children, his *sons*, would be accepted everywhere. Besides, he always slept well, the result of a clear conscience.

Except this night, his peace was broken by fitful dreams of a pair of gray-blue eyes and the possibility of scandal.

Chapter Seven

A rush of sunlight woke Blake.

He roared his disapproval and pulled the feather pillow over his eyes. "Shut the drapes," he snapped.

"I wish I could, sir," his valet, Jones, said, "but you are to go to church with the earl of Tay this morning."

Church?

"I never go to church," Blake mumbled into his pillow. His friends doubted if he would go to one for his own funeral.

It wasn't that he had anything against honest prayer. He'd been known to indulge in it a time or two, usually in times of great crisis and with very choice words. But the discipline of rising in the morning to listen to a man who was probably no more holy than he carry on about "should and should nots" was not high on Blake's preference of morning activities.

But then the word *"Tay"* registered in his still sleepy, and, yes, drink-befuddled memory. The first of his marriage banns was to be announced this morning.

He tossed the pillow aside and opened one eye. Jones was laying out the shaving equipment. The servant had also cracked open the window.

"What is that sound?" Blake asked.

"Birdsong, sir."

"I've never heard it."

"That is because you rarely leave London. The birds are quite happy this morning after our last few days of rain."

"We have birds in London."

"Pigeons and gulls, not songbirds."

"So you say."

"I do, sir. I like the sound of the thrush. Makes me content—"

"I should never have left the city," Blake declared, overriding his valet. Jones's talking of songbirds aggravated the foggy numbness in his brain. "Or drink with Tay. *Ever.* The man is a fish."

Blake had always believed he had a good head for spirits, but he could not keep up with Tay. He raised a hand to his pounding brow. "Good God."

Jones was an independent-minded chap and rarely refrained from letting his opinions be known. "Are you praying already, sir?"

"More than you can imagine," Blake muttered. "The last few days have been a bloody challenge. I'm pretending I'm a happy guest, but my patience is stretching thin." Especially around Tara.

In London, Blake had had business to attend to, and he'd only dealt with Tara during social obligations. She'd been a pretty bauble who had flattered his standing amongst his contemporaries and made his half brother Arthur jealous. He'd never spent too much time with her alone.

He now realized that his betrothed was a bit of a child. She was like Penevey's *legitimate* sons, with their slack jaws and vaunted sense of importance. They were coddled and cossetted and knew nothing of the world.

Ten minutes with one of them always made Blake thankful he'd grown up in the gutter. He'd learned in the hardest school any man could ever know how dangerous it was to waste time twiddling his thumbs or taking opportunity for granted. He valued purpose, something that

Tara did not seem to possess—although that was untrue of her sister.

Lady Aileen was apparently a cornerstone in country society. She seemed to be out and about visiting her neighbors and seeing to sick crofters and the like. A true Lady Bountiful.

He admired her industry, although he suspected her real motive was to avoid him—something she would not be able to do today. She had to go to church. It would be expected, especially since her sister's banns would be announced.

The thought of seeing her again was the impetus he needed to rise. He threw back the covers and put his legs over the edge of the bed to sit up. Immediately cold air hit his skin and he regretted the action.

"Would you shut the window?" he barked at Jones.

"Fresh air would be good for you, sir."

"And why do you think that?" Blake pushed back his hair with his hands and vowed to not drink one more drop of whisky with that devil Lord Tay.

"Stirs the soul, sir. Stirs the soul."

"I thought sermons did that," Blake grumbled. He stood, naked. Yawning, he crossed over to the screen to see to his morning business.

"They might," Jones was saying to him. "There is nothing like a rousing Calvinist screed read aloud to the uninitiated to vanquish dark and brooding natures."

"Sounds delightful." Blake pulled on a pair of breeches and turned himself over to Jones's services.

Using soap scented with oriental spices, Jones lathered the rough beard covering Blake's jaw before handing him a cup of strong tea from a tray on a side table. Letting the lather rest a moment, Jones prepared the razor.

Blake began to feel better, enough so that he noticed something out of the corner of his eye. "Jones? Did you lay out my dress coat for me to wear to church?"

"Yes, sir."

"And knee breeches and pumps?" Blake continued, incredulous. Though this outfit was part of every gentleman's wardrobe, Blake didn't even know why he had these clothes, as he avoided any stuffy occasion where he'd be required to wear them. *Once.* He'd worn them once. "I won't wear them."

"It's church, sir."

"It's a country church. In Scotland. Give me my boots."

"We aren't heathens, sir. You *dress* for church."

"*We?*" Blake frowned. "You are Scottish, Jones?"

"*Aye*, I am," Jones said, revealing a broad brogue. "Sir," he offered as an afterthought.

"Why didn't I know that?" Jones had been with Blake for over two years.

"You didn't ask, sir." Jones took the teacup and began applying the razor to Blake's jaw, but Blake caught his wrist and stopped him.

"But you haven't sounded Scottish, Jones, until this moment. And Jones is not Scots . . . is it?"

"A man can be a Jones and a Scot. There is no law against it. My father was a valet for an Edinburgh merchant, and I thought I'd find my fortune in London working for a fine gentleman. However, after several interviews I realized my accent was going against me."

"I would have still hired you if I had known you were Scottish," Blake said. "And we need to close the window. This country has a chill even in August."

"Your blood is too thin, sir," Jones said as he did as requested. "And you weren't the one who hired me. Your father's valet, Vernon, did. You and I settled in with each other after your brother Arthur gave me the sack."

"Oh, yes," Blake said, remembering. "I saved you."

"Or *I* saved you. Your wardrobe made me shudder with horror."

"It was a good bargain." Blake leaned back in the chair to be shaved.

"It was, sir. The marquis still tosses valets aside as if we are nothing. It was providence that my path crossed yours."

Blake chuckled. "Providence had nothing to do with it. You couldn't keep your tongue quiet, and Arthur doesn't like any opinion save his own."

"While you, sir, barely pay attention to half of what I say."

Blake's newly shaved skin tingled from the soap as he laughed at the truth in Jones's statement. But then he halted the shaving progress to say with complete seriousness, "It doesn't seem right you hide who you are. I know. When Penevey picked me up off the streets, I had to make the decision whether to pretend to be someone else or be the man I am."

"Once into the ruse, I couldn't stop."

"You stop now."

"Aye, sir."

"And because I am the man *I am*," Blake continued, "I will not wear those pumps."

But in the end, he did.

Jones insisted, and Blake was wise enough to listen to his valet, although his legs without boots felt, well, exposed.

"Your boots will be here for you when you return, sir," Jones promised, reaching up to tie a proper knot in Blake's starched neck cloth.

"So, tell me, Jones, what should I expect in church today?"

"Good people who are probably brimming with a curiosity about you, since Lady Tara is a local favorite." Jones often provided information to Blake, as did any servant worth the pay he received. He inspected his handiwork with the knot as he said, "You will have the attention of everyone in the kirk. They will watch every twitch of the eye and lift of the finger. *Gloved* finger," he emphasized, pointing to the kid gloves he'd laid out on the dresser. Blake hated wearing them perhaps more than he detested pumps.

Jones adjusted the knot a bit as he said, "If you think London is full of know-it-alls and busybodies, sir, wait until you experience country folk in Scotland."

Blake frowned. "Do you believe they will know that Lady Tara ran away from the marriage?"

"I've been listening for that, sir. I'm certain

Ingold and Mrs. Watson are aware, but if the other servants have an inkling, they have not breathed a word. They are very loyal here."

"Even about Lady Aileen's divorce?" Blake wanted to discover what he could about the incident.

"They are especially protective of her, sir."

That was unusual. In London, a story like Aileen Hamilton's would have been common gossip amongst the servants.

Blake held out his arms so that Jones could help him into his dark blue dress coat. "Keep listening. I'm interested in that regard."

His order was met by an uncharacteristic beat of silence, then Jones said, "Are you still going to continue with this farce of a marriage, sir?"

"I have no choice."

"There is always a choice, sir."

Blake smiled grimly. His man did not understand. "Not with any semblance of honor."

"Is your honor more important than having a wife who gives you comfort and sees to your needs?" Jones asked, offering Blake the gloves.

"A man's word is his bond." Of all the dictums he'd schooled himself on in his quest to become a "gentleman," this one rang truest. Even the scoundrels, pickpockets, and whores who had been a part of his early childhood understood a code of honor.

"Then perhaps it wouldn't be wise to ask more questions about Lady Tara's sister?" Jones suggested.

Blake bristled at the hint of disapproval, even while silently acknowledging Jones was correct. He should cool his interest in Lady Aileen. He should, but not quite yet.

Instead of responding, he took a bite of the bun Jones had included on the morning tray and finished the tea he had started while dressing. From outside the window, he heard the sound of horses being brought around. "I must go." He left the room, but Jones's admonishment lingered in his mind.

Penevey had said he needed a wife, and Blake had agreed with him. But finding a young woman from a suitable family had been difficult. In spite of the wealth he had created, the reputation he had established, and the duke's recognition of him . . . most doting parents did not find him completely acceptable for their precious daughters—not if they could land a young man with a less dubious history. The world might admire a self-made man, but the *ton* never would. They lauded tradition.

And Tara, too, had liabilities. For all her celebrated beauty, her father's drinking, womanizing, and general reckless behavior, compounded with the scandal of her sister's divorce, had seen her crossed off many a gentleman's list for a wife—at least from their parents' perspectives.

And Blake was no fool. He knew Penevey had approached him about marrying Tara Davidson because the duke wanted to save his heir from her. Arthur had been making an embarrassment of himself in his pursuit of Tara. She was the one thing Arthur appeared to want with a dedicated enthusiasm.

Considering all the mean-spirited pranks Arthur and his ilk had visited upon Blake when they had been in school together, Blake had taken great satisfaction in winning the lady.

And he promised himself that in spite of how silly he found Tara, he would be a good husband to her. This marriage would give his children legitimate bloodlines and social standing. It had already gained him great approval from Penevey, a man of whom he was never certain yet someone he wanted to please, as all sons, even bastards, wished to do.

God, he was even going to church.

"Ah, there you are, Stephens," the earl of Tay greeted him. The earl was standing in the front hall, his hat on his head. He wore knee breeches and pumps, and Blake silently prayed he cut a better figure in the clothes than the earl. "I was afraid I needed to send Ingold for you. The ladies are already tucked into the coach."

The *ladies*. That meant Lady Aileen.

Blake's step picked up its pace. He walked out the front door to the waiting vehicle.

The coach had a row of seats facing each other. Lady Aileen sat on one side; Tara on the other.

He dutifully took his place beside Tara, but he welcomed the opportunity to feast his eyes on Aileen.

Naturally, Tara looked fetching in a dress of soft white muslin trimmed in green silk ribbons. Her cheeks glowed with youth and country air. Green-hued pheasant feathers decorated her stylish bonnet.

At first glance, one would think Aileen was a dull duckling compared to her sister, but Blake found her handsome. Very handsome, indeed.

She wore a dark blue day dress with a neckline that was cut higher than her sister's and lacked any embellishment, but none was needed because the style emphasized her full breasts and trim figure, and the color highlighted the near perfection of her complexion. Instead of a bonnet, she wore a soft cap that reminded him of a painting he'd seen of an Italian countess. All she lacked was a strand of creamy white pearls.

Blake wondered if she realized that the blue in her dress brought out the gray in her eyes.

He found he longed to tell her.

But he couldn't, because Jones was right, damn him. No good would come from this attraction to Aileen Hamilton . . . other than to create another scandal, something Blake could not afford to do.

And yet he found himself wondering how much truth there was in what the gossips said about her. Everything about her demeanor was at odds with the accusations whispered about her. He could not picture her having an affair or being inconstant. The rumors struck him as inconsistent with what little he knew about her.

Tara beamed a becoming smile that brought a celebrated dimple to her cheek and asked, "Are you prepared for our big step?"

He assumed she meant the announcement of the banns. "Of course," he murmured. "For our 'Highland' wedding."

If Tara detected the hint of derision in his voice, she didn't comment.

But Aileen had noticed. The corners of her

mouth had tightened. She didn't say anything. She wouldn't.

The earl climbed into the coach and knocked on the ceiling for the driver to take off, while Tara began prattling on about her new plans for their wedding breakfast as if there wasn't any other topic in the world more important.

Blake pretended to listen.

He tried not to stare at Lady Aileen, yet every once in a while, their eyes met. In her expression, he saw confirmation of his belief that she had been evading him on purpose, and he wondered if perhaps she didn't feel some measure of attraction for him as well. What other reason could she have for not wishing his company?

It was a heady idea, especially since Blake had never experienced this mysterious pull toward one woman in particular. She aroused his hunting instincts.

He could even smell her scent. Light, slightly floral, yet there was a note of something deeper, something sensual—

Tara's hand touched his arm. "Don't *you* find it to be true, Mr. Stephens?"

Blake's mind scrambled. "Um, yes," he improvised.

"I though you would agree," Tara said, beaming happily.

Blake wondered what he'd agreed to, but instead of offering more explanation, she glanced out the window and announced, "Ah, we are here."

The coach had rumbled into the village of Kenmore. They passed what appeared to be a well-tended inn, a welcome sight to any man trapped at Annefield. The church, or kirk, was located on the banks of Loch Tay. The yard around it was filled with vehicles of all shapes and sizes, although they had the only coach and driver. The service would be crowded today.

When the coach rolled to a halt, the earl's footman opened the door and the earl stepped out with all the grandness of the Lord Mayor of London.

There were quite a few parish members gathered outside, enjoying a moment in the fine weather before going inside the kirk. A murmur went through them at the earl's appearance, then well-dressed and prosperous people rushed to greet him as if he'd been a returning hero.

Tay enjoyed the adulation. He grandly helped his daughters out of the coach. Blake was interested to note that Lady Aileen, a divorced woman, was not ostracized the way he would have anticipated. Why, in London, he doubted if anyone would have been pleasant to her. But here, she appeared accepted. Oh, there were a few prune faces, but there always were.

Tara was greeted with the welcome of a favorite child. They all gathered around her, surprised that she was there. Several women her age rushed up to her, wanting to know if she was married, and that was when Blake was presented with warm welcomes.

Their ready acceptance was a strange experience. The locals were more open than he had imagined. The people he was meeting refuted the image of dour-faced Scots. The men looked him in the eye and the women were gracious. Their words of greeting sounded genuine, and they introduced themselves by names he knew he would not be able to remember—but found he wanted to. These were good people, and not one of them demonstrated an undercurrent of "knowingness," the term Blake always applied for those who were overly aware of his dubious parentage.

The earl spoke in a carrying voice about how his daughter had wanted a Highland wedding. Many of the women nodded, as if they had already heard this fact. Blake played the dutiful husband-to-be, nodding and standing by Tara . . . while his gaze drifted to Lady Aileen—

No, he couldn't do that. He had to keep his focus on Tara, but the task was difficult.

The minister rang a bell, a signal that the service was about to begin.

Moving with his friends toward the door, the earl announced, "Stephens will know you all better on the morrow. We're holding a hunt. Everyone is welcome. Midday tomorrow. It's been a while since I've seen my hounds at work."

Heads nodded and smiles broke out. Several commented that the day would be good for hunting and promised to attend.

"What day will the wedding be?" a dowager in purple half mourning asked.

That question stopped conversation, as everyone seemed keen on the answer.

"We will be discussing that matter with Reverend Kinnion," the earl said, placing a hand on the minister's arm.

The well-dressed Reverend Kinnion, a thin man with a pale complexion and wispy brown hair, nodded agreement.

"I shall come round to Annefield to discuss the matter, my lord," Kinnion answered, adjusting the spectacles on his nose. "But now let us proceed inside for the service. The Lord awaits." He waved his hands, shepherding them in front of him.

Of course, the earl of Tay had his own pew in the cool darkness of the church. It was a narrow space, but the four of them managed to squeeze in, the sisters side by side, then Blake next, with Tay on the outside.

The Davidsons were also surrounded by family.

In the hurried moments before the service started, Blake was introduced to uncles, aunts, and distant cousins. It seemed a quarter of the congregation were relatives of the earl of Tay.

One woman who stood out was Miss Sabrina Davidson. She was the only child of the earl's younger brother, a ghastly, grim man who served as magistrate, a fitting role for him. Miss Davidson's demeanor was the opposite of her father's. A buxom brunette, she had a sunny smile.

It was obvious that she and Lady Aileen were great friends. Tara seemed equally pleased to greet her cousin, but Blake noticed that Miss Davidson's reception toward her was cool.

He also found he was growing out of his morning grumpiness. He had not considered that marriage would mean becoming part of a large extended family, one that appeared to readily accept him. He liked the thought.

His mother had no family that he knew of, or none that had stepped forward to take him in after she died, and his relationship with the duke was a delicate matter. His half brothers would have been happy to wrap him in a sack and toss him into the Thames if they'd been able to wangle it without being suspected.

So the Davidsons' easy acceptance of him into the family touched a deep chord within him. He found himself reaching for Tara's gloved hand. She raised surprised brows. He had never made such a simple, gentle move. He smiled and turned his attention to the service Jones had assured him would be instructive.

Actually, it was. He was no biblical scholar, so, on this Sunday morning, the story of a Good Samaritan was fresh to him, and meaningful. The idea that one man should help another for no reason other than it being the right thing to do resonated strongly in Blake. He'd always believed he had some responsibility to his fellow man, and Reverend Kinnion's words reinforced his conviction.

Furthermore, as he sat there among the congregation, a contentment he'd not known before settled upon him. In London, his goal was to validate himself. Always and relentlessly. But here, the knots of tension and determination loosened. He liked being with these people.

The time came for the announcing of the banns. Another couple was having their banns announced, and Blake was interested to realize that one half of the couple was Tay's horse master. He'd conversed with the man a time or two when he'd been around the stables. Jamerson was his name. He had the dark, brooding look that women always seemed to like. His betrothed was attractive in appearance but not stunning. This was their second announcing of the banns.

Reverend Kinnion had the couple stand.

Tara had removed her hand from his hold and had folded both hands in her lap. She studied them, so still she seemed not to breathe. Lady Aileen leaned toward her sister, offering . . . what? Support? Solace?

Was Tara anxious about this step toward marriage?

After all the prattling on in the coach, this stillness seemed out of character—unless she had been attempting to calm her nerves. He'd never noticed her to be ill at ease in public.

And then the reverend called for Tara and him to stand. The woman he knew, the one with the bright and studied smile, reemerged.

Blake placed his hand on Tara's arm.

Reverend Kinnion said, "I announce the banns between Mr. Blake Stephens and Lady Tara Davidson. This is the first time of reading. If any of you know cause or just impediment why these two persons should not be joined together in holy matrimony, ye are to declare it." He smiled at Blake. "Thank you, Mr. Stephens, my lady."

Tara practically fell to the pew as if her legs could not support her weight.

Blake sat down beside her, slightly concerned at her disquiet. Perhaps she was shy here amongst her people. Or more circumspect, which was not a bad quality for her to cultivate. After all, someday she would be the mother of his children.

Children, a dynasty. He had no use for a title. But he was building wealth, and if his other investments proved satisfactory, he would grow richer with time and need heirs to continue his legacy.

The service was over quickly then. Wellwishers kept them from leaving the pew immediately. Furthermore, the earl had caught the attention of a robust woman a decade his junior and was having a fine time teasing her. She was introduced to Blake as Mrs. Bossley, a widow, and she had obviously set her sights on Tay.

At last Blake was able to work his way around the earl and the attentive widow so that he could escort Tara and Lady Aileen out of the kirk into the warmth of the day.

Tara was quickly carried away by friends. Several gentlemen cornered Blake to discuss the upcoming hunt and make him feel welcome.

Lady Aileen had wandered away on her own.

After a few minutes, Blake caught sight of her standing by the kirk door, her brow furrowed in concern as she studied a point not far from her.

Curious, he followed her line of vision and realized she was focused on Tara, who, even though she was in the midst of friends, had her concentration on something else. There was a vulnerability in her expression, a yearning he'd not seen before, or, at least, certainly not when she'd ever looked at him.

He traced the direction of Tara's attention and discovered she was staring at Jamerson and his intended.

Inside the kirk, standing before the congregation, the couple had appeared happy.

Such was not the case now.

They acted as strangers, each slightly turned from the other, just standing, awkward and a touch sad.

And then Jamerson, a man whose physical attractiveness was such that he could set a thousand female hearts aflutter, glanced in Tara's direction before quickly looking away. In that single second, only the most hard-hearted could not have detected the anguish of love forlorn.

An expression mirrored in Tara's eyes.

Blake's mind reeled, staggered by a sudden revelation: He had believed Tara when she'd said her running away had been because of maidenly apprehension about marriage. Or had he just *assumed* that was her reasoning? She was lovely, she was female, she was vapid-headed, therefore why did she need a true motive for any of her actions?

But now he knew differently.

She'd not been running away from marriage, or even from him.

No, she'd run *to* someone else. She'd run to the horse master.

Blake had always trusted his instincts. They had served him well. They never lied to him . . . like people did. He knew he'd blindly stumbled upon a secret Tara wanted to keep, but she was doing a poor job.

And then the hairs at the nape of his neck tingled as if someone watched him.

Slowly, he shifted his attention from Tara to meet the level gaze of Lady Aileen.

She'd noticed. She knew he'd seen, that he understood.

Her avoiding him for the past couple of days now took on a different meaning, one that cut him like a knife. She'd pleaded passionately for Tara to not marry him because *she'd known* her sister loved another man.

It was all right there in front of him.

And, yes, Tara's passion for another man, one promised to another woman, was not comfortable.

But Blake discovered that what really disturbed him had nothing to do with Tara. He had convinced himself Lady Aileen was avoiding him because of their mutual attraction.

Now he realized she might have avoided him out of guilt. She hadn't wanted him to know the truth.

She might not have feelings for him at all.

And that, surprisingly, upset him in a way he wasn't certain he understood.

One of the gentlemen of the group he'd been standing amongst was jabbering about fishing in the river Tay. Blake discovered he needed time alone. He needed to think this matter through. He turned abruptly, knowing he appeared rude and mumbling some excuse even as he started to walk off to who knew where—

"Ah, there you are, Stephens," the earl of Tay said, coming up behind him. "I've invited company for dinner. The widow Bossley. What an interesting woman. We must be on our way so I can inform Mrs. Watson and Cook of my decision. Oh, look, the widow has already lined her rig up behind mine. I adore an anxious filly. You don't mind if I ride with her, do you now?"

The earl didn't wait for an answer but strode off in the direction of his new love interest. She beckoned him from her pony cart.

The earl appeared a sight in the small, two-wheeled vehicle pulled by a shaggy Highland pony, but he took the reins over from the widow and off they went.

Tara walked over to Blake. "What is happening with my father?"

"What always happens?" Lady Aileen said tartly, approaching from the other side.

Blake pressed his lips together. He could deal with Tara, but he found he was uncomfortable with Lady Aileen. No man wishes to appear a fool, and perhaps him most of all.

"Let's go," he ordered and walked toward the

coach without waiting for their responses. Of course they followed, Tara unaware she had been discovered.

And Lady Aileen? He didn't know what he thought, but he was not happy. Indeed, he was more disappointed in her than Tara.

As they traveled back to Annefield, Blake listened to the sisters talking. Their conversation was restrained and only about pleasantries. He now understood, and heard, what was not being said.

And with every turn of the coach wheel, he felt the bite of bitterness.

Chapter Eight

$\mathcal{D}$inner after church was an interminable ordeal for Tara. She was losing the ability to smile and pretend all was well. Tears hovered, and it stretched her sanity to hold them back.

Of course, she didn't need to say much at dinner. Her father was occupied with the widow Bossley, a schemer if ever Tara had met one. The two of them controlled the conversation with giggles and sly innuendoes.

Meanwhile, Aileen continued to be as insufferable as she had become of late. She was silent, disapproving, and acted as if she was the very model of propriety if one did not know her history. She judged Tara and found her wanting.

And then there was Mr. Stephens. During the church service, he had held her hand, but now he had returned to his taciturn self. His jaw was so tight that he must have been continually gritting his teeth. He was displeased about something, but she was not concerned. How could she be? Her mind was on Ruary.

She pushed the peas around her plate, pretending to eat while assuring herself she would never be happy again. It had been a herculean task to sit in that church and listen to Ruary's banns being read.

They had not seen each other since that disastrous meeting when she'd first returned to Annefield. But a part of her held on to a belief in the love they had once professed.

Yes, she had walked away, but he was hers. They belonged together. Besides, she had returned. That must count for something. She was willing to give up everything for him.

Of course, it was Jane Sawyer's fault. She was holding on to him, and Ruary was too kind a man to hurt her . . . or at least that is what Tara wanted to believe. But she also secretly hoped he would come back to her. He had to.

And in the meantime, for the past days, she had smiled and flattered and offered her attention to

Blake Stephens. Sometimes she hoped the servants noticed her attentiveness and reported back to Ruary how happy she was. Then perhaps he would be jealous and come for her like a Shakespearean hero, ready to face all dangers and defy all conventions for her.

However, seeing him standing next to Jane Sawyer in church had impressed upon Tara that Ruary would never be hers. She was going to lose him forever.

Aileen could chastise her and tell her that she was being ridiculous. But then, Aileen no longer believed in love. She had forgotten that the heart wants what it wants and no amount of practicality can ease the pain of loss.

Now Tara realized that this agony was what Ruary had experienced when she'd left him to go to London. No wonder he was so angry with her. She'd made the most foolish mistake of her life by leaving him. . . .

Tara set down her fork. "I don't believe I feel well. I need to go to my room and lay down."

"Is there something I can do?" Aileen asked with her air of motherly concern.

Tara felt her expression grow brittle. "Nothing. I will be fine."

Aileen reacted to the curtness in her tone, but hadn't Tara just said she didn't feel well? Did Aileen believe her such a ninny she didn't know how to take care of herself?

Tara set aside her napkin and rose from the table. Mr. Stephens also came to his feet out of respect, but she didn't look at him. She didn't want to. His very presence annoyed her right now. He was the reason she was so miserable.

Later, when she had a chance to take hold of herself, she would offer a pretty apology and he would accept it. He had no other choice. He was stuck with her . . . just as she was stuck with him.

In the haven of her room, Tara wandered over to her window. She needed peace. Her soul longed for it, and she didn't know how she could go on—

Tara broke her thoughts off abruptly and leaned toward the window, resting a knee on the window seat so she could be closer. She blinked twice to be certain her eyes did not deceive her.

They didn't.

Ruary was riding up to the stables. He dismounted, tied up his horse, and went inside the yard.

She straightened, her heart pounding in her ears. There was no reason for Ruary to be at the stables on a Sunday. It was not one of his training days. But back when she'd lived at Annefield, before she'd gone off to London, Ruary had often come on Sundays for the sole purpose of seeing her. Most of Annefield's servants were given time after dinner on Sunday for their own affairs. This had afforded the privacy she and Ruary had needed to meet clandestinely.

And here he was today.

Could this be a coincidence? She thought not. Ruary wanted to see her. She knew it. *Her heart knew it.* Perhaps the banns today had started him thinking about her? Perhaps he wondered as she did?

She stood only a moment in indecision before tearing off her dress and ransacking her wardrobe for her riding habit. In that outfit, people would understand why she was at the stables. She didn't want to ring for the maid. She didn't want to waste time. What if Ruary decided that he was making a mistake and left? She could not let him. This might be her only chance to speak to him with some privacy . . .

Tara heard voices in the hallway. Her maid, Ellen, was talking to Blake's man, Jones. Tightening the lacings of her habit, she leaned against the door to listen, waiting for them to leave.

Jones was saying, "My master has gone for a ride."

"Then you have time for me to show you the walk to the river," Ellen said, a woman's inviting warmth in her voice.

"I must be here when he returns."

"When did he leave?"

"A half hour ago."

"And he'll be gone how long? Come, Mr. Jones, don't make this difficult for me. A short walk. We'll be back before you can blink."

"I doubt that, Ellen."

She giggled in response to something he'd muttered only for the two of them, then there was the sound of footsteps. The door to the back stairs opened and closed, and all was quiet.

So Blake had gone riding, and where was Aileen? Probably reading, Tara hazarded to guess and opened the door to her room. No one was in the hall. She drew a deep breath, set her hat on her head at a rakish angle, and went down the front stairs.

Her father was in the sitting room, reading papers from Edinburgh and London and *sipping* his whisky for once.

"Going out?" he said as Tara made her appearance in the doorway. "You must feel better?"

"Yes, I do, thank you. I believe I'll enjoy a short ride."

"Stephens has already gone. It's a pity you couldn't have ridden with him."

"I hope to catch up with him," she answered.

"Ah, good," he said, beaming approval. "Keep that lad happy, Tara. We need him."

"Is the money so important, Papa? Could we not survive otherwise?"

Her father practically dropped his paper. He fixed her with a look that answered her question louder than words. "I'm done up," he said. "It's either marriage to Stephens or the duns will eat my liver. I told you how it was when I encouraged you to be open to him. But you have saved us, Tara, my girl. You and that pretty face. And now, if the widow Bossley's husband left her as much as it is whispered, we'll be doing fine."

"We would do better, Papa, were you not so fond of gambling."

In the act of raising his paper, he paused to deliver a cold look. "I don't gamble, Tara, I wager. There is a difference."

Not that she had noticed.

He seemed to hear her unspoken accusation.

He sniffed, frowned, and lifted his paper to hide his face. He *should* hide.

And she'd best be careful. Her father would not be pleased if she jilted Blake Stephens a second time.

*I*ngold was not at his station in the front hall. Tara slipped out the door, lifted her skirts and ran for the stables. Only when she was almost upon them did she slow to a walk, pretending a bit of decorum.

Walking through the stable's passageway, she took a moment to check the grain room. Ruary was not there, and his horse wasn't where she'd seen him tie it.

For a second she worried that he had left, yet she sensed he was here. She paused in the yard, listening.

Horses hung their heads out of their stalls, watching her with idle curiosity. Beyond their restless movements and the quiet munching of hay, she heard Ruary's low voice. It came from the one stall that appeared empty.

Tara silently walked over and looked inside.

Ruary had pulled a shoe off a big chestnut gelding named Dirk and was trying to file down the foot. Dirk nickered a greeting to Tara. Dirk had been born at Annefield, and she'd known him since he was a colt.

Ruary looked up, and for a moment he seemed frozen in place.

Tara glanced behind her. They were alone in the yard. Of course, there was always someone close at hand. She had to be careful. She let herself into the stall, closing the door behind her.

She smiled at Ruary, feeling giddy and tentative and shy, all at once, to be this close to him. He watched her, cautious, yet she knew he was not surprised to see her.

He wanted her here. She was certain of it, but instead of speaking her thought aloud, she said, "Did Dirk throw a shoe again?"

Ruary put down the hoof and stood, still holding the file. "You know him. He always loses it. But I found it in the paddock. I'll have it on in a moment." He reached for the worn shoe he'd leaned against the wall, replacing the file with a hammer. He bent to start nailing the shoe back in place.

Dirk leaned his nose toward Tara. She rubbed it with one gloved hand, and for a moment, it was enough to be here, in this space, with this man.

Ruary broke the silence first, not looking at her. "Congratulations on your betrothal."

"Congratulations on yours."

He grunted a response, his attention seemingly on the shoe he was nailing, but she knew differently.

"Where is your horse?" she asked.

"I put him in a stall. I didn't know how long I'd be here."

"And why is that?" Tara held her breath for the answer, waiting, wanting him to make the first move toward her.

He took a moment for two last taps of the hammer before he set down Dirk's foot. He tossed the hammer so that it landed next to the file. He did not turn to her as he said, "You have upset my world, Tara, by coming back."

There was pain in his voice. He was an honorable man in spite of his low birth. Indeed, there wasn't a gentleman in London who had his strong sense of what was right and what was wrong.

She studied the hay on the stall floor, knowing that she had to be careful with what she said. The strong connection they had once had was now a fragile thread. She feared breaking it. "I was wrong."

"Wrong about what?" He stood, turning to her.

"Oh, that is the question, isn't it?" she answered with a shaky laugh at her own culpability. "I may have been wrong to have returned and—" Her voice broke off as she realized she wasn't certain about what she'd been about to say.

"And?" Ruary prodded. His gloves were leather and were stained from the nature of his work.

"And it may have been the most right thing I have ever done in my life. I'm given Mr. Stephens good cause to doubt me. It will cost me dearly."

"Why did you really return, my lady?" he asked.

The question seemed to fill the air of the stall. Tara raised her gaze to meet his. "For you. I wasn't jesting when I said that I came back to you. I *had* to see you." This was harder than she had imagined. "I know I hurt you, Ruary. It was wrong—"

"Coming *back* was wrong," he said, interrupting her. He tossed the hammer and file into the wooden box in the corner that held his tools. His shoe on, Dirk turned his interest toward a pile of hay in the corner of his stall.

Ruary faced her. "It took me a long time to move past what you did, Tara. You took my heart when you left. I know I shouldn't have hoped, and yet . . ." His voice fell off.

"I was young, Ruary. I didn't understand what you meant to me."

"You are still young, my lady," he corrected, but there was no heat in his words. Indeed, he sounded tolerant, caring.

"Perhaps, but back then, I had to go, Ruary. I had to experience the world beyond Annefield. Now I understand that what we had between us was rare . . . and wonderful."

He shook his head, his brow furrowing. "I can't listen to this." He picked up his tools and started to pass her, but she stepped into his path, put her arms around his neck and kissed him.

It was an act of desperation.

Ruary immediately stiffened, so Tara kissed him all the harder. *Please, please, please,* she pleaded with him in her mind. *Please forgive me.*

No, what she was doing wasn't right. But in this moment, she wasn't thinking of anyone but herself.

For one second, his lips softened, and he kissed her back before pushing her away.

"No, Tara. No." His breathing had gone ragged, as if he battled within himself.

But she had no such conflict. She wanted to melt into him, to wrap him around her so completely that the world would not know where he began and she left off.

"*I love you.*" The words came straight from her heart. "I have always loved you, and I shall never apologize for it."

"We don't belong to each other," he said, as if trying to remind himself.

"We don't belong to anyone else—yet," she answered, her gaze refusing to waver.

They stood this way for a long moment.

"Tara, we can't go back to the past."

"Yes, we can." She tried to smile, willing him with her eyes, her mind and her heart to give her another chance. That was all she wanted. Just one more chance.

For a second, he stood in hesitation, one foot pointing in the direction of the stall door, and she wanted to cry. She couldn't lose him. She'd gone to such lengths for him—

Ruary dropped the heavy toolbox. He brought his arms around her like bands of steel and pulled her against him, thigh to thigh, hip to hip, her breasts flattening against his chest. He smelled of the late summer air, fresh hay, and the man she so dearly loved.

"This isn't good," he whispered.

"It's heaven," she answered, and he kissed her then.

This was no timidly eager kiss like those they had shared years ago. This was the kiss of a man who unashamedly wanted a woman.

She could feel his arousal. Knew it was for her.

An onslaught of desire and longing brought her arms around his neck. She clung to him as if to never let him go. *This* was what she had wanted.

This was the connection she had so foolishly tossed aside. Ruary Jamerson was a man like no other.

And Tara didn't care what his status was in life. All she knew was that for whatever reason, destiny had brought them together.

She'd tried to run once, to obey the rules.

She would not run again.

Chapter Nine

$\mathcal{B}$lake had needed to escape the house.

All through dinner, he had churned with anger and conflicting feelings. Tara would have jilted him for the horse master. *A horse master!*

Did she see Blake and all he'd worked for of such little consequence that she would lust after a man who was only a step above a servant? And the irony was that Penevey insisted Blake marry Tara because the marriage would supposedly raise his status in the world. Obviously, all he'd worked for was of little value to her.

But he felt it was Aileen who had betrayed him . . . and he couldn't quite define why. She owed him nothing. Her first loyalty should be to her sister. Still, he heaped on her the blame even while realizing he was being irrational.

And it was for that reason that as soon as the meal had ended—a dinner during which the only conversation had consisted of the earl and his lively widow's amorous repartee—he'd changed clothes and gone in search of exercise. He needed to clear his head. No good ever came from his losing his temper. He'd lost it recently when he'd learned Tara had run away, leaving him to public humiliation, *and now look where he was*—angrier, more lost and more unsettled than he had ever been in his life.

A fine decision it had been to go after her.

The horses in Annefield's famous stables were either young stock in training or hot-blooded stallions, all expensive livestock and not suitable for a Sunday's ride. There were only two geldings in the stables; one had thrown a shoe, so Blake had taken the other.

He now rode Thomas Aquinas, a strong bay Thoroughbred who wanted a run, which was fine with him. Blake was on the beast's back because he needed the wind in his face and the demons chased out of his being. He pulled his hat low and gave the horse his lead. Off they went.

For a good hour, all he did was ride. Thomas

knew his business, and he wasn't some ladies' mount. A man had to think when he was on this horse.

When Blake and Thomas were both out of breath, they began trotting down a sheep's path that soon led to a meandering road along Loch Tay.

In front of them, a boy was driving a shaggy beast of a bull with huge horns. The bull eyed Thomas as they passed, as if deciding whether he could take him on or not. The lad's stick and Thomas's snort of disdain seemed to make him think twice.

The boy pulled a forelock, an ancient symbol of respect. Blake nodded in return and, for a second, felt quite the country gentleman.

The air going through his lungs was sweet and clear, a striking contrast to London's thick soot. The views were astounding. The mountains made him feel as if he'd been cupped in God's hand, while Loch Tay's silver waters gave him a sense of freedom.

But then the road took him through the village of Kenmore and past the kirk he had attended that morning. His anger, his discontent, came thundering back.

If he was wise, he would ride this horse to London without a backward glance at Lady Tara

or Lady Aileen. He would return to the life he had
. . . yet he wasn't certain he wanted that either.

Indecision made him uncomfortable. He always
knew what he wanted. At one time, it had been
just to survive. Then his goal had become earning
Penevey's respect.

And now?

Why was he here? The question didn't pertain
to why he was in Scotland; it carried a heavier
weight—one his life had not encouraged him to
ponder until this moment.

He had everything most men would desire, yet
a part of him felt empty. Incomplete.

Blake was not a man given to introspection. It made him uncomfortable. And so he put
his attention to riding, to turning Thomas in
the direction of where he had no choice but to
return—Annefield.

He decided to abandon the road and ride across
fields. Thomas was game for it. All it took was a
touch of Blake's heels for the big horse to clear
the stone dyke edging the road and they were off
again, jumping fences and both of them enjoying
the independence of making their own way. Some
of the tension in Blake's shoulders started to ease.

When he was certain they were close to their
destination, he pulled Thomas into a walk to let

him cool down. The house came into sight, but Blake found he wasn't ready to return.

He stared at Annefield's stone facade. Beyond the drunk, self-seeking earl of Tay and his two headstrong daughters, the Scots he'd met had appeared willing to measure him by his accomplishments instead of his connections. That's when he realized that the disquiet, even the fury, he felt was directed at himself.

He had no love for Tara.

She was a bauble, a pretty thing that other men had wanted and he'd won. He'd been caught up in the gamesmanship in the chase for her. He also understood that his money had played a large part in her choice. Tay had driven a hard bargain, then asked for a considerable advance on the funds.

The money did not bother Blake. He would have risked it all to please Penevey.

However, he now understood he would never be accepted. Not completely. Arthur and his other half brothers had nothing to fear from him. They would always be the duke's first choice.

Perhaps the time had come for Blake to start pleasing himself first.

The idea was radical.

A lad needed a mentor, and Penevey had served the purpose . . . but perhaps the time had come when Blake should consider what *he* wanted out of life.

Discovering he still wasn't ready to return to the house, Blake directed Thomas to a path leading through the woods on the far side of the stables. They were about to come into a clearing a good distance from the house when Blake heard Lady Aileen's voice. Thomas had heard it as well and obviously liked his mistress, because his ears picked up, as did his pace.

As they came through the woods, Blake realized Lady Aileen was pleading with someone, begging that person to do as she asked.

Jealousy was a new emotion to Blake when it came to women. He'd never cared deeply enough for any one of them to be territorial. Yes, Tara provoked him. It was outrageous to have one's intended openly mooning over another man for all to see, but he wasn't jealous.

However, he discovered he envied the man who could make Lady Aileen plead with such open emotion and fond affection.

And he wouldn't be human if he didn't want to know to whom she spoke.

He nudged Thomas forward.

On the far side of the clearing, close to a line of trees, was a small, wooden-rail paddock of the sort that was hastily built and could be torn down quickly.

Lady Aileen, looking very attractive in a straw hat and serviceable day dress of a deep green, was trying to coax a lovely gray mare to come to her and eat from a small pail. The mare stood at the far end of the paddock, eyeing her mistress with disgruntled distrust.

Aileen was so intent on her task that she didn't detect Blake immediately, so when she turned from the mare in frustration, she was startled by his presence and almost dropped the pail.

"I didn't mean to alarm you," he said as an apology, urging Thomas closer to the fence.

She shook her head and pressed a hand to her brow. The action caused her hat to fall off her head, the green ribbon around her neck keeping it from tumbling to the ground. Her hair had come loose from her pins. She gave a discouraged sigh.

"Is there a problem?" he asked.

"My mare, Folly, she's angry with me. She is refusing to eat."

Ah, here was a problem Blake could help her solve. Blake swung down from the saddle. He tied the gelding's reins around a fence rail.

"Perhaps she doesn't like being alone?" he suggested.

"I'm certain she doesn't," Aileen said, "but I need to keep her separate from the other horses in the barn."

Folly trotted over to sniff noses with Thomas. "If you put a mate out here for her, she'll be happy."

"I know that," Lady Aileen retorted. "But all the other horses must be kept in their stalls in case the earl decides he wants a reckoning."

"Won't he miss this mare?"

"He believes Folly is dead," she said. The mare seemed to understand she was being discussed and eyed them with the disdain of an offended dowager at a party.

"He sent the order two months ago to have her put down," Lady Aileen continued. "He doesn't like feeding horses that can't earn their keep. Heaven forbid a penny is wasted that he can't gamble."

"Could she not have been sold?"

"*No*, she's mine."

Lady Aileen took an agitated step toward Folly and ran her hand along the mare's neck. "The earl doesn't believe animals have souls. He says they are put on this earth to serve man and when they are done, well, we have no obligation to them."

She turned stormy gray eyes on Blake and demanded, "Do you believe as he does?"

"I don't," Blake said truthfully. "I assume all creatures that feel pain or can show loyalty must have a soul." As if approving of him, or letting him know he'd like to graze, Thomas bumped Blake's shoulder with his head. But the gelding's response was nothing to Blake compared to Lady Aileen's approval.

"That is how I feel," she said, her earlier guardedness toward him vanishing. In its place was a vulnerable, troubled woman, the sort that would tug at any man's sense of honor.

"Then that is what you should tell your father."

Her response was an undignified sound of disgust. "If I thought the earl had any cares for anything beside himself, I would have. The last time he met Angus, our head groom, in Newmarket, Father questioned him about the horses in the stables *that he rarely visits* and sent word he wanted Folly destroyed. Angus knows what Folly means to me, and, of course, I countermanded the order. It wasn't hard to do. The servants are loyal to me. No one was worried. The earl's last visit was years ago. But now he is here, and Angus is most anxious that the earl not discover that his direction has been ignored, or else he could be sacked."

"Why would Lord Tay want to put down the mare? The animal looks fine."

In answer, Lady Aileen handed him the pail of grain and raised her arms, shooing the mare away from Thomas.

Folly's head came up and she snorted her impatience. This was no obedient animal. She had some spirit to her. Blake liked Tay's bloodstock. He preferred smart horses and used his elbow to shove away the nose Thomas was leaning toward the grain bucket.

Again Lady Aileen waved her arms, and the mare started to turn away with an angry swish of her tail. But instead of trotting, she hobbled a step or two.

"What is wrong with her?" Blake asked as she took the pail away from him.

"Age. In her hips, or at least that is what Mr. Jamerson believes, and he's usually right. She can't be ridden. She'd be in too much pain, so we just let her be." Unshed tears welled in Lady Aileen's eyes. "But now, alone, she is refusing to eat. She is such a stubborn mare. She'd starve to death just to spite me."

"No horse will starve to death. Put the pail down and leave it here. She will eat sooner or later."

"Not Folly. Not when she is in one of her moods.

She's upset being out here by herself. Every time I go after her with grain, she turns away. If I leave it, the pail remains untouched." With a distracted hand, Aileen brushed back a lock of hair that had fallen over one eye.

"Then let's find a mate for her," Blake answered. "Borrow a horse from the neighbors, a horse your father doesn't know."

"And run the risk of some neighbor mentioning such a thing to Father? No. He doesn't pay attention to anything at Annefield except the horses. They are his claim to fame. Since he arrived, he has walked the stables every day, counting the stalls."

The mare had lowered her head, looking like some aged crone stubbornly waiting to die. But she was also paying attention to the humans standing close by, as if she understood what they were saying.

"If she is in pain, letting her go may be the kindest thing for her," he suggested, trying to keep his tone tactful.

"Some days, yes," she agreed. "And then others, she acts like her old self, and I don't have the heart to take her life from her. I've prayed that she would die naturally and peacefully without any action required from me. I hope to come to her stall one day and see that she is gone, happy and content and all by God's will. But that hasn't happened yet, and I need her here. She is my mooring."

"In what way?"

"You will think me silly."

"I doubt that."

Lady Aileen looked up at the blue sky with its fat white clouds before confessing, "She knows my secrets. She has seen my failings, heard my fears, my doubts, and yet she has never betrayed me, unlike most people. She's always been faithful. Why should I not be at least half as loyal to her? See? She hears us. She understands. And I doubt if she *is* in pain. Putting her down would be an expedience."

Blake understood what she meant. How many times had he wished he'd had just that sort of support? His friends were boon companions and trusted . . . to a point. What Lady Aileen spoke of was someone closer than he'd allowed anyone in his life to be before.

"Where is the gate to this contraption?" he asked, meaning the fence.

"To your right. What are you going to do?"

"Make Folly eat," he replied as he led Thomas to the gate. "She's already shown a preference for Thomas."

"As long as he is on his side of the fence. She does not like them in her field."

"Perhaps a bit of annoyance is what she needs," Blake said.

"This will not be pretty, Mr. Stephens. She *really* doesn't like males."

He unhooked the gate. "Like her mistress?"

Lady Aileen made a sputtering sound. "I don't dislike men."

He hummed his different opinion as he twisted Thomas's reins, unhooked the throat latch strap and threaded them through it before fastening the latch again. In this way, there wouldn't be a danger of the gelding breaking the reins.

Blake turned Thomas loose into the pen.

Lady Aileen hurried to the gate, opening it so that she was out of harm's way. The paddock was small. "This is not a good idea," she warned, "Folly can kick, bad hips and all."

"I need the grain," he answered. He was not surprised that she had not followed his instructions and still had the pail. He took it from her, shaking it so that Thomas knew what was in it, as if the horse had any doubt. Indeed, the gelding fell into step behind Blake as he moved to the center of the enclosure, stretching his neck to nose the pail.

Blake set the grain pail on the ground and backed himself toward Lady Aileen, closing the gate behind him.

Thomas started gobbling away. Folly's ears perked, and she decided to assert her authority. Lady Aileen had not been jesting. The mare was truly offended by the gelding's presence, and she came at Thomas with her teeth bared.

"She will kick him with all her might," Lady Aileen warned. "She could break his leg."

"He's not that stupid," Blake answered. "He won't stand for it."

A ladylike snort was her answer.

Blake frowned at her. "He isn't."

"Men can be very foolish when it comes to something they want. He doesn't know the danger he is in."

"We all know we are in danger around women, my lady," Blake replied. "We just don't mind the risk."

Before she could answer, Folly kicked her back legs at Thomas with surprising force.

She missed, but she had come very close to Thomas's head in the grain pail. The gelding moved away, but Folly was not content. She stalked him.

"We need to stop this," Lady Aileen insisted.

She started through the gate, brushing past Blake, but he stopped her, grabbing her by both arms and pulling her back just as Thomas regrouped and made another foray toward the grain pail.

Folly began bucking without any sign of lameness, and Lady Aileen could have been caught in the battle.

Blake kept his arm wrapped around her, her straw hat crushed against his chest, and he wasn't about to let her go. She felt good this close to him. Very good.

"We must let it play out now," he said.

"He'll be hurt."

"He could be, but he's wise. Have you noticed the mare doesn't act all that lame now?"

"She'll be worse than ever on the morrow," was the tart reply.

"Folly won't overtax herself," Blake said confidently.

Thomas now trotted the paddock fence, his head up, as if challenging Folly to come after him.

Instead, the mare went right to the feed bucket that had been knocked over during her kicking and began eating for all she was worth.

"She's eating," Thomas pointed out, his mouth close to Aileen's ear. Her hair smelled of the summer flowers and Scotland's sweet air.

Lady Aileen didn't respond. She didn't move from his arms. Was it his imagination, or had her heartbeat kicked up a notch?

His had . . . as had another part of him. He wondered if she was aware.

An hour ago, he'd been furious with her. Right now, she was where he wanted her.

Slowly, she turned in his arms. Their faces were so close that he could see the laugh lines at the corners of her eyes, but she was not smiling. "That was dangerous," she whispered.

"No, they were doing just what animals do. It's all a game. Attraction, rejection, and on and on it goes." He waited, half expecting her to push away and praying she wouldn't.

He leaned forward. She seemed to move closer to him as well. The air around them hummed with excitement—

"*No,*" she whispered, her eyes troubled. "*No,*" she repeated, saying the word with more force. She pushed back from him.

He understood what she meant, but for a second, he was ready to pretend ignorance. He held her, craving her heat, and then he, too, let go.

She stumbled and regained her balance.

For a long moment they stood, facing each other. Tension whirled in the air around them, but its cause wasn't one of anger. No, they feared themselves.

"I'm not that woman," Aileen said before spinning on her heel and walking as fast as her legs could carry her toward Annefield. Her hands tried to bring order to her hair, and she replaced her hat with distracted, anxious movements.

Blake watched her until she was out of sight, and only then did he realize he'd been holding his breath.

God, his knees were even weak.

He moved, needing to make his senses work.

What had just happened both puzzled and embarrassed him. He prided himself on always maintaining control . . . and yet, with her, he was powerless, even over himself.

He glanced round. Thomas and the mare watched him. They stood side by side, grazing. Apparently *their* differences had been settled.

"Don't look at me that way, old man," Blake said to the gelding. "You're as stupid around them as I am."

Was it his imagination, or was there a glint of commiseration in Thomas's eye?

Blake walked over to the now empty grain pail and picked it up, shooing off Folly as he did.

If Aileen feared her father's discovering the mare's presence, and if the earl was as interested in his horses as she claimed, then having all grain pails accounted for was necessary. Folly ran with a hobbling gait to the far corner of the paddock. She'd used all she had on schooling Thomas and was once again a broken-down mare in need of a champion.

But Thomas would not be her defender. He had to be taken back to the stables.

Unlatching Thomas's reins, Blake led the horse out of the paddock and mounted.

Folly came running to them then. She did not want to be alone. She called after them, her lament of loneliness echoing in the clearing as Blake rode away.

Blake was disappointed he didn't come across Lady Aileen. She must have taken a different path. He had planned on showing her that he'd picked up the feed pail, that he had been thinking of her best interests. What better proof would she need?

Except she'd see through him to his true motives.

Just as he'd seen through hers.

Geoff Hamilton had done all he could to blacken her name. A woman scorned was no match for the temper of a man cuckolded. Blake had believed the stories. A woman having an affair in London was not a novelty. Having a husband angry enough to cry adultery was.

There was more to the tale. He knew that now, and he wanted to know her story, because he didn't believe she could be an adulteress. She was like him. She understood honor. She had a code. Moments ago, she had wanted to kiss him as much as he'd wanted to taste her, and yet she'd pulled away. She'd forced herself from him because of her sister, because of her family honor.

This was not the action of a woman who would cheat on her marriage vows.

When he arrived at the stable yard, not even the lad who had helped him saddle Thomas seemed to be around.

Blake led Thomas through the passageway and into the square. Horses stuck their heads out over their stall doors. Thomas called out to them, no doubt bragging about his time teasing Folly, and received several answers.

Blake placed the grain pail next to one of the stall doors before going about the business of untacking Thomas. He had removed the saddle and was rubbing down the horse when a stall door from the other side of the square opened and, to his surprise, Tara walked out.

She was dressed for riding.

Thinking that perhaps she had come looking for him, Blake called out, "Tara."

The woman jumped at the sound of his voice, her eyes wide, as if his presence shocked her.

"You didn't hear the horses calling to each other?" he asked, bemused by her surprise—and then he realized something was not completely right. There was a hint of worry in Tara's eye. Or was that guilt?

She also appeared softer to him, less tense than she had been over the past several days. Her complexion even had a rosy glow.

Then he perceived movement inside the stall. A man's white shirt.

Tara caught the direction of his glance and said, "I was going to ride, but Dirk had thrown his shoe."

That was true. Blake knew that.

"I called for Mr. Jamerson," Tara finished.

Jamerson.

The horse master with dark good looks came out of the stall.

"Mr. Jamerson's banns were announced this

morning," Tara was saying, her voice slightly breathless in that way she had when she was pretending very hard that all was as it should be.

Blake knew. He'd heard her speak that way often over the last three days.

"Yes, I know," Blake said, measuring his competition. "Congratulations are in order, Jamerson."

"As they are for you, sir," Mr. Jamerson said with humble diffidence, and Blake had a very masculine urge to pick the man up and toss him into a water trough . . . because he now understood what was different about Tara. She appeared more relaxed because her lips were rosy, full, swollen . . . well kissed.

And she thought him such a fool that he would not notice.

An anger he didn't know he had inside him erupted. "What the bloody hell do you think you are doing?"

Chapter Ten

*B*lake knew she had been kissing Ruary.

For a second, panic threatened to overwhelm Tara, but then pride took over. Pride in the man she loved.

Years ago she had denied Ruary. She would not do so any longer. She would not feel embarrassment or shame.

Only moments ago, she'd been so absorbed with finally being able to hold Ruary and be held by him that she had not registered they'd not been alone. She'd even lost track of time.

Now she found herself less than ten feet away from the man who would be her husband, and she knew she looked as if there had been intimacies, *but she didn't care.*

She loved Ruary. He was important to her. Their passionate meeting in the stall had served to convince her that she'd been right to run away. No other man had ever kissed her so fully or completely, and no other man ever would.

In truth, she'd been willing to offer all she had to him. Right there on the floor of the stall in the hay. Her desire, her need for him was that strong, and his response to her kisses had proven to her that he still cared. He would *always* care.

But Ruary had been the one to refuse to consummate their love. He had explained that he had to respect his betrothal to Jane. He must. At least until he and Tara had made a decision about their future. But first, he wanted to speak to Jane.

And his words, full of honor, had made Tara admire him all the more . . . especially when, for all his fine protestations, he'd not been able to resist kissing her again. And again.

With each kiss came hope. A love like theirs could not be denied.

A cold hardness came to Blake's eye as his gaze rested on her lips. They were still swollen from Ruary's kisses, and for a moment she had doubt. Blake was not a man to insult.

She braced herself for a confrontation, certain

Ruary would step forward. He'd come up to stand beside her.

Blake looked from one to the other. "What was going on in the stall?" he asked.

Ruary answered, "The horse in that stall threw a shoe. Lady Tara could not go riding until it was replaced."

That was true . . . although Tara had hoped for a more impassioned response from Ruary.

"I would imagine a farrier's duties beneath you, horse master," Blake said, his tone low, dangerous.

A tight muscle worked in Ruary's jaw. Tara held her breath.

"We don't stand on much ceremony here," Ruary answered. "The horse needed the shoe tacked on, and I was here to do it."

"The earl is fortunate to have your services," Blake responded, but there was an undercurrent of meaning in his words.

Ruary squared his shoulders, and suddenly Tara feared this confrontation. Too much was at stake. What if Blake went to her father? Ruary could be hurt, and Aileen's comment about the horse master needing a way to earn his living echoed in Tara's mind.

"I'm ready to walk back to the house now," she

said, interjecting herself between them. She kept her voice light, innocent, with just the touch of warmth that pleased men.

Contrary to character, Blake turned away from her. "I need to untack my new friend Thomas Aquinas."

"Oh, Mr. Jamerson can see to that, won't you, sir?"

A cloud darkened Ruary's face, an expression that said groom's duties truly were beneath him.

She smiled, pleading with her eyes for him to just continue the ruse a bit longer. After all, he expected her to do the same for him over Jane.

Ruary stretched his muscles, as if unwinding tension. "Yes, of course I will. I'm glad you like Thomas, sir," he continued, walking up to the horse. "He's one of the best in this stable. A grand personality."

"And another task outside your duties," Blake prodded. There was still an edge to his tone. "You Scots are a humble lot."

Ruary reached for the saddle. Blake had already unfastened the girth. "The stable lad went down the lane for his supper. I told him I would see to things while he was gone. I started off in these stables performing the exact same duties. In truth, there are times I miss it. Nothing like the day-to-day handling of a horse that tells you what you need to know about an animal. Makes them *respect* you."

Tara assumed that last was directed at Blake, and she decided to separate her men. "Come, Blake," she coaxed, pulling on his arm. "Let us go to the house."

"But of course, my lady. Lead the way," Blake answered.

She did not have to be asked twice. As she and Blake walked to the entryway, she could feel Ruary watching them, and she knew he was not pleased. She wanted him certain of her. She owed him that much, but still—a little jealousy was not a bad thing.

Tara began babbling to Blake about plans for the wedding day. She really didn't know what she was saying. As was so often the situation when she was with him, she just wanted to fill the silence and ease the tension. Here was a topic that she felt must interest him. Besides, it was easier to talk about menus and schedules than something of true substance—

Blake grabbed her arm and pulled her to a halt. They were halfway to the house, guarded by the line of beeches that separated the garden from the stable path.

"I am not a fool, Tara," he said.

"I would never call you such," she answered,

sounding convincing to her own ears. If he wanted a scene, well, this was as good a place as any. She braced herself.

He did not disappoint. "Why did you run away?" he asked. "And don't offer that nonsense of a maidenly fear of matrimony. I won't buy it—"

"It isn't nonsense," Tara said. "It was very real—"

He placed a hand on each arm as if he would give her a shake. "You went to great extremes and a good deal of danger to avoid marrying me, and then you turn around and act as if you are *happy* with our wedding? Then I catch you flirting with the horse master, and now you are on pins and needles as if daring me to make an accusation. What is this? What game are you playing? Why did you bolt? *Is* there someone else?"

A few moments ago, with Ruary beside her, she'd been ready to declare to the world her love for him.

But now, she found she couldn't. Blake's directness was unnerving.

At her silence, he said, "I'm not some callow youth, Tara. Things can be complicated between men and women. What I ask for, what I *trust*, is honesty."

She searched his eyes. He appeared serious, but she had heard these declarations before. People always claimed to want honesty, but when they had it, they were not pleased.

And sometimes she didn't know what the truth was.

She experienced that confusion now, because Blake was a good man, one who would be an excellent husband. She'd not been foolish in choosing him over her other suitors in London. Many a man had been willing to pay the price her father had wanted for her hand.

"Kiss me," she said.

"What?"

"*Kiss me.*" Tara lifted herself toward him. "Is that such an outrageous request?"

He appeared baffled by her demand, and it was Tara's turn to become surly. "Blake, you've kissed me before. I mean, you've kissed my hand and my cheek, but they were pecks, a mere brush of the lips. I don't think any one of them has ever qualified as a true kiss, do you?"

"Such as what Jamerson offered?" he countered.

Tara was not truly devious by nature, and she'd vowed never to deny Ruary, but for the briefest moment, her heart seemed to stop. *Was* she making the right decision?

And then she heard herself challenge him. "Why are you so insistent upon marrying me?"

His hands dropped from her arms. "Because—," he started and then stopped, as if there were no words to follow.

"Because *why*?"

"Because . . . I need a wife."

"Well, then, *any* woman would have suited your purpose. But why did you choose me?"

"I admire you?" he hazarded.

She almost laughed. "You don't sound certain."

"Is that terrible?" he said.

"It's not loverlike. Can you imagine Romeo doing all he did for Juliet simply because he admired her?"

"So I am to be tested?" he snapped. "You want to measure my kisses against a *servant's*?"

Ah, there it was. "Ruary is not a servant. He is a good and *noble* man—"

"And you wish to compare lovers," he shot back.

"He is not my lover," she said, heat rising to her cheeks. "And since you raise the question, let me say I am untouched. I am as you expect . . . but is it wrong, Blake, to start wondering if there isn't more to the idea of marrying than matching bloodlines or being sold off to the highest bidder?"

"There were others who would have bid more for you. *You* turned them down, remember?"

"Such as your brother Arthur?"

"My *half* brother Arthur, and, no, I was not referring to him. He could never have afforded the price your father put on you."

"But it gave you great pleasure to spite him and claim me," she answered, as clear-eyed as he himself. "But shouldn't marriage mean something more than a chance to prove yourself better than the duke's legitimate sons?"

"You know nothing of it," he muttered. He took a step toward the house, but Tara was not going to let him run from that statement.

She grabbed his arm and held on. She might be female and several stone lighter than he, but she did have strength, especially when she dug in her heels.

He whipped around. *"What?"*

"Why did you make an offer to me?" she pressed. "Say it. I'm asking for your honesty, Blake. Admit it, you don't care about me. You never did."

"Then why did you accept *my* offer?" he answered, true anger lighting his eyes.

"That is a fair question," she replied. She struggled to sort through her feelings, feelings she hadn't recognized having until that awful moment in London when she'd realized she had to find Ruary. Even after a week of considering the matter, many of her reasons seemed jumbled in her mind . . . but some things were clear to her.

Tara lifted her gaze to meet his. "I was flattered. They all wanted you, you know, all the women. You are handsome, but you are also aloof and perhaps a bit dangerous because of your past. And then there is your role as the duke of Penevey's black sheep. That he recognized you, that he might even prefer you over his legitimate sons, makes you very intriguing."

"I'm no rake."

"You don't have to be," she said. "Everyone knows the only gambling you do is the occasional wager, although your friends are out and outers. You aren't known for dueling or imbibing, although the one duel you fought, you won."

"That is no advantage to losing."

Tara had to smile. Blake had a quick wit. "What interested me most of all," she continued, "is that you *don't* need your father. Yes, Penevey played an important role in your life, but you are the sort of man who would have succeeded at whatever endeavor he chose. You can't imagine how jealous I am. I have so few choices."

"No, Tara, you can't blame your decisions on your father."

"I'm not," she replied, stung by his verdict. "I mean, Father is a trial. I recognized his vices and that he will never be a doting parent. But my choices are limited because I'm female. Perhaps if I was as bold as you or male, I could make my own way in the world."

"We all make our own way," he said, "but only the successful brag about it."

"Oh, please," she said with irritation. "You criticize me for not conforming to how I'm expected to behave, then chide me for not being more independent?"

"I chide you for wanting me to believe you are defenseless. There are mother wolves more defenseless than you, Tara. You always take care of yourself—"

"I have a heart—"

"And a reputation for playing fast and loose with it—"

"Are you going to claim your heart is involved now?" Tara demanded, stung by his accusation.

"I don't even know if I *have* a heart," Blake returned. "Certainly it has never been attached. A combination of luck and good sense has made me very wealthy, but I've had to work bloody hard, my lady, for everything I have. You asked why I courted you?" He laughed softly, a self-deprecating sound. "Of course it was because Arthur and all three of my 'brothers' don't consider me good enough to clean their boots. And because my father, a man who didn't claim me until I was ten, but claim me he did, advised me that I could change the future of my children with a good wife."

"Or Penevey wished me removed from the danger of becoming Arthur's wife."

"That as well," Blake agreed without missing a beat. "And don't think I didn't understand that fact when I offered for you."

"He needn't have feared. As you pointed out, Arthur is not wealthy, but also, I do have standards."

He shrugged his shoulders. "Then we have the same opinion of Arthur."

"But is that enough, Blake?"

"Enough for what?" he answered, his annoyance plain.

"On which to build a marriage?"

Blake backed away from her. "I don't know anything any longer." Again, there was a tone of self-criticism.

"Tell me what you are thinking," she asked, softening her voice.

"You wish to know what *I* think? I believe you consider me a fool. You left London without a care about what your jilting would cost me. If you jilted Arthur, a duke's heir and a marquis in his own right, he would have survived. But myself?" His eyes narrowed into hard glints. "If it was known that you'd bolted on me, I would have been a laughingstock. I would have lost respect. Do you know how hard I've had to work for every single thing I own? And that you would undo it all because of your flightiness?"

"But what if I love someone else?"

The words had just flowed out of her. A question that perhaps had not been wise to speak aloud, yet there it was: her very soul before him.

The set of his mouth turned grim. "I will not be cuckolded, Tara. I will not have a wife who shows no discretion. I may not be able to control you, but I can certainly make any other man think twice before he takes you."

"Even if it means we are both unhappy?"

"What does happiness have to do with honor?"

"Perhaps not very much," she admitted. "But it has much to do about love."

"And what do you know about love, my lady? What do any of us know? Love is a 'feeling.' A piece of nonsense to make us believe there is a deeper importance to our actions than what there is."

"Am I important, Blake?"

"Are you asking if I am as besotted over you as half your suitors? In a word, no."

"That wasn't what I meant," Tara countered, softly, stung by his bluntness. "I'm talking about love."

"And what is love then?" he challenged.

Tara thought of Ruary, of how she felt when she was with him—the racing of her pulse, the desire, no, the *need* to be as close to him as possible. "Love," she said, raising her gaze to meet his, "means doing whatever I must for the person I love. *Even* if my heart is hurt in the process."

He considered her a moment, then answered, "You are lovely, Tara. I mean no insult when I confess I do not love you."

"And yet you would object to my finding someone I genuinely love?"

"First, my lady, I can't imagine you being selfless. And secondly, I keep what is mine," he said.

"You *are* a bastard," she whispered.

"You force me to be," he countered.

Her response was to pick up her skirts and go flying for the house.

*B*lake watched Tara run as if she feared he would give chase.

She was wrong, of course. He didn't chase women. And Penevey was the only man to whom he had ever conceded his pride.

He was his own person. An island in a teeming sea of opportunists, charlatans and other selfish creatures. The only person he could trust was himself. To the devil with the rest of them.

Except now he was shackled to Tara Davidson. Damn her to holy hell.

She had taken what should have been a simple matter, a marriage, and turned it into a fight for his very self-respect.

Blake turned, looking in the direction of the stables, and discovered the horse master standing by the entrance, the reins of his horse in his hand. Chances were that he'd had a view of Blake and Tara arguing.

For a long moment, the two men took each other's silent measure.

If the horse master thought he would best Blake, he was wrong.

For a second, Blake toyed with the idea of calling the man out. However, there was no honor in dueling with a man beneath one's station in life.

Of course, the problem was, Blake didn't truly know what his station was.

The marriage was to solve that, he realized. The marriage would give him roots.

But if he didn't marry Tara, then what?

There were people who would adore a story of his fall from grace.

He could not let that happen. *He would not.*

It was a devil of a fix . . . especially since the woman he realized he wanted was not Tara at all but her sister.

Chapter Eleven

The earl of Tay had gone a-courting. On a Sunday evening, no less.

Aileen could barely contain her exasperation. The earl had left Annefield to call on the widow Bossley, and she doubted if any of them would hear from him until the morning or perhaps even the next few days. With this type of behavior, he'd become the talk of the valley, while she would be reproached for wearing her hem too short or some such nonsense.

Of course, he would be forgiven because men were always allowed freedoms with a knowing wink. A blind eye would also be given to Mrs. Bossley because she was widowed . . . and, well, no one cared about her.

But if Aileen stepped out of line, if she made a face at the butcher or indulged in even the mildest flirtations, she would find herself pilloried!

Worse, the earl had charged off without saying anything to anyone. She had discovered he'd left when she'd gone to knock on his door to let him know that a light supper would be served in the family dining room. His valet had informed her that he wasn't home. The earl hadn't even thought to pen a note to her.

It was already late in the evening. Supper should have been thought of earlier. Since Mrs. Watson always had Sundays off and Cook had left to visit her family after dinner, Aileen should have been the one doing the thinking, but she had been inca-pacitated. Yes, *incapacitated*. It was the only word she could think of that adequately described how she'd felt after her encounter with Mr. Stephens.

The man unnerved her. All he had to do was look at her a certain way or put his arm around her and ideas, yearnings and desires that she'd thought she'd grown too wise to entertain filled her head.

And it was not wise to have these thoughts. He was to be her *brother-in-marriage*—yet the attrac-tion she felt for him was real. It had been from the time she'd first laid eyes on him.

She was not some green girl. She'd danced with fire before, and she knew the danger. With Geoff and, later, with Peter, she'd betrayed herself over and over.

Only at Annefield had she finally achieved some measure of peace.

And then what did a benevolent God do? He sent a man with the power to stir up discontent and longings inside Aileen that were better left for dead.

But this afternoon, Mr. Stephens had made her realize she wasn't very alive.

Mr. Stephens also wasn't free.

He belonged to her sister, and Aileen had just spent a good two hours pacing the floor of her room and reminding herself of that fact.

Was it any wonder, then, that she embraced the annoyance of her father's slipping off for a lover's tryst with all the passion of an overtaxed martyr? Especially since he was leaving *her* to deal with Tara and Mr. Stephens alone?

Aileen crossed the hall to her sister's door and knocked.

"Who is it?" Tara's muffled voice replied.

"Your sister," Aileen replied with some impatience. "I had the kitchen girl set out a cold spread for supper. I always eat light on Sunday evenings."

She paused and said, "Father is not here. Apparently he is off to call on his newest paramour, at *this* hour of the night. I wonder when he'll return home?" Without waiting for an answer, she said, "I believe I will stay in my room this evening. I'm not feeling quite the thing. You need to see to Mr. Stephens."

There. She was done with the matter and would have run right back to her room save for Tara's answer.

"I'm not hungry. I'm not going downstairs."

Aileen turned back to the door. "Tara? Are you feeling well? Are you ill?"

"I'm fine," came the exhausted, disillusioned voice.

Aileen reached for the door handle. "Dearest, let me see you—"

The door was blocked from opening by Tara's hand. "I'm *fine*," came a more forceful response.

"Then why don't you want your supper?" Aileen said. "You need to entertain Mr. Stephens. He is your guest."

"I need time, Aileen." There was a hitch in Tara's breath as she spoke.

The door was still cracked between them, and Tara stood away from Aileen's line of sight. "Have you been crying?" Aileen demanded.

"Oh, please. *Enough*. I'm no longer a child. If I don't want to eat supper for *any* reason, then I don't have to."

That was true. But there was another hard truth at work: Aileen needed Tara to help her keep her distance from Mr. Stephens. "Mr. Stephens is *your* guest," she repeated.

"I know." There was a long, tension-filled pause, then Tara said, "My heart is breaking. I know you don't approve of Mr. Jamerson, but there it is."

"I'm not without feelings," Aileen answered, stung by Tara's verdict.

"But you *can't* understand. You have never been in love."

"I've—" Aileen wanted to protest but then stopped. What could she say? Had she loved Geoff at one time? Or even Peter?

Would she have done for either of them what Tara had been willing to do for Mr. Jamerson?

"Life goes on, Tara," she said, leaning closer to the crack in the door to whisper to her sister so that she could not be overheard. "It must."

"Blake knows about Ruary and me." Tara's words were edged in tears.

So here was the problem. "Did you tell him?" Aileen asked.

A portion of her sister's face appeared in the

door. "He found us together. Blake threatened he would destroy Ruary if I didn't go through with the wedding."

For a second, jealousy the likes of which Aileen had never known speared through her.

And anger.

She had not mistaken the emotions she'd felt in the field today, but she was convinced that Mr. Stephens had experienced them as well. How humbling it was to realize that only moments later he'd delivered such an ultimatum to her sister.

"Aileen? Are you still there?"

Crossing her arms against her chest, Aileen gave herself a mental shake. Geoff had never been faithful. Perhaps Peter hadn't either. And now Mr. Stephens was proving himself to be like all the rest. This was what God had wanted her to see, and she thanked her Almighty for this cold dose of reality.

"I'm here," she said. She shot a bitter glance in the direction of Mr. Stephens's door, then leaned closer to where Tara stood to say, "Men are territorial."

"I understand they are. I don't believe Blake wants me. He doesn't have any feelings for me. But if I can't have Ruary, I don't know how I shall go on," Tara confessed tearily.

"But you will," Aileen soothed. In truth, she didn't understand Tara's desire for Mr. Jamerson. Had she not left him once, years ago? "Darling, have you ever considered that what you feel for the horse master might merely be an infatuation? Or a way to accept the changes that marriage will bring?"

The answer was the door being slammed in Aileen's face so hard she could have lost her nose if she hadn't pulled back in time.

Pressing a hand to her almost injured nose, Aileen said to the door, "Tara, you would be wise to take this evening and work out what is in your heart and mind. The pain of regret is the worst you will ever suffer. If you do not wish to marry Mr. Stephens, don't. We'll see our way through this."

Silence was the only answer.

Aileen hated silence.

She was also disgusted that the earl and Tara both lived their lives according to their whims without a thought to anyone else.

But Aileen was not like them. She understood responsibility. They had a *guest*, and while Tara and the earl seemed determined to ignore him, Aileen knew someone must see to his expectations. It was the right thing to do.

She turned to his door. For a second, it seemed to glow and pulse with all sorts of imagined possibilities. Taking one step toward it was a risk.

She also knew nothing could stop her.

Straightening her shoulder, her heart pounding against the wall of her chest, her every nerve poised over the anticipation of seeing him again, Aileen crossed to the door and knocked.

Immediately, the door opened.

But instead of Mr. Stephens, Aileen found herself face-to-face with his valet. She could barely hide her disappointment.

"I wish to inform Mr. Stephens that supper will be light tonight, as it usually is on a Sunday eve. It has been laid out in the dining room. Of course, I would be happy to send up a tray," she added, wanting to come across as a hostess.

"Mr. Stephens is not here, my lady."

That was not the reply she'd expected.

"Not here?" Had he taken off as well without a word? Were all males without manners?

She knew the answer to that question.

"Where is he?" Her words sounded sharper than she intended, and the valet's brows rose accordingly.

"I do not know, my lady." In his tone was the reprimand that he didn't believe it was his position, or hers, to question his master's whereabouts.

"Very well," Aileen said, adopting her own hauteur. She walked away and went downstairs for a cold dinner *alone*. Just like every Sunday evening over the past three years.

Of course, eating alone had never bothered her until this night—and not because of the absence of her sister and father.

Reminding herself that Stephens was not hers to fuss and worry over did not take away the sting of his leaving without a word. He hadn't even left a message for her through his valet.

In the dining room, she picked up a plate from the stack of four left there. She used a fork to take a piece of cold sliced beef but found she didn't have the appetite for more. Simon the footman hovered like he usually did.

Aileen made a pretense of eating, but the food had no taste to her, and the meal was over all too quickly. Without conversation, eating alone was a practical ordeal, a matter dispatched with speedy resolve.

However, once she'd finished, she did not move. Instead, she sat in the dining room, the table lit by a single candle, and found herself wondering at the emptiness of her life.

She'd believed all was well. Now she realized

she'd been pretending. She was lonely, and her encounter with Mr. Stephens had forcibly made her aware that, all evidence to the contrary, she still believed in love.

The thought unsettled her. She was not as young as Tara, and life had taught her that Love—with a capital *L*—could not vanquish loneliness, fear and doubts. Love did not brighten her days or comfort her nights. Love would be steadfast, never wavering, and always accepting—but she'd never experienced it.

Life and marriage had taught her differently. She might as well believe in fairies and ghosties as to believe in Love. They seemed more sensible and real.

Meanwhile, Tara was upstairs crying over it and the earl was riding the streets of Aberfeldy wooing it.

And Mr. Stephens? Who knew where he was? Or if he even considered love a worthy emotion. A man like him probably believed only in himself, in what he could touch, see and smell. A rationalist. A modern man without the need of tender emotions—although she knew he felt lust. She had seen it in his eye this afternoon. She'd *felt* it as well. He could be very obvious in his desires—

"Are you finished, my lady?" Simon asked respectfully.

Aileen looked up, suddenly brought back to the present. She'd been so lost in the direction of her thoughts that his question had startled her. She stared at him a moment before fully comprehending what he meant.

"Yes, I'm done. Thank you." Dear Lord, she was almost ready for Bedlam. She must put all thoughts of Mr. Stephens from her mind.

Or at least always picture him standing dotingly by Tara, and not in the ways her overactive imagination was able to conjure him.

She rose from the table and lit a taper from the sideboard, placing the candle in a holder. "Thank you, Simon. That will be all for this evening."

"Yes, my lady."

Aileen walked out of the room, feeling herself at loose ends and not knowing why. This was her routine on Sundays. Her usual habit would be to return to her room and read a book until she fell asleep.

Except tonight the sameness of her days threatened to overwhelm her.

Chiding herself for low spirits, she decided to choose a new book from the library on a topic that would busy her thoughts. Of course, she'd already read all of them . . . but the time had come to reread them, an endeavor that failed to excite her—until she noticed the glow of light across the hall floor coming from the library.

It was unlikely Simon would keep a light burning. He usually longed to be done with his day and would have seen to all the nightly chores before supper.

Curious, she walked down the hall and stepped into the patch of candlelight. She was not surprised to discover Mr. Stephens sitting at the earl's desk. He was tilted back in the chair, his booted heels on the desk's polished surface. His hair appeared slightly mussed, and already the shadow of his beard was forming.

He held a glass of whisky in one hand. She glanced at the decanter on the liquor cabinet. It was almost empty.

Seeing the direction of her gaze, he said, "I assume there is more whisky to refill it?" He sounded sober, but there was a sharpness to his gaze, an anger that both warned her to be careful and beckoned her closer.

"There is always more whisky, sir."

"Another assumption I made," he murmured.

He studied her a moment through lazy, half-veiled eyes. His gaze fell from her face to her breasts.

She should leave.

But she couldn't, even as she felt her response to him. She had wanted his presence, and now she had him.

For the briefest moment she thought of Tara, but then he brought his feet to the ground, reclaiming her attention.

He stood, his movements slow, deliberate as he rose to his full height. His presence filled the room, reminding her once again of that impatient tiger.

"There is food in the dining room," Aileen said, falling back into the safety of her duties as hostess. "Or I can have a tray brought in here—"

"I'm not hungry," he interrupted her. He came around the desk, his empty glass in his hand.

"Whisky is best sipped on a *full* stomach . . . ," Aileen advised, her words fading away as she realized he was moving toward *her*.

He had loosened the knot of his neck cloth. To date, she had never seen him looking anything but impeccable. She understood the desire to always be perfect. When she'd been going through the humiliation of her divorce, she'd always taken extra time with her appearance, not wanting anyone to find a flaw about her if it had been within her control. He had to feel that way as well. Perhaps he, too, knew that people whisper, that they judge, that some condemn.

And no matter how well he dressed, he'd never be accepted. Not completely.

Oh, yes, she knew he understood that as well.

He stopped with not even a foot of space between them.

He was tall, foreboding . . . mesmerizing.

"Kiss me," he ordered.

For a second, she feared her ears played tricks. "I beg your pardon?" she said, even as her heartbeat kicked up a notch.

"Kiss me," he repeated.

He stood over her, more attractive than any other male she'd ever known. Proud, independent, a tiger of a man. He lived life on his terms, a trait that appealed to that part of Aileen willing to rebel against the constraints of her circumstances.

And she might have done what he wished if he hadn't sounded so matter-of-fact, so unemotional.

But before she could respond, he pivoted on his heel and walked away from her. "*See?* It isn't that easy," he said.

"I don't 'see' anything," she answered. "Was that a test of sorts?"

"Oh, yes, devised by your sister." He had reached the liquor cabinet and poured himself another drink, a very healthy one. "She holds hoops in the air and expects me to jump through them like I'm a lapdog. I don't even like her," he said into the glass he raised to his lips, speaking as if to himself.

"But you offered marriage," Aileen reminded him, her tone carefully neutral. "And in fairness, Tara is not treating you any differently than she would another man."

"Including the horse master?"

Aileen's mind scrambled to frame a response.

His smile held no mirth as he said, "I see my accusation does not surprise you."

"Oh no, I am not going to be dragged into this argument. What happens between you and Tara is not my concern."

"But *you knew*," he said, waving his glass as if it was an accusing finger.

"She ran from her wedding for a reason, Mr. Stephens. Did you not wonder why? Or did you believe her excuses of being overtaken by fear of marriage and all it entailed?"

"No, I didn't believe her. But it doesn't make a difference. I'm trapped. Damned either way I go." He took a drink.

"And so you shall numb your brain with whisky?"

"Is there a better solution?" he asked before taking another swallow.

For the briefest of moments, the words formed in her mind—*Yes, you could want me.*

They were insane words that should never be spoken aloud.

She didn't even know if they were true. They couldn't be. They mustn't be. *He was not hers.*

Aileen crossed her arms against her chest. "I can't believe this," she said. "My sister is upstairs, mourning the loss of what she *can't* have, while you are down here, carrying on over what you *can* have. It's almost laughable."

"I fail to see the humor."

"I can understand why. It's hard to see anything when you are feeling sorry for yourself."

If she had slapped him across the face, his reaction would not have been different. He slammed the glass down on the desk.

Aileen stood her ground, lowering her arms. "If you don't want to marry my sister, then tell her instead of drinking yourself into becoming a man like my father."

"That was unfair."

"Honesty has nothing to do with fairness." She took another step toward him, tempering her tone. "And you need to think clearly. If you don't like Tara now, you may hate her after marriage, and she doesn't deserve that."

"Can you imagine the uproar if *I* jilted *her*? It would have been more acceptable for her to bolt on me, since the wagging tongues, abetted by my brothers, had always believed she'd made a grave error in accepting my offer. Had they known the truth, they would have cheered her on."

"And your reputation for being 'the bastard' would be enhanced all the more."

His brows came together. "I take no pride in it."

"Perhaps you should," Aileen countered. "God knows I have made terrible mistakes in my life, but they have brought me to the woman I am today—and I rather like her. Yes, I do," she repeated as she recognized the truth in her words. "I prefer her over the clueless but well-intentioned person I once was. If you had been born with the social standing and opportunities your brothers receive, would you be the man you are?"

"I wouldn't have known any differently."

"But you do know *now*. You've been tested and can stand upright and look any man in the eye. Your whole presence is one of a person with a great deal of self-knowledge, and can we ask for anything more in this life?"

"Peace and quiet?" he said, muttering the suggestion.

"It is too late for that," she declared. "And you should know adversity makes us stronger. Our mistakes guide us toward being better people if we take the time to learn from them. For example, I now understand the price one pays for deceiving oneself. It is costly."

He raked a hand through his hair. "This is a devil of a fix," he mumbled to himself, then looked to Aileen. "Ever since I first learned who my sire was, I wanted to please him. Pathetic, isn't it?"

"Or a natural inclination," Aileen answered.

Mr. Stephens pushed the heavy inkstand on the desk over an inch before saying, "I was overjoyed to know that the man who is my father was not one of the sailors in the docks. God, I hated the tars. A foulmouthed, criminal lot. My mother was a whore with a taste for them. And the clergy. They paid her visits as well. She had bishops for lovers ... until she lost her looks. Drink," he added, nodding toward the whisky on the cabinet. "Gin was her demise. She claimed she loved too much and had to find solace when they left her, which they all did. I believe she just lost heart."

"It must have been difficult for you as a child," Aileen said.

He made an impatient sound. "It doesn't matter," he said. "I was too busy trying to survive to notice. She was *not* a doting parent. Penevey came into my life then and saw to my education. He changed everything about me, but he always keeps a distance. He watches from the back of the stage while I perform, but after a while, it isn't enough."

"Why is that?"

"Because," he said, turning to sit on the edge of the desk, "I want more. There is that inside me that wants everything. My goal in life became proving to him that I was a worthy heir. I'm older than Arthur by six months. In a fair world, I would be the marquis."

"In a fair world," she agreed, fascinated by his story.

"And what of you?" he asked.

His changing the subject caught her off guard. "Me?"

"Were you and Peter Pollard lovers?"

For a second, she was speechless. Those closest to her had never questioned her, yet he did.

For a long moment, they looked at each other, and she realized he was more sober than she had suspected.

"What do you think?" she asked.

He placed his hands on the desk beside his hips and eyed her with disappointment. "Is this how it is? I answer your questions and you refuse mine?"

"I just don't know why you should ask," she answered.

"Curiosity?" he suggested. "Is that not reason enough? Or perhaps my reasons mirror your curiosity about me?"

There was a challenge there.

Aileen eyed the door, then faced him.

"Peter was found guilty," she pointed out. "For most, there is no question."

"Peter Pollard was a good man. I knew him, remember?"

She had forgotten. "And Geoff as well," she reminded herself. She walked to the liquor cabinet and poured herself a nip. The whisky burned her throat. It felt good.

"Ah," he replied, holding up his hand for emphasis. "*Not* a good man."

"No, he was not." Aileen looked to him. Golden candlelight cast a glow over his features. The circle of light created an intimacy between them, as if all the world had faded save this place and this moment.

"I could have fallen into Peter's arms," she confessed. "He was willing to do whatever he must to help me, but he was a *gentleman*. There was nothing between us save for a deep, abiding friendship. He knew what my life was like. He understood how Geoff could be, and when the accusations started flying, Peter did not deny them, so I didn't either. Perhaps later, after everything was done, there would have been a chance for us . . . but it didn't work that way. He just wanted to see me free. It was such a gift, and the sad irony is they both died in the same battle." The pain of regret was sharp within her. "Peter paid a terrible price. He gave up his reputation and all because Geoff felt threatened. He was like that—uncaring unless someone wanted what he had."

"And what of you?" he asked. "Did you not pay a price as well?"

She waved a distracted hand. "Who knows? If I had just managed the marriage a little longer, then I would be a widow."

"Or you could be dead. Geoff never hesitated using force to gain his way."

The suggestion startled Aileen. She thought of the last time Geoff had attacked when she'd run to Peter for help. "I *could* be dead," she echoed in agreement. "I was never able to tell what mood he was in. For weeks he'd be pleasant and then go off into a rage."

"And your father wouldn't offer protection?"

She shot him a look that spoke volumes. "As far as the earl of Tay was concerned, I was Geoff's property. I turned to the earl once. I'll never look to him for help again."

"Instead, you allow people to believe you are a fallen woman."

"I'm a *divorced* woman," she corrected. "There is a difference. Not much of one. It is subtle."

He smiled at her note of irony. "You are right."

They thought alike. Their reactions to their challenges were the same, and Aileen liked being here with him. She trusted him.

"Would you truly destroy Ruary Jamerson?" she asked, uncertain.

The comfortable air between them vanished.

He came to his feet, but she forged on. "You don't want Tara. You've said as much. And you show little interest in her."

"This is none of your concern—"

"She is my sister."

"So you plead her case. What does *she* want?"

"I don't know. I'm not certain if she knows. She's young, Mr. Stephens, and spoiled. She's a very pretty girl, and perhaps life has been too easy for her. I don't believe the two of you would suit."

He did not argue that last. Instead, he said, "Why press this?"

"Because someone should."

He tapped the top of the desk with the fingers of one hand, an impatient gesture. "You have no idea how far I've come."

"I *do* have an understanding," she countered. "I know what is at stake. You understand the rules. You don't want to be guilty of bad form. The price is twice for you as it would be for someone like your brother the marquis. But I beg you, sir, to be wise. Marriage is difficult without the added burden of two people who do not trust each other."

He listened to her, his dark eyes somber. When she was done, he raked a hand through his hair, and she understood he was conflicted. "It is not easy being fodder for the gossips," she said in empathy.

"Especially when I'm the one who will most certainly be painted black."

"People will forget," she promised.

"Until my children go out into life. It is not myself I worry for, my lady. I am well aware of what a burden it is to carry the sins of the father."

She crossed to stand in front of him. "I can't argue against your position. You are within your rights. But the days when I felt I had to measure up to everyone else's opinion of me are past. Granted, I'm not a duke's son. But you see, even hours before my marriage to Geoff, I sensed that marrying him could be a mistake. He'd shown signs of his temper, usually when no one else had been watching. I wish I'd had the courage to cry off. My life would be different . . ." She let her voice trail off as she realized he was not paying attention.

Instead, his gaze had focused on her lips, and she realized how close she stood next to him. She'd been so anxious to convince him of her opinion that she had all but walked right into the tiger's arms.

Time came to a halt.

He moved first. He reached up and placed his hand against her cheek, his fingers winding themselves into her loose curls. His palm was warm.

A frown formed between his eyes as if he, too, was a bit surprised by his actions. She knew she should take a step back, but she couldn't.

This afternoon, it had felt good to be protected by his strength. She'd been wiser then. She'd known being close to him was dangerous.

But the hour was late and she had whisky in her veins . . . although she didn't need the excuse of drink. His body heat was a more powerful draw than spirits.

And this time, she didn't protest but leaned into him.

His lips met hers.

The spark between them became a flame. This kiss was not sane or wise. There would be a cost, but for right now, all Aileen knew was that from the moment they'd first met, she had seemed pre-ordained to kiss this man.

And now that it was happening, well, she could not hold back. Not when kissing him seemed as natural to her as breathing—

Tara's voice said from the doorway, *"What is going on here?"*

Chapter Twelve

*A*ileen jumped at the sound of her sister's voice.

Blake was equally surprised, but his immediate reaction was to protect Aileen. He stepped forward, pulling her behind him.

Tara stood in the doorway, her eyes alive with the outrage of an avenging angel. "What were the two of you doing?" she demanded again, as if it hadn't been obvious.

A good amount of whisky coursed through Blake's veins, but he was very sober right now.

"It is nothing, Tara," he said with a calmness he didn't feel. "Everything is fine. Return to your room."

"Are you ordering me about as if I was a child?" Tara craned her neck, as if she wanted to see her sister. Aileen started to move away, but Blake blocked her with his arm.

Tara shook her head with scorn. "You weren't happy to see me this afternoon with Mr. Jamerson, were you? What makes you believe I am happy with what I just witnessed? Or is this your way of treating me in kind?"

"We will discuss this later," Blake answered. "Calmly." But first, he needed to talk to Aileen. He knew enough of her character to understand this would not set well with her.

"We will discuss this *now*," Tara said, demonstrating the brattiness that had been so much of her character of late, a defect he could no longer ignore.

"*We* shall not," Blake said in a tone that made her take a step backward. "If you want to rant like an offended fishwife, you may do so. However, I'm for my bed, and your sister is as well."

"Obviously" was Tara's cheeky reply, and Blake was tempted to turn her over his knee.

Aileen tried to explain. "It really isn't what you think—"

"*Don't speak,*" Tara barked out. "How could you do this? You are my sister. I've trusted you with confidences of my heart and you've taken advantage of them."

"Tara—," Aileen started, but she spoke to air. Tara had run from the room, her feet pounding down the hall.

Aileen started to go to her, but Blake caught her arm.

"Don't. Let her be," he advised.

"I *can't* let this be. What were we thinking? What madness took hold of us?"

"It wasn't madness, my lady, it was—" He stopped, uncertain how to put what had happened in words. He hadn't planned on kissing her . . . well, yes, perhaps he had. The idea always seemed ever present in his brain whenever she was around.

"It was something that *shouldn't* have happened," she finished for him. "I have no excuse. I was wrong. It is *me*. It is my nature to ruin relationships—"

"You weren't alone in the kiss," he interjected, trying to reason with her. "And it was barely a kiss. Our lips had hardly touched." No, he wouldn't have classified that as a complete kiss at all.

"It was the whisky," she continued as if he hadn't spoken. "You didn't know what you were doing. We must tell her that."

"But I did know what I was doing," he answered. "In fact, I've been attracted to you since the first day when you argued so passionately against Tara being forced to marry me."

Aileen eyed him warily. "You should have been angry."

"I should have. I was tired, had spent two miserable days with your father in a coach driving as if the devil was on our heels. I also believed I was being played for a fool. But I've never known anyone to speak out for another person with as much intensity as you did. I could see you were surprised when Tara decided for the marriage."

"That is what is so ridiculous in all this," she said. "There isn't even goodwill between you and Tara. But that doesn't mean I want to be a part of any argument you have. Oh, no, I've had enough of scandal to last me a lifetime. *This* is not for me." She began backing toward the door.

"Aileen, no, don't be this way." He reached for her. "I didn't plan the kiss. You didn't either, but now that we know what is between us—"

"*What* is between us?" She gave a small, hysterical laugh. "There is nothing. *Nothing*. No-thing," she said. "What happened here was lust. Pure and simple and so insidious it wants you or me to believe that it was special, magical. *And it wasn't*. I've walked this path before. I shall not walk it again."

She was a step away from the door. In a second,

he would lose her. Blake caught her arm, meaning to take hold of her so that they could talk just a moment more. She shouldn't be so upset.

However, when he drew her forward, she came directly into his arms. Their lips naturally found each other.

This *was* a kiss.

She didn't want to kiss him. There was a hint of resistance, but it melted at his insistence. Her lips softened, and he pressed home his advantage.

His arm moved to her waist. She felt good against him.

The whys of this moment were complicated, but he didn't need to worry about them now. Instead, for the first time in his life, he tried to let his kiss say all she had refused to hear. He attempted to convey his understanding of her fears. He had fears as well. This was not something he had anticipated; how could she?

But he knew that if he let her go, he might be missing something very important to his life. Something of great value.

He leaned her back against the door frame. There was so much he admired about her. She was direct, passionate, and understood something of human weakness.

Certainly she would forgive him for his power-lessness over his character now—

She slipped from his arms and escaped, moving out into the hallway.

Holding up her hands to ward him off, she whispered sadly, "I can't. I'm not brave enough to pay the price. Not anymore."

In the next beat, she was dashing down the hall.

Blake leaned an arm against the doorjamb.

For a moment, she had been his and he'd wanted her very much, but not in the way of rutting lust. Aileen touched something inside him no one had ever moved before. There was a connection between them, one he didn't understand, and he could not turn away.

He picked up the candle from the desk and went upstairs to stand in front of her bedroom door. He knocked lightly. There was no response. He hadn't expected one.

But in that way he was becoming accustomed to sensing her presence, he knew she was there, right on the other side of the door.

"Don't close me out," he said, keeping his voice low, aware that Tara might be listening and ready to create another scene—and then where would he be?

He thought he could hear Aileen breathing, could catch the scent of her, more potent than any perfume. "We aren't done with this," he promised. "We will talk."

She did not answer him.

Blake walked to his room, and once he was there, he doubled his fist and slammed the door shut with it.

Pain shot up his arm, but he didn't care. The action relieved some of the tension pent up inside him.

Jones was waiting up, snoozing in a chair by the room's wardrobe. He came awake with a start at the sound of wood cracking and frowned as he pieced together what Blake had done. Unruffled, he said, "Did that do the trick, sir?"

Blake turned. "No, *no.*" He pushed his hair back with one hand. He looked at the valet and confessed, "I think I may have found the one thing I want in life."

"Truly, sir?" Jones said, crossing to help Blake remove his jacket. "Is that why you are hitting the door?"

"It was either hitting the door or hitting myself." Blake paused a moment and then said, "I believe I'm falling in love."

For a second, that last word sounded alien to

his ears. He was a practical man. He'd given no credence to love before. However, the more he considered this revelation, the more real and true it became.

"Can it happen that quickly?" Blake wondered aloud. "And without good reason?"

"What would be a good reason, sir?"

"I don't know. I haven't really thought about love."

"Most men don't" was Jones's reply.

Blake frowned, trying to reason out his feelings.

His mother had been a victim of love. He'd watched numerous men go in and out of her life. After one disappointment, she'd warned him that the only person who could be trusted was oneself. It was simpler that way, and he had believed her.

Still, her attitude hadn't stopped him from searching for approval from Penevey. Blake had stretched himself to be all he could to win his father's respect—and was that not a form of love?

But what he was feeling—*at this moment*—was something entirely different.

It was as if he'd discovered in Aileen a part of him that he'd never known. There was something about her presence that felt right. And, of course, she had the other qualities he noted in women. She was not a stunning beauty like her sister, but he liked looking at her. And he enjoyed her intelligence. He respected it. When he spoke to her, he could talk as an equal. She didn't have missish ways, nor did she feign silliness. "There is substance to her."

"I beg your pardon, sir?" Jones said.

Realizing he had just spoken aloud, Blake turned to his man and said, "I *am* in love."

"Very good, sir," Jones answered, sounding slightly befuddled by Blake's meanderings.

"Yes, it is," Blake agreed. "But I am in love with the *wrong* sister."

Jones's lips formed a round and heavy "*Oh.*"

"Yes," Blake confirmed. "I am falling in love with Aileen Hamilton . . . and there will be hell to pay."

"What are you going to do, sir?"

"I don't know."

"Sir, there are plans being made for your marriage to Lady Tara."

"Thank you for stating the obvious, Jones." Blake frowned, considering his options. "Tomorrow. I'll to Lady Aileen. We'll work this out," he said and felt a sense of expectancy, of the rightness of his feelings.

He also needed to speak to Tara. That conversation would be the difficult one. Now he was glad he'd caught her with the horse master. The man was welcome to her.

Sleep didn't come immediately. He didn't count on good things just happening to him. Everything he had, he'd worked hard to attain.

However, this was one of those rare times when he let himself believe that he was meant to be here. He had been destined to meet Lady Aileen. Her reputation didn't put him off. Indeed, he had a reputation of his own. They might have been made for each other.

When he did finally sleep, it was deep and dreamless. His mind and body were content. He woke refreshed and filled with determination.

He was going to make Aileen his wife. He would speak to her, and then together, they would discuss this with Tara.

All would be well.

*B*lake went down for breakfast as early as he could, hoping to catch a moment alone with Aileen.

Dishes had been freshly set out, but according to Ingold, none of the family had been down yet.

"Not even Lady Aileen?" Blake asked.

The butler hesitated a second before saying, "No, sir."

It was that hesitation that didn't set easy with Blake.

He went about serving himself from the dishes on the buffet but found he had little appetite. Something was not right, and he didn't feel better when the earl came lumbering in the room, looking the worse for wear. His clothes were rumpled. He had been shaved, but that only made the circles under his eyes seem deeper.

"Good morning, my lord," Blake said.

A grunt was the reply.

"I assume you slept well," Blake said. He planned on this man blessing his union with a different daughter. He believed Tay would come around, although Blake was certain it would cost him a pretty penny.

The money was no matter. He was willing to pay the price. He'd never been more certain of anything in his life than he was of his feelings for Aileen.

The earl forked sausages onto his plate. "I need ale for my breakfast," he mumbled to Ingold. He then toddled over to the head of the table and sat down. Pushing back his sleeves, ready to tuck into his plate of food, the earl said, "Sorry I'm not better company."

"I understand," Blake said, steeling himself for Tay's story of last night's adventure. Men like the earl always bragged.

"Aileen woke me out of a sound sleep and ordered me home. Can you believe that? She had me on the road and back to Annefield before I realized my eyes were open."

"This morning?" Blake said, uncertain if he understood.

"Aye. Aileen pounded on the door of Mrs. Bossley's house. She was so loud, she could have woken the dead." He popped a sausage in his mouth and reached for the tankard of ale a footman had delivered.

"Why did she do that?" Blake asked.

The earl wiped the grease from his mouth with the back of his hand. "Who knows? She insisted I return to Annefield immediately. In the wee hour of the morning and when I was very comfortable, if you know what I mean."

"I do, but what was her reason?" Blake pressed, his patience growing thin.

"So I could chaperone you and Tara. Aileen has been called away suddenly. She said her cousin Sabrina, you met her in church, has taken ill and needs her. Aileen said she may be absent from Annefield for a good long spell."

"Do you believe her?" Blake demanded. This was too convenient. People didn't go running around in the night to tend to sick relatives. Aileen had left because of him. Because of the kiss.

"Why should I not?" the earl asked. "Are you suggesting she wanted to leave her home for another purpose."

"No, of course not," Blake said, realizing that no good would come of declaring himself without Aileen present. He sat back in his chair.

She'd left—without a word to him.

And he didn't know what to do about it.

Love was new to him. Did one chase love? Or respect the wishes of a woman who obviously wished to keep a distance between them?

Blake didn't know.

Growing up, he'd learned in life not to rely on people. They walked away—his mother, the duke . . . those who made him work a hundred times harder than his half brothers for the same respect. Money could keep them close. Money could buy anything a man wanted.

Except this was different, and it didn't make sense.

Aileen wasn't like any other person in his life. The kiss they had shared had held a promise beyond sex, a promise for something Blake didn't know if he could trust as real.

But he did believe he was in danger of losing someone very important to him, and he was powerless to bring her back.

$\mathcal{T}$he sight of Blake and Aileen kissing had sent Tara's mind into a frenzy. It had taken her hours to find sleep, and then it had been restless.

Everything was out of control. *Everything*.

But then she'd realized that she could use catching Blake with Aileen to her advantage.

She would tell Ruary what she'd witnessed. He would want to protect her in the way Blake had Aileen. Ruary would understand, at last, that she was free to give her heart to him. He could love her without fear of recriminations.

And if Mr. Blake Stephens kicked up a fuss, then Tara would tell the whole world she'd seen Aileen in his arms, and *all* would understand her position.

Because Ruary started his work early with the exercising of the horses, she'd slipped out of the house shortly after dawn, to find that Ruary was not scheduled to be at Annefield that morning. A well-placed question to the stable lad who was saddling Dirk had yielded the information that Mr. Jamerson would be working for Laird Breccan that morning. Breccan Campbell's estate was over beyond Kenmore and was not a far ride.

She did not waste any time setting out. She wanted no questions or having someone like Angus catch her leaving and demanding she have a groomsman ride with her.

Laird Breccan was a distant cousin of the earl of Breadalbane. He was a tall, giant figure of a man and not well liked in the valley. Then again, few Campbells were. They had a bad history, and a canny Scot knew better than to trust one, perhaps Laird Breccan more so than the others. By nature, he was a lone wolf. He rarely participated in the local society and seemed intent on buying all the land he could, even if that meant taking advantage of others' misfortunes.

Apparently he also planned on building a stable to rival those at Annefield.

Tara drew this conclusion as she trotted up to the new stone-and-timber structure on the laird's estate. Laird Breccan was said to live in a modest home built in the last century and not improved upon since—but the stable was, even to Tara's eye, a magnificent building.

The stalls were laid out in long rows. Paddocks marked off the property. The laird apparently had a good thirty horses. Tara knew how high Annefield's expenses were, and she could not imagine how much the laird was spending to breed and maintain this many racing animals.

On the far side of the paddocks was a training field, where a group of riders exercised their mounts. Seeing Ruary's horse shut in one of the stalls, Tara assumed he was over with the riders.

A stable lad saw her approach. He knew she was Quality and hurried forward with an awkward bow.

Tara suddenly felt nervous. Perhaps she was being too bold?

"Is Mr. Jamerson here?" Tara asked.

"Aye, my lady, he is," the boy said.

"Tell him Lady Tara Davidson wishes to speak to him. It is imperative."

The lad ran to do her bidding.

Tara helped herself down from Dirk's back. She was curious about the stables, and, after tying her horse to a post, she couldn't help but pry a bit. She stuck her head into one of the stalls, impressed how large it was.

Her investigation came to a quick end when she heard male voices and realized she was not alone. She crossed to Dirk in time for Laird Breccan himself to come around the far corner of the row of stalls across from her.

He was talking to a lad who was leading a sleek, well-bred Thoroughbred. Tara could recognize good horseflesh. Annefield didn't have a horse like this one in the stables.

Trailing in Laird Breccan's wake was a pack of the mangiest dogs Tara had ever seen. They were in all shapes and sizes, a striking contrast to Annefield's hounds, bred for their uniformity and good looks. Seeing Tara, they came racing up to sniff her boots.

One hapless creature stood off to the side and howled Tara's presence as if the laird could not see the visitor himself.

Tara sidled back. She didn't mind dogs. Her cousin Sabrina had one, but these animals were rude with those noses. She pushed them away. They also weren't obedient until Laird Breccan whistled. Then they all went running to his call, their tails wagging.

"Sit, you bastards," Laird Breccan said. The dogs immediately went down on their haunches, tongues hanging out.

Noting Tara with a nod, Laird Breccan finished his instructions to the lad before giving him a leg up and sending him off to exercise with the others. He watched the rider a moment, then turned his full attention on Tara.

She held her head high, pretending it was not unusual for her to be there.

He approached.

"My lady," the laird said in greeting, "to what do I owe this pleasure?"

He had a deep voice. He was also, she was surprised to note, younger than she had assumed. Of course, she'd never paid very close attention in the past, and with his shaggy dark hair and unshaven jaw, she wasn't about to pay mind to him now.

He wore work clothes, woolen tweeds locally sewn, and heavy boots that were good for marching through muck. He was brawny enough that he needn't worry about padding or tailoring, although he would never be mistaken for a tulip of the *ton* or a Corinthian. Just the thought of him in a yellow waistcoat almost made Tara laugh.

"I have a request from Father for Mr. Jamerson," she said in her imperial voice, the lie coming easily to her.

He laughed, the sound not pleasant. "Do you truly expect me to believe Tay sent his precious daughter, the one whose marriage portion will keep him gambling for life, on a mere errand? I'm no fool, lass. You'd be best to remember that."

"I needn't remember anything, Laird," Tara answered, "since it is not you I'm here to see."

He did not like her saucy response. Tara didn't care.

"You'd best mind your tongue," he murmured.

"Or the Campbells will be after me?" She laughed. "There is nothing you can do to me, Breccan Campbell, not if you want to give a pretense to being civilized."

Anger lit his eyes, and she was surprised to note they were gray, icy gray like Loch Tay on a winter's day. Well, she didn't care if he felt insulted. She had matters other than humoring him on her mind.

And fortunately, Ruary came riding up on one of the exercise horses. He dismounted and said with some urgency, "My lady, what is it? Is there a problem at the stables?"

She hadn't thought he would equate her presence with being a matter for alarm, although it did work to her advantage, so she used it. "Yes, Mr. Jamerson. We need you. Can you leave with me right now?"

Ruary looked to Laird Breccan. She couldn't help but notice that Breccan was taller than Ruary by almost half a foot. "The lads are doing fine," Ruary said. "May I leave?"

"Will you be back later?" the laird said, his words clipped. He was obviously not happy.

"If you wish, Laird."

"I do. I expect all that I'm due for the money I'm paying you."

"Are you not pleased with the results I have delivered, Laird?"

Instead of answering, Laird Breccan glanced at Tara before he cautioned Ruary, "Be careful of that one."

Tara didn't know whether to be offended or to laugh. She decided to ignore him. "Are you ready to leave, Mr. Jamerson?"

"Aye, my lady." He helped her mount Dirk, then gathered his own horse. Within minutes they were on the road.

When they were out of sight of Campbell's stables and alone on the road for Annefield, Ruary asked, "What is the problem? Why did you come fetch me?"

In answer, Tara rode off the road into the shelter of trees beside a racing stream. She slid off Dirk.

Ruary, too, dismounted. "What is it?" he asked again.

She answered him by throwing her arms around his neck and kissing him with all she was worth.

Chapter Thirteen

For a good long moment, Ruary was distracted by the kiss. Tara had that much power over him.

Tara Davidson was more than just a lovely woman. She was his first love, and she had returned for him. What man would not be flattered?

Since yesterday afternoon, memories of her kisses had threatened his sanity.

He wanted her; he didn't trust her.

She'd almost ruined him once and had left without a backward glance. And now? She felt good in his arms.

Their kisses had always been deep and sweet. The driving force, the need to possess, beat in his loins.

Ruary didn't know where he found the power to break free of her kiss.

"What is this about?" he managed to grind out, his voice harsh with his internal struggle.

"*Us*," she said, her eyes shining with happiness. "I am not going to marry Mr. Stephens."

Ruary took a step back, needing some distance from her warm, willing body so that he could think. "What do you mean?"

"I caught my sister in his arms." She said this with the joy of a child sharing a successful prank.

But it didn't make sense to Ruary. "Lady Aileen and your intended?"

Everyone in the valley liked and respected Lady Aileen. She had shown herself to be a good and caring woman—and few who had met her husband, an English officer, had admired him. When word had reached Scotland of his death, a few had predicted darkly that his own men must have shot him.

"I'm surprised," Ruary said, his sense of honor offended. "Your intended has not wasted his time."

"*Exactly*. I'm so upset," she confessed, tears welling in her eyes. He instinctively reached out to comfort her.

She went to him willingly, wrapping her arms around his waist. She leaned her head against his chest. "I am thankful I have you." She gave him a squeeze and said, "I will instruct Mr. Stephens to cry off. He will do as I wish, or I will tell all the world of what I saw."

"Why would *you* not end the betrothal?"

Tara lifted her head to smile up at him. "Because it is better this way. People will think the worse of him and favor me. When we go to London and I introduce you, people will think well of you because you were my rescuer."

"Go to London?" Ruary wasn't certain he understood her meaning.

"Isn't going to England something you always planned to do?" she asked.

"Aye, to work horses. But I've been to London a time or two, and I'm not fond of it. I'd probably be in Newmarket when the races are."

"And I will be there with you," she said eagerly. "I've thought this out. I have connections now, and your reputation is growing. We are no longer what we once were, too young to know of the world. People admire you, and I will see that all doors will be open to us. You will become famous. And I will be your happy wife."

She made it sound simple.

It wasn't.

"What of Jane?"

Tara shook her head. "Look at us. Look at how we are standing." She leaned forward so that her breasts flattened against him. The tone of her voice warmed, silkened as she said, "Be honest, Ruary, you love me. And you are the only man I would sacrifice everything for. Haven't I proven that? Would you be as happy with Jane?"

The devil himself could not be more persuasive.

Ruary was tempted to put his hands on her trim waist, to cover his lips and give in to the greedy hunger in his loins. She was an exciting woman. He could picture her in his bed, waking beside her every morning, seeing his bairn being held in her arms close to those luscious breasts she generously pressed into his chest—

God help him. He couldn't think.

"I want you, Ruary," she whispered. "You are my man. Do you ken? You are *mine.*"

He wanted to be hers. He did.

So it took a strength he never knew he had to place his hands on her arms and push her away while he took a step back.

He needed the room to breathe and allow his brain a moment to think.

"You would blackmail your sister for what you want?" he asked.

Tara had been leaning toward him, held back by his hands. She had a dreamy expression on her face, and he knew she believed in the picture she'd been weaving for him . . . so his question startled her.

She frowned, annoyed. "Blackmail? That is an ugly word."

"It is an ugly thing you want to do," he said.

"How so?" she demanded, the spark of anger in her eye. Now she was the one to take a step back, shaking his hands off her arms.

"You plan to make your intended cry off, a dishonorable action if ever there is one. The world will frown on him."

Her response was a shrug. "Is it better to say I caught him in my sister's arms?"

"I know the ways of the gentry. They would turn a blind eye—"

"And you believe *I* should as well?"

"Most wives in your class do," he said.

"Are you testing me? Are you wondering if my affections are true or not? Well, I'm *not* like most women, and I would think *you* would know that."

Her temper was rising. Tara could be as sweet as honey, but she had a sting as well.

"I do, Tara. I know you very well, and what you are planning is not the action of the woman

I know. Your sister would be destroyed if you tell people what you saw—"

"*What I saw is what happened.* I didn't ask her to kiss Mr. Stephens—"

"She is *not* a light skirt, and well you know it."

"You are defending her?" Tara said.

"Aye, I am. I like her. She's a good woman. She has always been fair to me."

"Yes, she is a good woman, unless she is left alone with another woman's man—"

"Oh, please, Tara, you have no feeling for Stephens. You have been all over me since the day you arrived at Annefield."

"I love you—," she started, but Ruary would have none of it.

At last he had clarity. He understood. "You *don't* love *me*." Those words were surprisingly hard to say. They had been part of a fiction that he had wanted to believe and now realized was false.

Tara reacted as if he had physically assaulted her. "How can you say that? Look at what I've done to prove my love to you."

"It would be so easy to believe you. Indeed, I think you believe yourself."

Her brows shot together. "How can you doubt me? Ruary, I don't want to live without you."

He shook his head. "And do you think I am the

sort of man who believes it is all right to threaten people to have my way? Especially family?"

"I just want us to be together."

"Tara, there is no *us*." The truth of those words rang through him. "Years ago, we were both too young and too naive."

"I've apologized. I didn't realize what I was tossing aside—"

"Yes, you did, Tara. You were the wise one. If we had run off the way I urged you to, then life would not be good for us. I would have given up everything I worked for and wouldn't be able to support a dog, let alone a wife and bairns."

"You would be a wonderful husband."

"Aye, you are right—but not a wonderful one for you. The 'what ifs' would have destroyed what we felt for each other. And if I agreed to this scheme of yours, then maybe not now, but soon, what you'd done to your sister would play on you. I've watched you and Lady Aileen for many years. You are close. And take it from a man who doesn't have family—blood is important."

Tara's lips turned mutinous, but she did not challenge his words. She turned from him, staring off into the distance at what only she could see. He waited, caring enough about her to give her time.

She swung her gaze back to him. "What was yesterday?"

"The kissing? Wishful thinking."

Slowly, she lowered her head. For a moment, he thought she wept, but when she faced him, she was dry-eyed, and resigned. "What do I do now?"

"Go back to Annefield and learn to be a good wife to Mr. Stephens. You've put the man through his paces, Tara. You owe him that."

"I don't think he likes me overmuch."

"You have been a trial."

"I'm not talking about recently." She shifted her weight. "He has never been particularly devoted to me. He certainly hasn't kissed me in the manner he was holding Aileen."

"Then he is a fool."

She smiled as if agreeing with him. She was not a woman men said no to very often. He doubted if she'd ever heard the word until this last twenty-four-hour period. That would be hard on anyone.

"Do you truly love Jane Sawyer?" she asked.

"Yes," he answered, realizing another truth. "I do. I didn't at first. I still missed you, but as time passed, I've come to care for her very much."

A tear escaped the corner of Tara's eye. She swiped at it with a gloved hand, looking away as if embarrassed, then said, "Well, then, you'd best be going."

"What of you? Can I escort you back to Anne-field? Campbell expects me to go there with you, and he has demonstrated a shrewd ability to know everything that happens in the valley."

"I suppose we must then." She walked over to her horse. "I don't like him. He has no manners."

"Breccan doesn't care what you think."

"He cares about having a better stable than Annefield's. Do you think it loyal that you help him?"

"I go where a man is willing to pay for my talent, Tara, nothing more, nothing less. Of course, it is always easier to deal with horses than it is men like Breccan and your father."

She nodded, and Ruary moved to help her mount. This was how it had begun for them. He'd been the stable lad who had held her horse. For a second, the poignancy of the moment gripped them both. She looked down at him, and he felt transported to that innocent time long ago when he'd first begun to dream of a life beyond his station.

She broke the moment first. "Be good to Jane," she whispered.

"I will. You be kind to Mr. Stephens. He'll have his hands full with you."

Tara laughed, the seriousness of the moment broken. "We shall see."

Ruary mounted, and they directed their horses out of the haven of the trees and back onto the road just as a rider came cantering from the direct of Laird Breccan's estate. The rider pulled up at the sight of them.

"Jane," Ruary said in recognition and also in a moment of surprised guilt.

Her horse pranced a step as she took in the sight of Ruary and Tara together. She'd seen them emerge from the trees.

Indignation rose to her cheeks in two bright red spots, while the rest of her face turned pale. "Laird Breccan said I would find the two of you on this road."

"We are going to Annefield—," Ruary started to explain, but she cut through his words.

"Stop it. *Don't say another word.* I'm done with it. You want her? Then have her. No more sneaking around and thinking folks don't see. Well, I have pride, and I'll *not* marry a man who is *unfaithful*."

She threw the words at him before putting heels to horse and galloping off.

For a second, Ruary sat, stunned, then he charged after her.

Ruary chased Jane all the way to her father's smithy on the outskirts of Aberfeldy, but she would not see him. She went inside her house and refused to come out.

Ruary pounded on the door. Finally her father came to him, iron tongs in his hands, and said, "You'd best leave, Jamerson. She's done with you. Go back to your lover."

He spoke as if Ruary had been a stranger.

Not only that, but Ruary's shouting and beating on the door had gathered a crowd of villagers. He could tell by their expressions they had heard about his meetings with Tara.

Too late he remembered there were no secrets in the valley.

They had formed opinions and found him guilty. He'd lived amongst these people for a good twelve years of his life. They had treated him well. They had given him opportunities he would not have found anywhere else.

But they now stared at him coldly.

Their loyalties were to the smith and his daughter.

Ruary left the doorstep, his heart heavy.

*T*here is talk in town about your sister," Sabrina said, entering the morning room, where Aileen was reading a book. Or rather, she was *attempting* to read it. She'd been studying the same book for the two days she had been at her cousin's and had not made any progress. She had too much on her mind.

Her uncle, Richard Davidson, was the local magistrate. His wife had just passed the year before. Her death had been hard on him and Sabrina. After the divorce, he'd not been accepting of Aileen's friendship with his daughter. However, she was kin, and he would never completely turn her away.

Besides his daughter, Richard had two sons, both serving in the military. Consequently, he relied on Sabrina as a hostess and housekeeper, since his portion was vastly inferior to his brother's, the earl of Tay.

Aileen had often suggested to the earl that he should increase his brother's circumstances and offer him a living from the estate. However, the earl was not inclined to be generous. Not if he needed the money for his gambling.

"Talk of Tara?" Aileen repeated, quickly forgetting the book.

"I wasn't certain whether to say something to you," Sabrina said. She sat on the edge of the chair opposite Aileen. She had just returned from a walk into the village and still wore her wide-brimmed straw bonnet at a rakish angle.

But right now, her manner was very serious.

"Say something about what?" Aileen's first thought was that Tara had denounced her. It was what she deserved. She should not have kissed Mr. Stephens, not in that manner.

"They say she has been meeting the horse master. The one that works at Annefield."

"Oh." Aileen couldn't think of another word that was safe to say. Tara had been caught.

Sabrina lowered her voice as if sharing a secret. "You know he and Jane Sawyer were having the banns read, but now she'll have nothing to do with him. I saw Mr. Jamerson in the village. He was standing on the bridge. One can see Sawyer's smithy from there, and they say Mr. Jamerson has been there day and night, just staring." Sabrina focused her gaze, mimicking Mr. Jamerson's expression. "They say he hasn't moved."

"What does he want?"

"I suppose to see Miss Sawyer, but Helen Dinwiddie told me she will have nothing to do with him. Everyone is worried about her. She is not eating. She refuses to come out of her room. Her heart is broken—and they hold Tara to blame."

Aileen sat very still, trying to comprehend this turn of events.

"Jane Sawyer must be acting a bit like you," Sabrina observed.

That comment cut the confusion in Aileen's mind. "What do you mean?" she challenged, even as a guilty flush warmed her cheeks.

"I don't pry," Sabrina said, "but you are not yourself. Something happened to bring you to our door in the wee hours of the morning. I wouldn't push you to discuss it, but with the gossip in town, well, perhaps you need a cousin to confide in?"

Aileen started to refute any hint that something was wrong, but then realized protests were fruitless. The evidence was too damning. She had not stirred from her uncle's. Her only concern at Annefield was for Folly's care and keeping. Other than that, she'd not mentioned her home.

Furthermore, she could use a confidante,

and she trusted Sabrina. Her cousin had been a staunch ally throughout the Crim Con trial and divorce. She'd even traveled to London to be with Aileen, something the earl hadn't been willing to do. He'd been absent from London during that time, and Tara had been too young to have been of much help. Nor would it have served her well if she had sided with Aileen.

But Sabrina had come without a care of the social costs or her own father's disapproval.

"My mind is a knotted maze from trying to sort everything out," Aileen confessed. "And I don't know why. It should be so easy."

"What should be so easy?"

"My feelings for Blake Stephens."

"Wait," Sabrina said, tilting her head in confusion. "Mr. Stephens is betrothed to Tara."

"And they should have married in London, but she bolted. She jilted him."

"But he is here now." Sabrina drew her brows together. She adored a mystery. Indeed, she enjoyed her role as the magistrate's daughter because it gave her access to all of what she called the "very best details."

"Aye, he is here," Aileen agreed, "and I believe I've fallen in love with him." She put a hand up to her mouth, shocked by her admission. She looked to her cousin. "I couldn't be in love with him. I didn't mean what I said. We have only just met."

"And," Sabrina said, equally surprised, "he is to marry your sister."

"That is why I had to leave. I couldn't stay in the same house with him. He's dangerous. Like a tiger."

"A tiger?"

Aileen shook her head. "It is how I imagine him. He can behave like one of those beasts. There is power around him and he never seems ruffled by events, although he can be annoyed." Oh, yes, she had seen that side of him many times.

"Is there merit to the gossip in the village?" Sabrina asked.

"About Tara and Mr. Jamerson? I'm afraid it is true."

Sabrina brought her hand down onto the chair seat as if afraid she would fall out of it in amazement. "Tara? With the help?"

Aileen nodded.

"He is a handsome man, I'll grant you that," Sabrina said. "But so is Mr. Stephens."

"The horse master is an uncommonly handsome man, but I actually prefer Mr. Stephens's looks over Jamerson's."

"Yes, I imagine you would," Sabrina said with a small touch of irony.

The insanity of her admission pierced Aileen's sense of right and wrong. She let out a horrified groan. "What have I done? Why can't I just be normal? Why couldn't I have married a man who wasn't a monster? Or had enough sense to not search for love from Peter who was so weak?"

"Mr. Stephens is not weak," Sabrina pointed out. "He's a tiger."

"You will never let me live that down, will you?" Aileen said to her cousin.

"I'm afraid I can't. That description was too good to ever forget," Sabrina assured her with just the merest hint of regret.

"I didn't mean to be attracted to Mr. Stephens. He belongs to Tara. They are going to marry."

"Which sister is *he* attracted to?" Sabrina asked.

"His preferences don't matter," Aileen countered. "Not once he spoke for Tara." She came to her feet and paced a few steps, thinking, before saying to her cousin, "In truth, Sabrina, I don't know if he cares for me at all. It is possible he just wished to teach Tara a lesson."

"He knows about Jamerson?"

"Yes, he found out. He was upset, and I was

close at hand. Then Tara caught Mr. Stephens and me kissing, and I knew I had to leave."

Sabrina sat back in her chair with a sound of revelation. "And here I assumed you were living a quiet life."

"This is not a joking matter," Aileen warned. "And discussing this with you, I realize I may have made too much of the situation. He could have been using me to strike back at Tara."

"Which I do not believe speaks well for him," Sabrina returned stoutly.

"Perhaps not, but it means that I have allowed feelings I should not have to influence my best judgment."

"Aileen, think on it, love is a strong word. Perhaps you just have a high regard for him. Or maybe, what with Tara and this disturbing liaison with Mr. Jamerson, you might empathize with Mr. Stephens and, well, be your caring self. You might not like him at all. Not truly."

"And imagined I'm in love?"

"You have known Mr. Stephens—what? A week? One can't fall in love that quickly."

Sabrina was right. "Geoff courted me a year before I had feelings for him. And I'd known Peter most of my life."

Sabrina held up a hand as if to stave her off.

"Please do not compare Mr. Stephens to Geoff and Peter. He'd be better served if you compared him to my dog Rolf than those men.

Hearing his name, there was the click of nails on the wood floor as Rolf jumped up from his cushion in the corner and came running. He was a small pup that weighed less than a stone.

He leaped into Sabrina's lap. Sabrina laughed and kissed Rolf's front paws. Her cousin had rescued the pup from some boys who'd been teasing it.

"Thank you," Aileen said.

"For what?" Sabrina asked in surprise, looking up from her pet.

"For helping me sort out my troubles. I may have read too much into my own feelings, let alone those of others." She started walking toward the door.

"Where are you going?"

"Back to Annefield. If rumors are going around and Mr. Jamerson is standing on the bridge pining for his betrothed, Tara needs me. My being here will only add to the tongue wagging."

"What of Mr. Stephens?"

Aileen paused. "He doesn't have feelings for me. You are right."

"I didn't say anything," Sabrina said, holding Rolf back as he tried to lick her face.

"But you gave me a chance to reconsider. If Mr. Stephens did have strong feelings for me, wouldn't he have shown some sign, such as coming to me? Or at least writing a note?"

"Or standing on the bridge, staring at your uncle's house? That would be a sight, with both Mr. Jamerson and Mr. Stephens on General Wade's Bridge."

"That it would, but tigers don't wait, not for anyone. They either act, or they don't. Thank you, Sabrina." Aileen came back in the room to give her cousin a kiss on the cheek, needing to push aside the wiggly Rolf to do so.

"Good luck to you," Sabrina said. "And don't worry about the rumors. I've already denounced them and will keep doing so."

"I shall see you at Tara's wedding," Aileen called as she left the room.

*I*t did not take long for her to pack. Emory, her uncle's man, drove her back to Annefield in the pony cart.

The sun was setting when she arrived, and the lamp over Annefield's front step had been lit. Ingold opened the door in greeting. "It is good to have you return," he said.

"Is all well?" she asked as Simon took her luggage from her and carried it up the stairs.

Ingold leaned forward. "Lady Tara has taken a tray in her room. Mr. Stephens ate with his lordship but has returned to his room."

"And the earl?"

"In the dining room."

Which meant he was drinking.

Aileen did not want to see him. "I shall go upstairs," she said. "Please send a tray to my—"

"Daughter!" the earl's voice rang through the hall. He came marching toward her. He had removed his coat, so he was only in waistcoat and shirtsleeves.

Aileen drew a deep, fortifying breath and plastered a smile on her face. "Hello."

"Good to have you home," he said and then, in the next breath, "Ingold, my coat, my hat. Send someone to have a horse saddled."

"Yes, my lord." The butler motioned for Simon, who was halfway down the stairs after having carried Aileen's bag to her room, to fetch his lord's clothing. Ingold himself then went down the hall to send someone out to the stables.

"You are going out?" Aileen asked, puzzled. "At this hour?"

"I am indeed. Thought I would go half mad

stuck here in the country. Had to keep up appearances, but you are here now, and you can chaperone the lot." He confided, "You won't have to worry much. Stephens and Tara are a bit like oil and water. They don't mingle."

Aileen did not like the way her heart gave a happy little start at the information. "Does that bode well for the marriage?" she couldn't help but ask.

"The marriage bed will stir them up fine," the earl predicted. "And if it doesn't? Well, not my worry."

"Where are you going?" Aileen asked.

The earl did a little jig. "The widow Bossley needs me for a wee visit. She's been lonely."

"Oh, I'm certain she has been," Aileen murmured.

Her sire's response was to laugh. "She sends me letters with fulsome promises for breakfast, supper and dinner. I am most ready to take her up on her offers." He tapped an impatient foot, a sign he was anxious to be off. "We had a good hunt the other day," he said as if making conversation.

Ah, the hunt. After all that had transpired Sunday evening, Aileen had forgotten about it. She was certain that Ingold and Mrs. Watson had seen to matters. They usually did. "That's good," she murmured, as anxious for him to leave as he was to go.

Simon came down the stairs with the garments. The earl smiled and held out his arms for help with the wool jacket in a very stylish bottle green. He tugged on each sleeve, then stopped, as if struck by an idea. "I should tell you, Stephens is interested in the stables. He discussed building his own."

"Oh," Aileen said, not trusting herself to say more on the subject of Blake Stephens.

"He asked about one of my mares." He reached for his hat and stepped in front of the small looking glass by the door to check his appearance as he put it on. "You know the mare. You used to ride her. Folly is her name."

Aileen stopped breathing, suddenly afraid.

"Old thing," her father was saying. "She was a good breeder, but her best days are behind her."

"What about Folly?" Aileen's first thought was that Mr. Stephens had exacted the perfect revenge. If he was angry with her for the other night and for leaving the house, there was no more perfect way to hurt Aileen than to tell the earl that his order to put Folly down had been ignored.

"He bought her," the earl announced. "Told me he was interested in breeding stock and had heard of the mare." He paused and frowned. "I'd thought I'd ordered the mare put down, but fortunately, I have her." He turned to Aileen. "And let me tell you, I bargained hard with Stephens. He hardly countered for the price. I sold that mare to him for three times her worth. He'll be keeping her here until he sets up his own place."

Aileen thought she would faint from relief. She reached for the stair bannister to steady herself.

If Aileen had wanted a sign that Mr. Stephens cared for her, she could have asked no better.

There was a knock on the door. Since he was standing right there, the earl opened it to the stable lad with his horse. The earl shot Aileen a parting grin. "Don't expect me home, daughter." He left.

Had she told Sabrina she "believed" she had fallen in love with Mr. Stephens?

She now *knew*.

Love was not what she'd expected. It wasn't gallant and noble. No, it was a heady rush of emotion based upon the realization that here, at last, was someone who cared about her as much as she did him.

Here, at last, was a man she could trust.

Aileen went charging up the stairs. She bypassed her room and went straight to Mr. Ste-phens's door. She did not knock but walked right in.

He'd best be ready, because she was going to do more than just unceremoniously reenter his life. Oh no, she had come to love him.

Chapter Fourteen

*B*lake had been feeling as if the world was a bleak place.

Tara had been doing her best to be pleasing the past two days, and without the artifice of pretention. It was as if she truly wished to marry him.

But he saw through her now. She was lovely, a fine specimen of the female species . . . but he found he wanted more. He wanted a woman who spoke her own mind and understood that passion for anything had to be genuinely felt for it to matter.

But that wasn't the woman he was going to marry.

Word had been passed around London about

his Highland wedding. His cronies and Penevey had sent word that they would be present. The worst moment was when Blake had read in Penevey's letter that Arthur would be his traveling companion. The time to cry off was past.

Blake should have let Tara run when she'd first bolted . . . and yet, if he had not given chase, he would not have met Aileen. He would not have learned that his heart was capable of being moved or that he, too, like every other mortal man, yearned for the connection only love for a woman could provide.

Life had been a shallow experience before he'd met Aileen. Meeting her had been like discovering another half of himself.

And when this was all over, he and Tara would return to London and the life that *would* have made sense to him two weeks ago.

The prospect filled him with emptiness.

And then the door to his room opened.

Aileen marched into his room and back into his life.

She shut the door. For a second, he feared he was conjuring her out of his imagination, and then she smiled. She rushed toward him, threw her arms around his neck and kissed him with the ferocity of a tigress.

He had no choice but to kiss her back. It was as if his dreams had come to life.

She felt good in his arms. She fit so well against him. She was soft and accommodating in the places he was hard—and he was hard.

Even the scent of her drove him to madness.

This kiss, the touch of her skin, and the taste of her tongue, tickling and teasing his, set his every nerve on edge. He'd never wanted anything in his life as much as he did Aileen.

Still, when her hands tugged free the edge of his shirt from his breeches, when she began unbuttoning those breeches, Blake broke the kiss.

His breathing was labored and deep. His desire for her was very real and obvious between them. "Do you know what you are doing?" he asked.

A slow, *knowledgeable* smile curved her lips. She slid her hand between their two bodies. She placed her palm on the length of his erection pressing against his breeches.

Her boldness stole his breath. With what little sanity he had left, he demanded, "Why?"

She moved closer to him to press her lips against the line of his jaw. "Because there isn't another man in the world like Mr. Stephens," she whispered. "And I am in the mood to make you very happy."

There comes a point for a man when blood can be in only one of two places—the big head or the little one. He can think, or he can react. He can't do both.

Blake had hit that point. Did it matter what drove her? He wanted this woman, and he would have her.

He backed her onto the bed, the covers thoughtfully turned down by Jones. He attempted to finish unbuttoning his breeches, but his fingers were clumsy.

Thankfully, Aileen's weren't.

She helped, and he could finally spring free. He pulled her skirts up, tore at the thin lawn of her undergarments.

The heat of her against his fingers pushed him beyond reason. She had reached the same point. She did not shy away but offered herself to him.

Sweet, merciful heaven.

He could not wait another moment or he would disgrace himself. Blake lifted her legs with his forearms. She was completely at his mercy.

"You are so beautiful," he whispered, meaning the words as he'd never meant them before.

"If you don't do something right now," she answered, reaching her arms out for him, "I shall scream in frustration."

Blake heard himself laugh. She'd surprised him. And delighted him.

Her desire matched his. She was not afraid to demand action, and he felt himself a very lucky man.

With one strong thrust, he buried himself to the hilt.

For a moment, he went still, reveling in her heat, feeling her body stretch, encase and embrace him. This was more than just the primal need of a man for a woman. There was magic in this joining and a sense that, at long last, he'd found where he belonged. *With* her.

Beside her.

In her.

Her cry let him know he was exactly where she wanted him. And if he released, he knew she would be happy.

But he wanted to make this a moment that would never be forgotten. So he held himself tight, an act of unbelievable restraint, then slowly began moving inside her.

Aileen was a vocal lover. Her sighs and well-pleasured moues were the finest encouragement he'd ever received.

The heat between them built. He found he

needed more. He no longer held her legs. She had wrapped them around his waist, holding him to her. He took her by the hips. His thrusts became bolder, more demanding. Her arms gripped his forearms. She was beautiful, she was magnificent, she was glorious. Together they moved toward the moment of completeness, toward fulfillment.

Conscious thought was beyond Blake's ability. She had him. He was hers. He pushed and pushed, wanting, wanting, wanting—

In one shimmering moment, they were together, and then, in the next, he felt her go over the edge of release. She cried his name, his *first* name, half sob, half blessing. He pressed deep, reveling in the sensation. Her muscles clenched him, holding him.

No woman had ever given herself so completely, so generously to him—and he allowed himself to follow her. He was so rooted inside her that their bodies felt fused together.

Blake's physical sense of being disintegrated, blending into her in a way he'd never experienced before. They were completely one, bound by a force stronger than any he could have imagined.

He clung to her, silently vowing never to let her go. She was his salvation, his purpose, his meaning, his life. For a man who had never felt as if he'd belonged anywhere, this was a gift.

Her arms held him just as tightly.

Blake wanted to hold this moment forever. But eventually, his heartbeat began to return to normal. He became aware of his surroundings and realized his breeches were around his knees and her dress up to her breasts. "If anyone walked in right now . . . ," he started.

Instead of her being embarrassed, a smile lit her face. She placed her hand against his jaw. "They would know we had a good time," she finished.

I love you, he wanted to say, but he held the words. Everyone professed love after what they'd just experienced.

He wanted that declaration to mean something to her when he said them, and a simple "I love you" would not be enough. For the first time in his life, he understood why men were moved to write poetry.

She ran her hand down the arm that still bore his weight over her. Her blue gray eyes looked up to him. "Would you like to undress completely . . . and perhaps try it again?"

Her suggestion had an immediate impact. He hardened. She had that complete power over him.

She'd noticed his reaction. She scooted back on

the bed, her legs exposed to him. "I take that as an 'aye,' Mr. Stephens."

"Oh, *aye*," he assured her.

Aileen laughed and began loosening the laces of her dress, which was already hopelessly mussed. Blake didn't waste time removing his own clothes. His boots were particularly stubborn, or was it that he was clumsy, with proof of his desire so evident?

She was already naked and pulling the pins from her hair. Seeing his difficulty, she set the pins on the table beside the bed and slid off the mattress to kneel before him. She grabbed the heel of his boot and pulled, almost falling over, to her delight.

Blake loved the sight of her breasts, with her hard pink nipples, bouncing with her laughter. She was so beautiful to him.

Yes, Tara had the perfection of a goddess . . . but Aileen was a woman, warm, caring, gracious. Her flaws were part of her charm, part of what made her unique and valuable to him.

He had to touch the shining mass of her hair, tangling his fingers in it. She dropped the boot in her hand and looked up at him.

"So lovely," he whispered.

Her brows came together. "I'm not, Blake. Not

if I stop and think about what we are doing with Tara close at hand."

"She has no strong feeling for me, or I for her."

"I know."

"But I care about you," he dared to say.

The sadness left her eyes. "I know that as well. You bought a horse."

So his purchase of Folly had done the trick. "It was the only thing I could do that would have meaning for you."

"It did, Blake." She closed her eyes a moment, as if making a wish. When she opened them, there was a peace in their depths. "No one has ever cared enough for me to discover what truly holds meaning for me . . . but you did. I don't know why events happen the way they do, but right now, I've never felt happier."

And then, before he could answer, she leaned forward and kissed him in the most intimate ways a woman can a man.

All words were wiped from Blake's mind as her kiss robbed him of sanity. And he realized words didn't matter. She was right. What was between them was powerful. It defied explanation. Defining it would be futile.

But their actions . . . ? Ah, yes, the way they

touched, the way they made love told them louder than mere words what they meant to each other.

And Blake was perfectly content to let her have her way with him . . . as long as he could happily return the favor.

Aileen was in love.

She didn't leave his bed until the wee hours of the morning, before the servants stirred. Other than a few hours napping in Blake's arms, she hadn't slept. Who needed sleep when one was in love?

Her worries the day before for Tara evaporated. It was midday before she remembered the gossip about her sister that had driven her to return to Annefield. But now, the needs of her sister did not excite the same concern. Love had that ability. It insulated lovers from the daily fears of ordinary people. Or was it that love put those fears in their proper perspective?

And that night, after all had gone to bed, Aileen returned to Blake's bed. He was waiting for her. Eagerly.

Making love to him made her feel whole. And so she went to him the next night, and the next.

The weight of time and regret that had at one time plagued her gave over to the wonder of being exactly where she should be.

Had she once prayed for peace? For her life to have meaning?

Her prayer was answered now. The twists and turns she'd made had been the only way she could have waved her way toward Blake Stephens.

One afternoon, she came across her journal. The last entry had been written shortly before Tara had arrived home.

Reading those words, Aileen could only smile. She took the journal to the kitchen and threw it into the fire.

"What is that?" Cook asked, obviously surprised by Aileen's actions. Why should she not be? Aileen valued books.

"It is my past," Aileen answered.

Cook smiled. "Ah, well, then it is a good thing to burn."

"Aye, it is."

Of course, Aileen didn't mention love to Blake. He was not hers to love, something that, after their first few nights of slaking their lust for each other with wonderful sex, began to bother her.

Blake didn't speak of a future for them. He seemed to keep his own counsel, although she knew he cared. She could tell by the way his touch lingered, as if she was something precious to him.

During the day, his gaze would often wander to meet hers, especially if something was said that he knew would amuse her. She cherished these moments as small gifts. For the first time, she understood what was possible in a loving relationship.

And they played chess. Hours and hours of it, when they weren't making love. Blake had moved the chessboard and table up to his room. She doubted if Tara noticed it missing from the sitting room. Aileen couldn't beat him at the game, although she tried mightily, and he praised her for it.

In fact, Tara seemed oblivious to the new companionship between her betrothed and her sister. They took great care to appear distant from each other during the day, but also Tara spent hours at the stables. Thinking of the rumors, Aileen made some discreet inquiries and learned that Mr. Jamerson had not been at Annefield since the week before.

Aileen also noticed that there had been no callers to Annefield. No locals with good wishes for a soon-to-be bride.

Of course, plans were being made for the wedding celebration, and Aileen was assuming Tara was making them. The wedding ceremony itself would be a small family affair, but there would be guests for the wedding breakfast. This celebration would not be as grand as what Aileen had heard had been planned for the wedding in London. Still, accommodations needed to be organized for the few guests who would be arriving for the event, especially since one of them would be a duke.

The earl couldn't be called upon to do anything. He hadn't returned home since he'd gone after the widow Bossley four nights earlier. His absence made Aileen's trips to Blake's room easier.

Blake and Aileen did not talk about the wedding. She sat beside Tara, with Blake on Tara's other side, as their banns were read a second time. There was no third reading of the banns for Miss Sawyer and Mr. Jamerson. Nor was the couple in church.

Aileen wondered what Tara thought, but she did not ask her. Indeed, the two sisters rarely spoke to each other.

That night, in bed, was the first time either Aileen or Blake mentioned Tara.

They lay entwined in each other's arms. Aileen's head rested on his chest. He'd propped several feather pillows behind him, and she was very comfortable. She enjoyed snuggling bare skin to bare skin with him.

He had a loose arm around her waist. Sometimes they read books like this. Other times they just talked. So far, to Aileen's knowledge, the servants didn't know of their liaison, although occasionally she noticed a speculative glance.

Was she sensitive to her past and what they might say?

She tried not to think on it.

"I wish to talk to your sister about us," Blake said. "I must stop this farce of a wedding before it goes further."

Aileen raised her head to look him in the eye. "What are you going to say?"

"I will ask her to release me from my offer. Honorably."

"Why?" Aileen asked, knowing in her heart the reason. She'd known when she'd heard he had purchased Folly . . . but she wanted to hear him say it.

He tightened his hold on her, pressing a kiss to her forehead. "I will not speak, not yet. I am not free to do so. I know you well, Aileen, and I believe you know me with the same understanding. Let me talk to your sister."

"May I be there?"

"I don't believe that wise. You have nurtured her a good portion of your life. The decision she has to make must be hers alone. You must step back."

"But what if she refuses to release you from your marriage offer?"

"What would you have me do?" he asked.

She did not know the answer.

For a long moment they studied each other, and then she leaned forward and kissed his eyelids, his nose, and the curve of his mouth as it stretched into a smile of anticipation.

"Don't think on it," she whispered. "Not now. Not yet."

His response was to roll over on the bed, his weight on top of her, and love her until she was senseless.

Chapter Fifteen

For a few days, Ruary had not come to Annefield. Nor was he in church on Sunday.

Miss Sawyer and her family were not in church either.

Then Tara overheard the stable lads discussing rumors. They said that Miss Sawyer would have nothing to do with him. They said Ruary had stood for days on General Wade's Bridge, staring at the smithy's house.

That information ate at Tara. *Had he no pride?* Did he not understand that she waited for him with open arms?

It was one thing for him to pine but another for him to make a spectacle of himself.

She would feel better if he would come to

Annefield. Then they could talk and she could remind him of what he meant to her. She would not treat him the way Miss Sawyer was. He needed to know that.

And, in spite of the words they'd spoken in the wood that day, this rift between Ruary and his intended gave Tara hope. Here was a sign he was meant to be with her.

On Tuesday, in spite of the rain, she went into Aberfeldy on the pretext of visiting her cousin Sabrina. She never made the call. What she'd really wanted to do was see if she could catch sight of Ruary. He lived in a slate-roofed cottage close to the village. She hoped her presence would make him realize she still cared, that she was there for him.

However, he was not on that bridge or anywhere in the village that she could see. She kept riding around, knowing she was hard to miss on top of Dirk and with an Annefield groom as her escort. At last she gave up and went home.

It was a sad ride, until she began making excuses for Ruary. She'd been silly to believe he would approach her in Aberfeldy. People expected her to marry Blake. The horse master would be sensitive to her reputation and what creating the wrong impression would mean for both of them.

He was right. They had to be careful, but Tara was nothing if not impatient.

She toyed with sending a note, then rejected the idea.

And so she waited, expecting him to appear at Annefield at any moment.

But he didn't.

The next morning, she sat in her bedroom window with its good view of the stables and watched the lads take the horses out to exercise. No horse master appeared to watch the work.

Tara didn't know how long she'd sat there waiting. Time had ceased to have meaning. The only thing that brought her back to the present was Ellen entering her room.

"Are you wishing to dress, my lady?"

For a second, Tara couldn't form an answer. She was that adrift in her own sadness. She raised a hand, a gesture Ellen took for assent.

The maid began making the bed. "Did you hear that Miss Sawyer, the blacksmith's daughter, is leaving the valley?"

Tara swung around in her chair by the window to face her. "What did you say?"

"Jane's mother is my aunt," Ellen said, smoothing the counterpane. "She told my mother that Jane has asked to be sent away for a spell. It's a pity she won't marry Mr. Jamerson."

Tara's heart danced at the news. "Does anyone know why?" she asked, trying to keep her voice calm.

Ellen seemed to be concentrating on fluffing a pillow as she said, "Jane and her family are not ones for idle chatter. They have not said. My mother has asked, but it is to no avail. All they will say is Jane is leaving on the Mail for Glasgow, where my uncle's family lives. She'll be leaving today. Of course, she'll probably meet a fine young man there. Then again, few can match Mr. Jamerson with the looks. What dress would you like to wear today, my lady?"

The deep desolation that Tara had been experiencing vanished. *Jane Sawyer was leaving.* Ruary could be hers.

"The blue," Tara said, choosing the cheeriest color in her sparse wardrobe. Perhaps Ruary was waiting until Jane was truly gone to pay a call?

He was right, if that was his plan. They should let the talk die down before they said anything to anyone.

In no time, she was dressed and ready for anything. She wore her hair pulled back and curled around her shoulders. The blue brought out the color in her eyes, and she knew Ruary would appreciate it *if* he came to call. And if he didn't call today, she'd wear the dress tomorrow. Anything to charm him.

When she came down for breakfast, Ingold informed her that the earl had returned home that morning. Tara didn't care. In London she'd grown accustomed to her father coming and going as he pleased. Her sister was not home either. Apparently Aileen had just left to help deliver charity baskets to the sick in the kirk.

Tara broke her fast with a bit of toasted bread and tea, then set about the task of keeping herself occupied while she waited for that one thing she wanted most of all—a decision from Ruary.

A few hours later, Tara was attempting to work on a needlework piece that really had no purpose other than to rest her anxious mind when Blake found her in the morning room.

He gave a light rap at the door frame. "May I join you?" he asked.

She gave a guilty start. Her mind had been so focused on Ruary that she had paid scant attention to him. Then again, he hadn't seemed to need any. She didn't know what he did with his time, but he didn't appear to be at loose ends.

She'd almost forgotten catching him kissing her sister. The whole incident had ceased to be of importance once she'd learned of Miss Sawyer and Ruary's fight.

Besides, from what she could see, he and Aileen barely spoke to each other.

"Please join me," she said, setting aside her needlework and moving over on the settee to make room for him.

Instead, he pulled a chair up to sit directly opposite her. His action didn't bother her. Blake could do what he wished. There was only one man who concerned her.

"Have you been making yourself useful?" she asked, giving him the smile men seemed to like most from her. The one that never touched her eyes.

"I have."

She smiled again.

He didn't smile. In fact, he had a grave expression on his face.

"Blake, you seem as if you have something to say."

He met her eye. "I do."

"Well, what is it?" she prodded.

"I've fallen in love with your sister."

At first, Tara didn't believe she'd heard him correctly.

Blake rightly considered her silence as shock. He plunged on. "It was not her fault. Not mine either. It is something that just happened. Tara, you don't care for me. I beg of you, release me from my promise to marry you."

For a second all Tara could do was blink, but she quickly found her wits.

"My *sister*?" she repeated, the surprise in her voice unfeigned.

"You must not blame her. Or if there is blame, then it rests on both of us. Tara, I have never felt this way about another person in my life. I never knew there could be a bond this deep and strong between two people. I'd like to handle this matter honorably. In truth, Aileen would have no other way. She cares for your feelings and understands how sensitive you might be right now." He leaned toward her. "I want Aileen to be my wife. I can't imagine my life without her. And let us be honest, there isn't anything between you and I save for mutual respect."

Tara released her breath slowly.

What was happening to her?

First Ruary had not come immediately back to

her. And now, Blake was telling her he preferred Aileen over herself.

"Isn't mutual respect enough for a marriage?" she heard herself counter.

"Not for the marriage I want," came Blake's answer.

Tara sat for a moment, her mind a jumble of feelings.

This was the declaration she wanted from Ruary.

She could not begrudge Aileen. Her older sister deserved happiness.

Still, it would not appear well to the eyes of the world that Blake had chosen Aileen over her, and Tara cared very much for what the world thought. She knew how difficult London society could be. One misstep and doors slammed shut.

Blake knew as well.

"Do you not realize what will happen if you marry my sister?" Tara asked. "Everything you worked for will be gone. Especially since she is a divorced woman."

"I'll have my business affairs," he answered, his tone hardening, as if he was not pleased with her mild observation. "And my friends will stand beside me. I would have nothing to do with those who would reject Aileen."

"What of your father? Will he approve of such a match?"

"Are you raising objections out of concern for your sister?" he asked coolly. "Or do you have your *own* reasons?"

His question was a good one. Tara wasn't certain how she felt.

Instead of running away the way she had, he was being decent and asking for her understanding. Furthermore, this involved Aileen. Perhaps they had grown apart over the years, but they were still sisters, and Tara did love her.

However, Tara had come a good distance from those days when she'd been completely dependent upon her oldest sister. Much had happened.

What did she owe Aileen now? And didn't allegiance go both ways? "I can hear the whispers," she said. "They will talk about one sister stealing another sister's future husband. It might be different if you weren't who you are. There will be a great deal of speculation."

"I know." He shrugged. "I sense what is going through your mind. You are right to be concerned."

"Concerned?" Her voice sounded a bit shrill. She swallowed. "This is not some comedy where lovers are passed around and all's well that ends well. There will be a price."

"I'm willing to pay that price."

"And what if I say no?" she asked.

Blake sat back, the set of his jaw hardening. "I hope you won't, for Aileen's sake as well as mine."

"But if I did, would you honor your commitment to me?"

He considered her a long moment before saying, "Yes, I would. Mainly because your sister would not have me without your blessing."

Her blessing.

And, Tara wondered, what did she want? She wanted Ruary. If he came back to her, then she didn't care what Blake did.

"I need to consider the matter," she said. "Will you let me have a bit of time?"

Blake's gaze narrowed. "Our banns will soon be announced for the third time."

"I am aware of that. How good of *you* to remember."

He did not like her jibe. He stood. "I mean nothing to you, Tara. But Aileen means the world to me. I'm not a begging man, but I ask you now to free me of my pledge."

"It isn't just my decision to make," she answered. "We are bound by the conventions of society—"

"*That is rubbish.* You were willing to bolt on me without a thought to 'society.' "

"I'm wiser now," Tara said, her tone equally steely. "And a woman has more to lose. Men don't like being second choices. And I don't want Aileen's lot. I don't want to be left in the valley to just rusticate. The life I desire is in London. You know that."

"And what of your horse master?"

"What of him?" she challenged.

Blake didn't continue on with it. Instead he shook his head with disgust. "You are a child."

"I was woman enough for you at one point. But this isn't easy, Blake," she said, rising to her feet. "It is like we are all marionettes. There is a limit to what we can do freely."

"What limits? The conventions of society? To the devil with them, Tara. Do what is right."

"And what is that, Blake. Ruining myself?"

"How would you be ruined? Cry off and let me carry the blame."

"But all will know you chose my sister over me."

"And that is the heart of it, isn't it? You don't want to be left behind."

"You are right," she admitted with complete honesty. "I don't want to be pitied or abandoned." She'd experienced that once when Aileen had left her and gone to London.

No, Tara had not liked that at all. She'd understood then that the important did not stay behind.

"Well, understand this," he informed her. "Your sister and I are lovers."

His words were hard. Piercing. For a second she wanted to blame Aileen . . . and yet couldn't. "You would risk breeding subject bastards?"

"Yes," he said, as if just considering the thought. "I could wish no mother better for them than Aileen." He left the room.

No mother better . . .

His words were a cruel cut. She'd not thought of what it would mean to be a mother. She'd not considered it. Childish of her . . .

She sank down onto the settee.

Ruary. She had to focus on Ruary. He was her only hope for a life of love. Closing her eyes, she repeated the prayer that had been in her mind for days, "Please, Ruary, come for me."

Jane had left him.

Ruary was stunned by the knowledge.

Even though she had not let him close to her for the last six days, he had desperately hoped they would work out their differences. He'd never imagined her running.

Hannah Menzies was the one to tell him. She was a young widow with two small lads and had eyed Ruary as a father for her sons for a good time now. She had not been pleased when Ruary had started courting Jane.

Catching Ruary while he was preparing to stand his vigil at the bridge, she couldn't wait to tell him the news that Jane had gone off to Glasgow.

There had been only one day when he'd not been at the bridge. That had been when Tara had come searching for him. It would not have served to have Jane see him speaking to, or being anywhere near, Tara.

He'd hoped to wear Jane down. He'd seen her a time or two in the window of her house, watching him. He had expected that she would finally listen to him when he said he loved her. She would forgive him for his lapse with Tara. He'd been a fool.

Instead, she'd gone to Glasgow, and the news surprised him.

He'd seen her father almost every day, although the two men had not spoken. Sawyer wouldn't even make eye contact. The smithy was protective of his daughter and only child. Ruary expected him to take her side, although the two men had rubbed well together in the past. Sawyer had been pleased when Ruary had asked for Jane's hand.

Now it was as if Ruary was completely cut out of their lives.

"You must be feeling sad, Mr. Jamerson," Hannah Menzies said. "Perhaps having a good dinner at my table will help your spirits."

Ruary took a step in one direction and then another, confused. How could she just leave?

"I've stewed a chicken. Do you like stewed chicken, Mr. Jamerson?" the widow Menzies continued.

Ruary frowned, not understanding. But there had been something she'd said that made sense. "Glasgow?" he repeated.

"Aye. They said on the coach out of Kenmore."

That coach would have left an hour ago.

The widow smiled hopefully at him. She was missing two of her teeth, one for each child, they say.

For a second, Ruary was tempted to rip the bridge into pieces. He was that upset. He'd done a great deal of thinking over the past days. He'd watched Tara looking for him. He knew he could turn to her and she would welcome him with open arms . . . until something or someone else caught her eye.

Or she grew bored being a simple horse master's wife.

Yes, he knew Tara better than she did herself. They'd been very young together, and the ties between them were strong. He had no doubt that she loved him as well as Tara could love anyone. She still had much to learn. He understood that now. For whatever reason she had run to him, he knew *he* wasn't the answer for her.

He also knew she was his past.

Jane had been his future, a future that had once been filled with everything he could have ever wanted—and Ruary reached a decision.

He had done this all wrong. Everything wrong. He'd expected Jane to come to him. Or he'd thought he could knock on her door and she would forgive him.

Ruary had no doubt that Jane loved him, but he also knew she needed to be certain of him.

And he didn't have much time to make amends.

But he could. *He had to.*

"So what do you say, Mr. Jamerson? Will you be coming for dinner?"

Ruary placed his hands on the widow's arms to move her out of his path as he said, "Thank you, Mrs. Menzies. I wish I could be eating with you and your sons, but I have to go fetch Miss Sawyer. I must have Jane."

"But she left you," the widow protested.

"All the more reason for me to chase," Ruary said, already moving toward the field where he kept Marcus. His saddle was in his cottage, but there was no time to fetch it. The widow tried to follow.

"You are a fine man," she was saying to him. "I don't believe a man like yourself should chase after a woman who doesn't want you."

"Then you would be wrong," Ruary threw out at her. "Although I am deeply in your debt, Mrs. Menzies, for the knowledge."

"I don't want you in my debt," she pouted. "I *want* you at my table."

And in her bed.

But that wasn't for Ruary.

Years ago, Tara had left him, and it had taken him almost two years to overcome her rejection. But Jane was different. Jane loved him. He knew that all the way to his soul.

He also understood that she would not tolerate his playing fast and loose with her, and he had needed that lesson. He'd let his head be turned by a past love, but he was seeing clearly now. He knew which woman he wanted. The question was—did she want him?

As if reading his mind, the widow said in a singsong voice, "She's left you. She doesn't have a care for you." She sounded like the harbinger of doom, but Ruary didn't care.

He mounted his horse and smiled down at her. "You may be right, Mrs. Menzies. But I can't let her go without doing everything in my power to win her back." He put heels to horse, and they were off.

After days of inactivity, Marcus was ready to go. Because of his work, Ruary knew all the paths and byways between the different villages and stables. He now used the knowledge to his advantage.

Man and beast ran as one, and within the hour, Ruary rode up over a knoll and saw the Glasgow Mail on the road below him.

He charged down the hill. Marcus landed on the road in front of the coach. The driver had no choice but to pull his horses to a halt.

The guard blew his horn for Ruary to move out of the way, while the driver punctuated the sound by shouting, "You bloody fool."

Ruary ignored the order. "I need to see a passenger. A Miss Sawyer."

Several passengers craned their necks out the window for a look at what had caused the delay.

They passed on this information to those inside the coach.

"Move out of the way," the guard shouted, setting aside his horn and reaching for his blunderbuss.

"Go ahead and put a hole in him," the disgruntled driver said, holding his stamping horses. "Either that or I'll drive over him—"

"*Jane*," Ruary shouted. He called for her again, and again, until the coach door opened.

Jane climbed out. For a long moment, she stared at him, her features tight and unyielding. She wore her best dress, a brown one with black trim, and her bonnet was one she had designed herself—and she looked beautiful to him.

He had her attention now, and he didn't know what to say, because if he said the wrong words, she would be gone from him.

So he did the only thing he could think to do that would make her understand how sorry he was to have hurt her—he sank to his knees, right there in the road, in front of everyone.

Chapter Sixteen

*J*ane had been dreaming of him.

In the tight confines of the mail coach, she'd been crushed between a wool merchant and a grandmother who smelled of onions. She had closed her eyes against them and her sadness. In her mind, she could see the handsome man who had won and destroyed her heart.

Her father thought Ruary a good man. As the days had passed and Ruary had kept his vigil for her, her father had suggested that perhaps she should give him another chance.

He didn't understand.

Ruary wanted her to believe there was nothing

between himself and Lady Tara, but Jane knew differently. Lady Tara would not give up, and Ruary didn't have the will to walk away from her.

The incident also brought home to Jane that Ruary was the sort of men many women would try to entice. His looks commanded attention. She, herself, always felt a little giddy whenever she looked at him. Many a time she had wondered what he saw in her. He could do much better.

What she had come to face was that she did not want to live her life ruled by jealousy. There would be no peace.

Besides, she was still not convinced that Ruary loved her.

He cared for her. He liked her. But *love* was not a word he mentioned to her.

Her father had explained to her that when a man asked a woman to marry him, it was the same as saying he loved her. He just didn't use the words. Her father didn't understand. The words mattered.

However, now Ruary was on his knees in front of her.

"I'm sorry, Jane. I'm so sorry." He bowed his head. "I know the pain I caused."

"How do you know that?" she asked.

"Because I feel it." He touched his heart. "I know."

She believed him.

Slowly, she walked toward him. Marcus nickered a greeting. It made her smile.

She stopped in front of Ruary, then sank down on the earth in front of him. She placed her gloved hand on the side of his face. Looking into his eyes, she said, "I'm not beautiful."

"You are to me."

"I *was*—"

"*You are*. Jane, I was flattered by Lady Tara's attention, and in some ways I'm glad for it, because now I know that you are the woman I need in my life."

"You hurt me," she admitted.

"I know. I was wrong, Jane. Can you forgive me?"

Could she?

Her answer was to place a kiss on his lips. They hadn't kissed often. Jane was shy and Ruary courteous.

However, this kiss was different.

For once, Ruary did not hold back. He allowed her to see his passion.

The thought went through her mind: Had this been the way he'd kissed Lady Tara?

Ruary broke the kiss. He caught her hands and

held them as he looked into her eyes and said, "I love you, Jane. I will always love you and only you."

Those were the words she'd yearned to hear.

Tears came to her eyes. Jane leaned forward, throwing her arms around him. "I loved you," she whispered against his neck. "I adored you. This has hurt me so much."

"I know, I know, and I never wish to hurt you again."

She believed him.

The guard blew on his horn. *"Do you mind?"* the driver shouted when he had their attention. "We have a schedule to run. Either climb in or go to the nearest inn."

Ruary jumped to his feet, pulling Jane with him. "Let us have her bag," he said. "We are going to elope. No more waiting banns and the like. And then, after I make you truly my wife, Jane Sawyer, we're off to England. Will you come with me?"

Off to England. There had always been talk that he would go sooner or later, but Jane had believed that there couldn't be very much of the world beyond Aberfeldy. This decision to go to Glasgow had been a huge one.

But now Ruary was *asking* her. And this was

what marriage was about. A woman left her family and joined with one man to become his.

"Aye, I'm for England, and a *grand* adventure it will be," she said. The pride in his eye was all the validation she would ever need. She loved this man and now knew he would always take care of her.

"Then would you remove yourselves from the road," the coachman roared and lifted his whip.

Ruary took Jane's hand, and together they sprinted out of the way of the coach. The onion-smelling grandmother leaned out the window and waved a farewell as she went by.

"Are we truly going to elope?" Jane asked.

"Aye."

She faced him. "Because you are afraid to return to Annefield?"

Ruary shook his head. "No, Jane, because you are mine and you always will be. I don't need the reading of the banns to tell me that."

"Then let us go," she whispered.

He climbed onto Marcus's back and reached down his hand to pull Jane up to sit in front of him. It didn't take them long to marry. In Scotland, outside of the church, all that was needed were witnesses. They were easy enough to find.

And that night, in a small, cozy inn beside Loch Awe, Ruary made her a wife . . . and she would never question his love again.

Nor would he give her cause.

*T*ara didn't know how she felt toward her sister or the knowledge that Aileen and Blake were lovers.

Should she be angry at Aileen? She didn't know. And the more Tara thought about it, the more confusing everything seemed.

From her earliest memory, she'd always had a certain power over men. It wasn't anything she did in particular. They just liked to look at her.

And men weren't the only ones. When she'd been presented, it had been women who'd approved of her and begun inviting her to the balls, routs and soirees that were so much a part of London society—and that was with the scandal of Aileen's divorce still fresh in the air.

But she also understood that her physical beauty could take her only so far. There were lines one didn't cross. Aileen had crossed with her divorce, and, after witnessing what had happened to her, Tara was always cautious.

But now Blake wanted to cry off. If people discovered why, tongues would wag from Scotland to London. Tara would be humiliated.

And if she cried off, well, there would still be disapproval.

The key to all of this was Ruary. If he came to her, then Aileen could have Blake and all would be happy, just like the ending to one of Shakespeare's comedies.

And that was how she wanted it to end— without her having to make a hard decision.

She went down for dinner that evening but did not linger. Finally she saw what anyone not wrapped up in her own worries should have noticed: Blake and Aileen shared something very special.

Aileen pretended to keep her distance from Blake, but it was futile. They made a handsome couple. They were both of the same age and shared similar temperaments. There was a courteousness between them, a caring that spoke volumes for their regard for each other.

Aileen did try to corner her for a moment of conversation after dinner, but Tara was not in the mood. "I'm tired," Tara claimed. "Perhaps in the morning we can talk."

"I didn't mean for this to happen," Aileen persisted, following Tara to the stairs.

"But it has," Tara countered.

"Yes."

For a second, the two sisters took each other's measure.

"What happens next is your decision," Aileen said. "I won't push the matter if you choose to hold Blake to his promise."

"And why would you back away?" Tara wondered.

Aileen shook her head as if recalling memories that were unpleasant. "I can't go through another scandal, Tara. I won't let that happen to Blake or to you. It's too painful."

On the tip of Tara's tongue was the admonishment that Aileen should have thought of that before she'd laid claim to Blake's affections. But before she could let loose that barb, Aileen said, "I know what you must think. I have made terrible errors of judgment in my life. I've tried to live it for other people and do what was expected. You see where I am now." She placed her hand on Tara's arm. "You are my sister. I value and love you. I will not harm you. The decision is yours."

"And I'm to feel no pressure?"

"There is pressure," Aileen conceded. "I don't want to give Blake up. I love him."

"I thought you'd decided that love is a myth," Tara said, reminding her of the discussion they'd had when she'd first arrived home.

"I know," Aileen said. "And this is a devil of a fix." She reached over and, placing her arm around Tara's shoulders, gave her a squeeze.

The gesture reminded Tara of the day her sister had left to go to London. Her sister. She'd worshipped her.

And now that Aileen was asking for something, Tara didn't know if she should give it. Or if she could. "Good night," she murmured and started up the stairs, but Aileen stopped her.

"If Mr. Jamerson does choose to marry Miss Sawyer, if he doesn't come for you, what shall happen then?"

The possibility was repugnant to Tara, and yet very real. "I don't want to lose at love," she confessed, then turned and ran up the stairs.

*A*ileen watched her sister hurry to her room as if being chased by demons.

Blake came up behind her. "How did it go?"

"Not good."

"You had to do better with her than I did this afternoon. She's had time to think about it."

Aileen turned to this man she loved. "Were you gentle with her?"

He hesitated a moment, then said, "I was direct with her."

No wonder Tara was so quiet. "It is her decision to make," Aileen insisted. "I will not impede a marriage between you."

"Don't I have something to say about this?"

She took two steps away from him, glancing down the hall to ensure they were alone. Of course it didn't matter how much distance was between them, she could feel his presence and identify immediately the scent of his shaving soap. "I don't want regrets," she whispered.

"You may be asking too much," Blake answered.

Aileen shook her head. "You think we can brazen this out. Perhaps *you* could . . . I couldn't. I already have one reputation—"

"A completely false one, and I shall shout it to the world."

Aileen smiled, knowing differently. "But what if we have children?"

"They shall survive, as I did," he said.

"Funny, but I believe that saving your children from being outcasts was the reason you asked for Tara's hand in the first place."

Now it was his turn to move away. "You

changed me," he said. "It is you I want to please. No one else but you. I love you."

His declaration caught her by surprise. She'd been waiting for it. Wanting it, expecting it, hoping for it. She knew how he felt, but hearing him say it was all she wanted. "And I love you, Blake, but this is so hard."

"Don't make it so." He took Aileen's hands, raised them to his lips and kissed the back of her fingers. His breath was warm on her skin. "Whatever happens, we shall see it through. I am your protector."

"And I am yours," she said. "I will not let any harm come to you."

"I can take care of myself."

She nodded. She knew differently.

Doing what one wished always sounded easy until one had to pay the price.

She went up to his room with him then. He held her in his arms and whispered vows that all would be well. He would see to it.

Aileen listened, but she did not believe. And halfway through the night, unsettled while he slept peacefully, she rose from his bed and returned to her own. Her sheets were cold. They lacked the warmth and scent of his body.

However, hers was a wise decision . . . because

the next morning, a Sunday and the announcing of the third banns for Tara and Blake's marriage, the gossip before the service was of Mr. Jamerson giving chase to Miss Sawyer as she left the valley on the Glasgow Mail.

Had he caught her?

They had their answer when her father stood up at the end of the service and announced his daughter had married. "She is now Mrs. Jamerson," he said with a note of pride.

Chapter Seventeen

$\mathscr{S}$itting in the church pew, Tara's first inclination was to deny Mr. Sawyer's announcement.

Around her, heads nodded with approval. There were even smiles on faces.

Tara sat very still, trying not to scream.

Was this how Ruary had felt when she'd left him three years ago? As if he had been betrayed? Was this the way he was paying her back?

If it was, it was remarkably effective.

Aileen reached over and placed her hand over Tara's. Her empathy at this moment was not welcome.

And then people turned in their seats in her direction, looking at her. She was confused until she realized that Reverend Kinnion had just asked her and Blake to stand for their banns to be announced a third time.

Blake didn't move.

Aileen had taken back her hand. She sat quiet. Composed. Tara wondered what she was thinking. She'd had fine words for her last night . . . but they had been meaningless. The truth was her sister had been finding love with Blake while Ruary had chosen another.

Anger eased the overburdening pain of a broken heart.

Nor did Tara feel she had any other choice than the decision she must make. In this moment, she hated the valley. She wished she had not come back here.

London was where she belonged, and she could not return there disgraced. She would not allow anyone to ridicule her.

She shot to her feet.

She smiled with a confidence she did not feel.

Slowly, Blake Stephens rose to stand beside her, and Tara knew Aileen had urged him to honor her decision. She could feel the tension in him. Hot tears stung Tara's eyes. She opened them wide, willing herself not to show emotion.

Reverend Kinnion smiled and read the banns. When he was done, Blake and Tara sat down together. She did not look at him. She knew he was angry. Well, she, too, was disappointed. They'd have to see their way around that. Many couples did. And what was disappointment when compared to pride?

The rest of the service ended quickly.

Tara rose, ready to leave. Aileen and Blake came to their feet as well. Their forward movement was blocked by the earl, who was charming two elderly ladies.

Aileen turned to Blake and whispered, "Apparently the widow Bossley is not in favor."

Tara looked around the church and saw the sprightly widow standing off to one side, her expression both resentful and yearning as she watched the earl laughing and enjoying himself with others. Last week, she had basked in the earl's attention.

This week, he didn't even cast a glance her way.

Having lived with her father in London, Tara knew his ways. He'd enjoyed Mrs. Bossley, but he was done.

Was that *always* the way between men and women? Tara was beginning to think so.

The earl moved, and Aileen and Blake anxiously slipped around him and hurried off without a backward glance to Tara. They would probably put their heads together and discuss what to do next. Tara had no illusions. She would be the topic of their conversation. Blake would be just as happy to brush her off his hands like dust on a windowsill. Aileen would argue, and in the end she would win . . . because he loved her.

Tara looked over her shoulder at the widow Bossley. She had friends around her now. Tara had no one.

Her father finished his conversation and turned to her. "Shall we go, Daughter?"

"Yes," Tara agreed, moving out of the row of pews.

The earl placed a hand on her elbow. "It's good to be in the valley, but I can't wait to return to the city."

Her sentiments exactly. "Do you believe it wise to raise Mrs. Bossley's hopes the way you did?" The widow and her friends had already left. In fact, Tara and the earl were the last to make their way out of the nave.

"Ah, now, Tara, Mrs. Bossley knows what she is about, and so do I. Don't worry your pretty head about her. Say, did you notice Breccan Campbell sitting in the service?"

Tara frowned. Her world was ending. Her

heart was breaking and she was in the process of making an enemy of the man she was to marry. She hadn't had time to notice who was coming to church.

Fortunately, as usual, her father didn't need an answer. "I tell you, I'm surprised the roof didn't cave in on that devil's head. You could see the shock on people's faces. I'm certain there are Campbells who go to services, but I'd not thought to see Breccan there. He's a big, ugly man, isn't he? He has a good two stone on me and maybe four inches, but his hairy face—" He shivered his opinion. "The man needs a razor, although I doubt if it would help his looks."

Tara gave her father her back as she said something pleasant to Reverend Kinnion, who was standing by the door.

"Less than a few days until your ceremony," the reverend reminded her with a smile. "I imagine you are anxious with excitement."

"I'm looking forward to it," Tara answered, forcing a smile.

Her father stepped up to repeat his comments about Breccan Campbell alarming the Almighty by his appearance in church. "You know how some lads are about the Campbells," the earl said.

"We're lucky they didn't spit on the floor in his direction." Tara didn't linger to hear the clergyman's response.

Instead, she scanned the churchyard for sign of Aileen and Blake. They stood by the coach as if waiting for the earl and her. They were obviously in deep discussion. Blake was arguing for something, and Aileen was shaking her head no.

Tara realized she'd best stake her claim on Blake before he convinced Aileen otherwise. She needed to walk over and interrupt them. She set off with that purpose but was waylaid by her cousin Sabrina. They did not know each other well. Sabrina was her sister's age and often annoyed Tara by treating her as if she was a child, but they were friendly enough.

"Well, you needn't worry about gossip any longer," Sabrina said. "Not now that Mr. Jamerson has made his choice."

Tara felt her feet root to the ground. She frowned at her cousin, pretending not to understand. "What are you talking about?"

"The rumors about you and the horse master."

"What rumors?"

"The ones that made Jane Sawyer shut him out. He made a good choice. I like Miss Sawyer."

"Whereas you don't always like me?" Tara challenged, discovering herself ready for a fight.

Sabrina smiled evenly. "No, I don't dislike you, Tara, but you are selfish. I understand why. If I had your looks and your father with his own special type of benign neglect, I might behave the same. It is probably not entirely your fault."

"Why, thank you, Sabrina. How kind of you," Tara replied, sarcasm in her words. She started walking toward the coach, but her cousin was not done. She reached for Tara's arm, catching her attention.

"You have an opportunity," Sabrina said, "to become a good person. I'm glad you didn't destroy the regard Miss Sawyer and Mr. Jamerson had for each other. It would have been sad if you had."

"And what of me, Sabrina? Aren't I entitled to happiness? Or is my face such a curse you would wish the very worst on me?"

"I don't wish that, Tara. I'm hoping you have a meaningful life. The kind that understands you don't have the right to take another woman's man just because you have the ability."

For a moment, Tara wasn't certain if Sabrina referred to Miss Sawyer and Ruary or to Aileen and Blake. "Did Aileen tell you about Ruary and me?"

"Your sister is loyal to you. But are you so naive that you think you can meet Mr. Jamerson, a man of a lower social order, for trysts and no one will notice? Or that you can ride aimlessly around Aberfeldy and it will not cause comment?" Sabrina leaned closer. "If so, you should be wiser, Tara."

"I loved him." Tara said the words, but the excuse was beginning to sound hollow.

"He wasn't yours, lass. And let me tell you something else that might surprise you. Looks don't last forever. Men are different, especially if a man has a title. He can be a fool and thrive." She nodded at Tara's father as she said this. He was laughing loudly with two other men. Probably telling them his weak jest about Breccan Campbell in church.

"But we women," Sabrina continued, "we have to rely on each other. We need friends, people who will stand behind us when things are not good."

"I have friends."

"No, you don't. Not here, not after the whispers about your chasing Mr. Jamerson. And I doubt the debutantes in London have shed a tear at your absence. You are alone, save for your one staunch supporter—your sister."

"You think she's perfect," Tara said, letting her anger show in her voice.

"None of us are that."

For a second, Tara was tempted to denounce Aileen and Blake. Then Sabrina might understand Tara's side of the story.

At the same time, Sabrina's words had pierced Tara deeply. She had never thought of herself as being disliked. She'd never worried about it. There were women who were jealous of her, but they didn't dislike her . . . did they?

In some ways, she realized, she was a bit obtuse, like the earl. And few people liked him.

The thought did not rest easy with her. However, when Tara felt threatened, she backed away, which was what she did now.

Her cousin watched her, a slightly superior smile on her face. Tara would adore the opportunity to wipe it off her—except Sabrina might have been right. Tara turned and walked away.

Aileen and Blake had apparently settled the argument they'd had. They were already in the coach, sitting so that they faced each other.

Simon helped Tara into the vehicle. She hesitated a moment, then chose to sit by her sister.

There was a moment of quiet, then Aileen said, "You two must marry."

Blake looked out the window at nothing.

Tara sat very still. She had no answer. None at all.

Chapter Eighteen

Aileen returned to Blake's bed. She could only stay away from him for one night. She'd promised herself that she'd give him up and prayed that she could.

Then again, they didn't have much time left to be together, a fact borne home as guests began arriving for the wedding the very next day.

There would not be many. A few of Blake's friends made the journey and took up residence in the Kenmore Inn. Of course they expected Blake to join them in drunken revelry. He did but returned to Aileen at an early hour each evening. They thought he left them to see Tara and teased him unmercifully.

"I let them think as they wish," he told Aileen as he slid into bed beside her.

"I understand," she murmured, snuggling up to his body heat. His valet, Jones, knew she was there, and perhaps Tara did as well. Aileen believed the other servants were not aware of where she spent her night. "However, their disappointment is expected," she said. "They have come a good distance for your company."

"Aileen, I don't have that kind of time to waste. Not when I want to be here with you." He pressed his lips against her temple. "You must let me cry off the wedding—"

She cut his words off by placing her fingers over his lips. "I won't." The words physically hurt her to say. "I love you to the depths of my being. I'd want nothing more than to be with you forever. And we'd be happy for a while, Blake. Yes, we would. Of course, we couldn't live here. Even the people of the Tay Valley have a limit to their goodwill. Betraying my sister by stealing her man would make them wipe their hands of me for good. And certainly London would not welcome us, except as a curiosity. Even your friends would find it difficult to recognize us."

"There are other places."

"Where?" Aileen asked, raising up on one elbow and resting her other arm on his chest so that she could look into his eyes. "Manchester? York, Bath, Aberdeen? Do you believe we could escape such an infamous story?"

"Amsterdam?"

"New York? The Indies? The world can be a small place for gossip. And I won't live that way, Blake. I also wouldn't want to bring children into that sort of world. You know yourself the weight of a parent's mistakes."

"I survived. I might not survive losing you."

"*You will*," she promised. And she meant those words, although as she wondered how she would ever go on.

*B*lake was furious with Tara, even as he recognized himself as the buffle-headed fool who had offered for her. He should have put more thought into choosing a wife instead of just desiring to best his half brother.

He couldn't bring himself to speak to Tara. She didn't appear interested in talking to him either. This was the life he had ahead of him, he realized—one of resentment.

Aileen urged him to overcome his disappointment.

He wouldn't. Not ever. He'd had a taste of what life could be like with a woman who fulfilled a part of him that had been empty. Why should he settle for anything less?

The duke of Penevey arrived on Wednesday. The wedding would be on Friday.

Penevey did not come alone. Besides his servants, he was accompanied by Arthur, marquis of Tynsford, the one who had originally offered for Tara and been rejected. It was as if the man wanted to hear the marriage vows for himself before he would believe Blake had won her.

Blake was pleased that Aileen took an immediate dislike to Tynsford. His half brother was six months younger than himself and almost silly in his jealousy of Blake. Then again, one had to look at what Blake's own arrogant spite had cost him.

For the first time, Blake realized how much his own sullenness and, yes, jealousy over not being his father's heir had cost him. Aileen's love had freed him from all that. He now had a sense of what was truly important in the world.

Indeed, over dinner, as he listened to Arthur plump up his consequence by bragging upon himself to the other guests, Blake had a glimpse of what his presence in Arthur's life had done to the marquis. Blake had always nipped at his heels. He'd had a fanatical need to prove himself better than his father's legitimate heir, and he had.

If Arthur excelled in a sport, then Blake would take it up and be better. If Arthur put himself to his studies, Blake would apply himself harder and outshine him. If Arthur wanted a woman, then Blake would claim her.

Of course, Blake could only be so sympathetic to Arthur. It was obvious he was here because he truly couldn't believe the beauty would choose being the wife of a bastard over being his marchioness.

Still, the recognition of his own culpability humbled Blake. Arthur was obviously still moony-eyed over Tara. She appeared oblivious to him. And Blake wasn't completely free of harsh judgments, because he wanted to hold Arthur's infatuation against Tara as well.

And of course, later that night, in bed, while they discussed the day—an activity that was Blake's favorite after making love to Aileen—she pointed out that Tara could not be held responsible for men choosing to fall in love with her.

"Few even know what love means," Aileen said.

"Most are like Geoff, anxious to possess without an appreciation for deeper meaning."

"Guilty," Blake said.

She smiled at him, rubbing her foot down his leg. "It is the way God made you."

"Not all of us. Some men are not as vain as I was."

"I've never found you so."

"I am," he assured her. "I'm a selfish one. But you make me better. You make me wiser."

He made love to her then. He'd found that this act of connection spoke louder than mere words the depth of his feeling for her. She, too, responded in a way he understood.

But their nights together were coming to an end. Blake knew without asking that Aileen would not come to him after he married.

Too soon he would lose her.

𝒯ara had plenty to keep her busy. Since Aileen was *obviously* distracted, the majority of the preparations for the wedding festivities fell upon Tara and Mrs. Watson.

Not that it shouldn't. But Aileen had always been in charge. Even when she'd been married, the rules and organization of Annefield that she had created had held sway. Now Tara had to make decisions.

The servants were excited in anticipation of the big day. Almost everyone in the valley, with the exception of outsiders like Breccan Campbell and the like, was invited, as was the custom. There would be the wedding breakfast inside the house, but a great feast outside.

A huge pit had been built for roasting sides of beef and mutton. Cook had been busy preparing side dishes of all varieties, and extra staff had been hired to help her. The smell of baking bread started Monday morning and would not stop, not even into Friday morning.

If anyone noticed that Tara and Blake did not speak to each other, they did not comment.

Tara assumed he was furious with her. What surprised her was that she wasn't angry in return. Instead, as the excitement started to build toward her wedding day, she felt more and more trapped.

It was obvious that he and Aileen were in love.

Love wasn't just a word thrown about between them or bandied about by Blake in a poem penned to Aileen's earlobe. No, Tara could see their care and affection in the respect they showed each other.

Their company or the earl didn't seem to notice,

but Tara witnessed the small touches, the looks, the kindnesses between her sister and Tara's intended. In a way, these observations puzzled her.

Her only experience with what was called love was her passion for Ruary. Aileen and Blake's love didn't seem all consuming. There was trust between them. And understanding.

In fact, Blake even treated Tara with respect. She had expected his anger. Instead, out of love for Aileen, Blake was doing what she asked. How many men would be that giving?

Few Tara knew.

And how many sisters would accept what Aileen was accepting without bitterness or rancor?

Tara began to wonder what it would be like if Blake had that same regard for her. Marriage wouldn't seem so stultifying then.

Right now, she didn't know what to expect.

She'd accepted his proposal because she'd been afraid of being unimportant. He'd been everything she'd counted as needful in a husband. He was wealthy, and willing to pay her father for her hand, he was handsome, and he was popular. People respected him.

But was that enough?

Certainly, her father had never set a good example of what men and women of good sense should search for in a spouse. Her mother had died right after she was born. Aileen had been her parent, and nothing about her marriage to Geoff had made Tara anxious for the wedded state.

However, now, watching Blake and Aileen, Tara wondered if there couldn't be something finer about marriage that should not be missed.

And she was beginning to question if she knew what love was.

Was it the side glances and whispers that Aileen and Blake shared? Or the contentment that seemed to have become a part of them, even when they were away from each other?

Tara didn't know. And in truth, what happened between a man and a woman was still a bit of a mystery to her. The marriage act, as she understood it, did not sound pleasant. Once, a young matron had warned her it was messy. Tara had been afraid to ask her why.

If it was those things, they didn't keep Aileen from stealing into Blake's room each night.

And what would happen when *she* was married to Blake?

Tara found she didn't care if he touched her or not.

And of course, the tension inside her was building. On Wednesday afternoon, while her father was self-importantly entertaining the duke and the boring Arthur, she searched for a moment of peace with a ride.

The thought of exercise and fresh air seemed like a piece of heaven.

She entered the stable yard to come upon a very angry Blake holding his friend Sir Nolan Ogilvy by the scruff of the neck and the seat of his pants. He was ready to fling a flailing Sir Nolan into the long horse trough.

The scene was almost comical. Blake was a head taller than the redheaded Sir Nolan and weighed more. He appeared as if he could juggle the man if he so desired.

Angus and the stable lads had grins of approval on their faces as they watched—however, upon her arrival, their attitudes changed immediately. Angus cleared his throat as a warning and sent a pointed look in her direction.

Blake caught sight of her and put Sir Nolan on the ground. "Hello, my lady," he said.

Sir Nolan, his balance wobbly, tried to bow and muttered a greeting.

Tara approached them. "What is going on here?" she demanded.

"Nothing, my lady," Sir Nolan said. "Just a disagreement between friends."

In truth, she didn't like Sir Nolan. He had a pompous sense of his own importance, but then, most men in government did. He had pursued her once. She had used all her wiles to avoid his making an offer, but he had been persistent. He'd proposed and she'd said no—a decision that he had not accepted kindly.

She supposed it should have been to his credit that he was here for the wedding. He was Blake's guest, not hers.

Tara looked to Blake. "This is the way you treat your friends?"

"I beg your pardon, my lady." His tone was cool, derisive. "I no longer count Sir Nolan as one of my friends."

"Oh, please, Stephens. I was just having some sport."

"In what way, Sir Nolan?" Tara asked.

Dull red stained his cheeks. "In a man way."

"A man way?" Tara queried.

"He made a rude comment about your sister," Blake said. "About the sort of woman he thought she was."

Tara's temper flared. "Indeed, Sir Nolan?"

A wise man would apologize.

Sir Nolan was not wise.

"She is not like you, my lady," he said. "I have the highest respect for you."

"And for my sister?" she prodded.

His shoulders tightened. "Her reputation is not the best," he insisted. "This should be no surprise to you and certainly does not reflect upon my regard for you or Stephens."

"I see," Tara answered, and she did. She saw very clearly.

With both hands, she pushed Sir Nolan in the chest. He fell backward and splashed into the horse trough.

A cry of approval went up from the stable lads, who had not taken their eyes off the exchange. Sir Nolan spit water and sputtered. Tara had no sympathy for him.

She picked his hat up off the ground and threw it at him before ordering, "Angus, bring Sir Nolan's horse over here. He is leaving."

Then addressing Sir Nolan, she said, "Your invitation to the wedding breakfast was obviously a mistake. Ride back to London, sir, and tell everyone how you've been treated. And let them know that if *anyone* thinks to say a word against *my* sister in my hearing, they shall receive the same treatment."

On those words, she went marching for the house, so full of steam it was a wonder she didn't fly. She'd reached the line of beech trees when Blake caught up with her. He took her arm and swung her around. Only then did she realize he'd been calling her name.

"What do *you* want?" Tara demanded crossly.

"Nothing," he said, holding his hands out as if to show he meant no harm. "Except to say that was excellent, Tara. I did not know you had that in you."

"Had what?" she said, placing her gloved hands on her hips.

"That love for your sister."

That remark struck right where she felt the most guilt. And she was not going to discuss it with him. She started to walk away, but he hurried to place himself in her path.

For a moment they stood. She refused to look up at him. He seemed to wait.

Hell would freeze over before she would speak.

He broke the silence first. "Thank you. Aileen means everything to me. I might have killed the man. My intent was to drown him in the trough."

"And been hanged for it. How anyone thought to knight Nolan Ogilvy is a mystery."

He laughed, the sound genuine.

She shifted her weight and glanced toward the house, her plans for riding forgotten. "Is that all you wished to say to me?" She'd brought haughtiness back in her voice, knowing it would annoy him.

Blake stepped back, his disappointment in her change of attitude clear.

Tara took a step past him but stopped. "Guilt is an uncomfortable emotion. I don't enjoy it. I'm usually very honest with myself and others."

"Of course," he murmured.

He was so handsome standing in his riding clothes. At some point he'd lost his hat, so the wind ruffled his dark hair . . . and yet his looks did not move her the way Ruary's had.

"I want to cry off, Blake—"

His eyes lit with happiness.

"—but I can't," she finished. "I know I've treated you shabbily. This whole state of affairs is my fault. If I hadn't bolted on you . . . ?" She left the question up in the air to say with a new understanding, "I've probably disrespected *many* men in the worst way. Although I will not apologize for rejecting Sir Nolan."

"Completely understood," Blake said. "I'd not seen that side of him before. Not until he had the stupidity to speak of your sister with disrespect."

"You would have seen it if you'd been female. He is quite aggressive." She sighed, heartsick. "If I don't marry you, then they shall talk of me the way they do Aileen. They already call me a man eater." She shrugged. "But this will be different. Sometimes the expectations in London are very high—"

"You don't need those people, Tara."

"What do you want me to do? Stay here in the valley, waiting for time to pass before I can return to town?"

"You could do worse, Tara."

"But if I wait, I'll be too old to return. I am already growing too old."

Blake tilted back his head and laughed. "What are you, all of one and twenty? Tara, you have a life ahead of you." He took a step toward her and placed his hands on her arms. "Don't make a decision out of fear. There is too much at stake. Not just for Aileen and myself, but for you as well."

She shook him off, backing away, not knowing if she trusted him.

Not knowing if she trusted herself.

She hurried to the house.

*T*ara spent the night before her marriage alone in her room.

Most weddings in the valley were cause for days of celebration, including a few rowdy tricks played on the bride and groom before the wedding night. They were a preparation for the most raucous of pranks, when the guests would carry the bride to her groom on that special night of all nights.

It was all in good fun, but Tara had let it be known she wanted none of that. No, her wedding had taken on a definitely more somber tone.

Still, the servants were excited. Ellen worried over what dress her mistress should wear, and should Tara's hair be styled up or left to curl around her shoulders?

But for Tara, that night before her wedding was one of deep introspection.

She remembered when Aileen had left for London. Losing the sister she had depended upon for so much had been frightening. But Tara had overcome those fears. She'd also taken on some resentment, she realized. Yes, she had let Aileen go, but she'd started to assume then a feeling that she would always be left behind.

Tara sat in the middle of her bed, her legs crossed, stunned by the possibility behind those revelations.

"Perhaps I want someone who is wholly devoted to me?" she whispered. The words sounded magical in their meaning. But then, no one had ever been that way toward her. Not Aileen. Not Blake. Not Ruary.

In truth, there was only one person who could save her.

The next morning, when Ellen came in to prepare Tara for the wedding, she was surprised to see her mistress already up, dressed and anxious to go to the church.

Chapter Nineteen

Aileen was to ride in the coach with Tara. Blake
had gone to meet the duke and marquis at the
Kenmore Inn and would be waiting at the church
when they arrived.

The duke had actually expected Blake to stay
with them. Blake had refused, which had surprised Aileen. She had told him she did not feel
comfortable in his bed the night before he married, but he'd informed her that he still needed to
be close to her. In the end, she had not been able
to resist.

They'd spent a good long time last evening
playing chess—and she'd beaten him for the first
time.

But it would be the last time they were together.

The earl had happily decided to spend the night at the Kenmore Inn as well. He had become fast friends with Blake's cronies. They were gamblers at heart, and, of course, he had to be amongst them. He left it to Aileen to see that Tara arrived when she should.

Little did he know how much he asked of her.

Over the past week, there had been moments when Aileen had feared she was so disconsolate her heart would stop. It took all the courage she possessed to hold her head high and go through the motions of living. The only time she'd been truly alive had been with Blake.

The day of the wedding was a good one. A warm breeze gently blew fat white clouds in the sky. It had rained a bit the day before, and the world was green and fresh.

Aileen waited in the front hall while Mrs. Watson went upstairs to fetch Tara. The servants were lined up to see the bride. Even the stable lads were out on the drive, lined up by Angus to pay their respects to the youngest mistress.

There was a sound at the top of the stairs. Those in the hall looked up as Tara came down the stairs, moving with such grace that she seemed to float toward them. Ellen and Mrs. Watson followed her.

Aileen had never seen her sister look so beautiful.

Tara wore a snowy white muslin dress trimmed in layers of her favorite Belgian lace in her favorite hue of blue. She held a prayer book in her lace-gloved hands, and her hair was styled high on her head. Small flowers, fashioned from the same lace, pinned her curls in place. The white brought out the vivid coloring of her hair and the lace the cornflower blue of her eyes.

But what truly caught the eye was the look of serenity upon Tara's face. She appeared happy and relaxed in a way Aileen had never seen before.

"Aileen, you look lovely," Tara said when she came off the last step.

"You are a beautiful bride," Aileen answered and meant the words. "You outshine all of us."

Indeed, there was no way Aileen could ever compete with her sister, although she had tried to look her best. She wore a dress of layers of soft green muslin. The gown was from her married days. Her hair was braided and fashioned into her usual knot at the nape of her neck. She wore a straw hat trimmed in green ribbons a shade darker than the dress.

However, Blake would not notice her when confronted with the spectacular vision Tara made.

And that was as it should be, she reminded herself.

"We'd best be going," Aileen said, shepherding her sister toward the coach. Tara seemed as if she was in no hurry but was rather enjoying the moment. She smiled and teased the stable lads, who blushed just looking at her.

Then, piled into the coach and with a crack of the whip, they were off for Kenmore Kirk.

They were surprised to see folks lined up on the road, hoping for a glimpse of Tara. She didn't disappoint. She smiled and waved to everyone.

"This is like London," she said. "When we went to big events, there was always a crowd."

"Well, you will be back there soon," Aileen said.

Tara didn't answer. Some children ran along the side of the coach, calling out, "My lady." Aileen was surprised when Tara pulled out a small bag of halfpennies. "I always wanted to do this," Tara said as she threw coins to them. "It is for good luck. Here, throw one."

Aileen did. The coin was caught by Hannah Menzies's oldest son, a lad of twelve. "Let me have another one," Aileen said, holding out her hand.

"It's fun, isn't it?" Tara said, giving her sister two coins.

"I feel like a princess," Aileen answered, forgetting her sadness for a moment.

Tara laughed.

Too soon, they pulled up in front of the kirk. Reverend Kinnion waited at the door for them. The marquis of Tynsford and two of Blake's friends who had come from London, Lord Gibbons and Mr. Markwell, lingered in the yard talking amongst themselves. Presumably Blake, the earl and the duke waited inside.

At the sight of the coach, the gentlemen came forward. "I imagine they are hoping to catch sight of you before Blake does," Aileen suggested.

Tara shrugged.

The coach came to a halt. Simon jumped down from the box and proudly opened the door for them. Across the road, in front of the inn, another small group of people had gathered, hoping to catch sight of Tara.

Simon helped Aileen out. She shook out her skirts as Tara exited the coach.

The reaction of the men waiting for her appearance was all any woman could wish. Tynsford's jaw actually dropped. Mr. Markwell nudged Lord Gibbons out of the way and offered her his arm.

Tara waved him away. "I'm with my sister," she

said. "You gentlemen go join the others so I can make a proper appearance."

"Lady Tara, any way you wish to make an appearance would be *more* than proper," the marquis opined.

It was an awkward compliment. A bit silly. After a few days with Tynsford, Aileen could understand why Blake thought himself so much better than this half brother. Arthur was a thin man, with arms that seemed too long for him, much like his father's. Blake definitely had a better physique.

"Go on," Tara chided him, waving them on with the hand holding her prayer book. "Go inside."

The men reluctantly did as she ordered.

Tara watched them disappear into the church before she faced Aileen. "Now, I want you to walk in with me. We shall go up the aisle together."

"Why?"

"Because it is what I wish," Tara said. She didn't give Aileen time to argue but took her arm and directed her toward Reverend Kinnion.

"Are you ready, my lady?" he said, smiling with appreciation at Tara.

"I am, sir."

"Then let us be about it. Follow me." He pivoted on his heel and led them into the church, his head high, in keeping with the importance of his office. It wasn't often one of the local gentry married, and he was the sort of man who would make the most of the occasion.

Aileen would much rather have sat in the back or in the family pew by the earl, who, to her surprise, was asleep and snoring softly. He must have enjoyed himself too well the night before.

Tara's hold on her arm was tight. Perhaps Tara needed her emotional support. The moment reminded Aileen of when Tara was little and had been frightened of crowds. She'd always clung to Aileen's arm.

Blake waited at the front of the church. He wore formal clothes, including his detested pumps, and had combed his hair back in a severe style. His gaze was not on Tara but on Aileen.

Aileen swallowed hard, struggling to keep her composure. She loved this man so much. She prayed Tara would be a good wife to him. She knew that if he was hers, she would devote everything she had to him.

As Reverend Kinnion reached Blake, he turned and motioned that all present should rise. There were not many people to serve as witnesses. Marriage ceremonies were intimate gatherings. The wedding feast was where guests joined in celebrating. Aileen was certain many were already arriving at Annefield. They might even start the drinking before the ceremony was finished.

Aileen and Tara stopped in front of Reverend Kinnion. Blake stepped to Tara's other side. Aileen started to pull away, but Tara tightened her hold.

Reverend Kinnion frowned. Aileen's presence in front of the altar was unusual. But since Tara would not let her go, he began. "We are here today to join one woman and one man in the sacrament of holy matrimony . . ."

*A*s the reverend opened his prayer book and set about his business, Tara knew the time had come.

There had been a moment when she'd had doubts over whether or not she could see this through. But then she'd seen how Blake had looked at Aileen coming up the aisle, and her reservations had vanished.

"Wait," she said, interrupting Reverend Kinnion. "I wish to make a change to our marriage vows."

"A change?" Reverend Kinnion echoed. He held up his prayer book. "There is no change to this book."

"No, the change is to the *people* who are marrying," Tara said, a comment that caused a great deal of surprise. She turned to Blake. "I admire you, Mr. Stephens. I think highly of you. Please treat my sister with the love and respect she deserves."

Aileen gave a start. "Tara—?"

"No, Leenie, this is not the time to argue. I know you love each other. I'm glad you have found happiness. I *must* cry off. My selfish concerns are unimportant in the face of what the two of you truly mean to each other. I don't want to marry Blake. He doesn't want to marry me. But if you'll have him, Aileen, then we'll have a wedding."

For a moment, Aileen appeared too stunned to speak. "I'm crying off," Tara said softly, prodding her sister. "I don't want him."

"*Of course* I will have him," Aileen answered. She hugged Tara with all she had, tears of relieved joy streaming down her face. "Thank you. Thank you, *thank you*, thank *you*."

"You are welcome," Tara answered, feeling happy tears in her own eyes.

Blake didn't speak. He acted as if it had taken all he had possessed to appear composed. Now, he reached for Aileen. Their hands found each other. He laced his fingers with hers before giving Tara a brotherly kiss on her cheek. "Words fail," he managed, his voice hoarse with pent-up emotion.

"It is as it should be," Tara whispered. "Like one of Shakespeare's plays."

"Excuse me?" Reverend Kinnion said. "You can't change brides on a whim."

"Oh, it isn't a whim," Tara assured him, stepping back. "We are very certain."

Aileen and Blake laughed their agreement. They had their arms around each other as if they would never let go.

"*The banns*," Reverend Kinnion interjected. "The banns have not been read for this couple."

Tara had anticipated this objection. "We live in Scotland, sir. All they need to do is declare themselves in front of witnesses. Mr. Jamerson took Miss Sawyer to wife in this manner, and it is recognized by all. We have witnesses. More than two, in fact. Are you ready to perform a marriage, or shall we go in search of a blacksmith to say the words over the anvil for them?"

Before the reverend could answer, the duke stood. "I object to this marriage. Blake, this woman is not suitable. If you marry her, you will never succeed in society."

"I have no desire to please anyone but myself, Your Grace," Blake responded.

"Even if it is your father's decision?" Penevey said. "I will not have a divorced woman in my family."

"Then we part company, Your Grace." Blake didn't even flinch from speaking those words.

Tara was so proud of him.

The duke straightened in surprise. He took a step into the aisle. "You know what this means?" he threatened, as if offering Blake one last opportunity to repent.

"That I shall no longer be expected to lend you money?" Blake returned.

That was not the answer Penevey had expected. Or anyone else, for that matter.

For a wild moment, the duke appeared ready to explode into a tantrum. Instead, he turned on his heel and went marching for the door, throwing the words, "Come, Arthur," over his shoulder.

The marquis rose, but he was not ready to go. "I could marry Lady Tara," he offered to the room at large. "That would make things right."

Penevey looked at his heir as if he had grown two heads. "*Nothing is right*." The duke walked out the door, setting his hat on his head.

The marquis lingered a moment. He sent one longing look in Tara's direction. "Go on," Tara said. "Your father expects you to obey, and truly,

Tynsford I would not make a good wife. You would not be happy when people start whispering about all this. Then there will be rumors about me and a horse master . . ." She let her voice trail off, allowing him to draw his own conclusions.

The marquis hurried to join his father.

"I say, Stephens," Lord Gibbons said from his seat in the pews, "you know how to host an entertaining wedding. We'll dine on this story for a month. Considering Penevey's reaction, perhaps longer."

His reminder of society seemed to make Aileen nervous. "Will it be all right?"

"Yes, love," Blake said. "Penevey has no say in my business interests. He may try to make matters difficult, but I've gone up against him before." He looked to Reverend Kinnion. "We would like to marry now."

Reverend Kinnion seemed to debate for a moment but then said, "Very well. Let us have a wedding. And, as a matter of opinion, Mr. Stephens, I believe you are taking on a fine wife. In spite of what happened in London, we stand beside her."

"Thank you, Reverend," Aileen said.

"Now, can we *marry* them?" Tara said, wanting to hurry the matter along. "There is a feast the likes of which this valley has not seen in many years waiting for us."

"Yes, Lady Tara, we can," Reverend Kinnion said, and with that, he set to work.

The ceremony did not take long. The kiss Blake gave Aileen to seal their pledge took longer. Much longer.

The earl of Tay woke up in the middle of the kiss. He looked around, then whispered to Lord Gibbons in a voice loud enough to carry, "Is Stephens kissing the wrong daughter?"

"No, he's kissing the right one," his lordship answered.

"The one he married?" The earl was very confused.

"Go back to sleep, Tay," Lord Gibbons ordered. The earl didn't obey but sat with a confused expression. Tara would have to explain it all to him later.

She doubted if he would be pleased, but what could he say? She tapped Blake on the shoulder. "Enough, my brother-in-marriage. We are tired of watching you be so happy."

The kiss ended then, Blake and Aileen laughing. Arm in arm, they left the church. Blake's friends fell into step behind them, anxious no doubt for the feast. Reverend Kinnion even joined them, and he seemed rather proud of himself. Tara understood.

Doing the right thing was freeing.

Today, she had done something meaningful, and she'd done it for someone else. For the first time, Tara was proud of an accomplishment. She felt good.

Her father had not moved from the pew. He appeared thunderstruck. She walked over to him. "Come, Father, you must drink to the health of the bride."

He did not move. His face was pale, and he looked as if he felt ill. "Do you believe Stephens will let me keep the money he paid me for you?"

Ah, money. Always money.

"I'm certain, Father."

He released his breath as if he'd been holding it. "Right. Well then, let us go to the house." He stood and offered Tara his arm. They walked toward the door. "That was a foolish thing to do, Daughter. Penevey is angry."

"But not at me."

"Ha!" he answered. "Do you believe it will not come back on you? Or me? We've insulted a powerful man."

"We'll manage," Tara said as they stepped out of the kirk.

"Tell me that three months from now," her father muttered as they stepped outside. "*Then* we'll see if we are managing."

Mr. Markwell and Lord Gibbons approached them. They had been over at the coach, seeing Aileen and Blake inside.

"You will save a dance for me today, won't you, Lady Tara?" Lord Gibbons asked.

She knew him. He had written a poem to her shoe. It had been terrible writing. "I will, my lord."

"And for me?" Mr. Markwell said hopefully. She'd gone through one whole season of his watching her from covert places, behind the potted plants or lurking behind her at soirees or appearing out of nowhere when she was shopping.

"Of course I will dance with you," she said.

"Perhaps two dances?" Mr. Markwell queried.

"One apiece, gentlemen. One," Tara answered, holding up her finger for emphasis. Oh, yes, she was going to be fine.

For a moment, she had to stand and look over Loch Tay. It would not be so bad being here for a spell. Few places on earth were this beautiful.

And she would return to London again. When she did, then maybe she would find a love as strong as Blake and Aileen's.

"All right, all right," she heard her father say

from the coach. "No more of that lip locking until after we reach Annefield. I've no choice but to ride with the two of you, so behave yourselves."

Blake and Aileen's response was to laugh. He climbed into the coach and called for his youngest daughter.

Yes, all would be good, Tara thought as she went to join her family, and she was right.

The wedding feast, with the tale of two brides, was one of the merriest in anyone's memory. When the bride and groom were that much in love, then the guests couldn't help but be happy for them.

And as for Tara, she was the heroine in the valley, for the day, at least. She knew they would be gossiping about her on the morrow. Such was life in the valley.

But her future was in London. Penevey's anger aside, she would return. And when she did, she would find love.

She'd not settle for anything less.

Epilogue
The Bride Said Maybe . . .

October, 1816

The hour was late when her father summoned Tara to the library.

He had not talked to her in weeks. After the initial goodwill and euphoria of the wedding, he had begun to realize exactly what the duke of Penevey's threat meant. They would not be returning to London any time soon. The word from what few friends they had there urged them to stay in Scotland a while longer. Perhaps for a few years.

Even Aileen, who was in London with Blake, settling their affairs there before deciding where they would like to live, had written and warned Tara as much.

She had expressed regrets that Tara had sacrificed so much. In truth, Tara was a bit perplexed. Everyone in the valley had celebrated her decision. Could those she knew in London be so close-minded?

Apparently so.

That her father had sent for her also had to mean that perhaps he was over his snit and they could talk and reach an understanding.

She knocked on the door.

"Come in" was the abrupt order.

Tara turned the handle and entered the room.

Her sire sat at his desk, mounds of ledgers spread out before him. She rarely saw him like this. Aileen had been the one to keep the books and accounts in order.

A lamp had been lit, and its yellow light highlighted the sheen of sweat on the earl's pale complexion. He did not wear a jacket, and he had loosened his neck cloth.

The bottle was no longer on the liquor cabinet but sat on his desk, close at hand.

"You sent for me, Father?"

"I did. Sit."

She took one of the upholstered chairs around the small table. He came around from his desk, shut the door and faced her, placing his hands behind his back. For a long moment he stood, his lips pressed together sternly.

Tara tried to sit still, to wait. At last she could stand the silence no longer. "If you are going to berate me, start on it. I'm tired and ready for my bed—"

"We are done up," he interrupted.

"Done up?"

"Broke, gone, bankrupt."

The air seemed to leave the room. Tara forced herself to be calm. "How can that be? Didn't Mr. Stephens pay a marriage portion even though I was not the one he married?"

Her father's scowl deepened. She waited. At last, the words almost bursting out of him, he said, "I spent it."

"*All* of it?"

He snorted his amusement. "It was gone before we left London."

Tara grabbed the arms of the chair as if they were lifelines. "All of it," she repeated in amazement.

He nodded and sank into the chair opposite

hers. "There were a couple of fights, and I wagered on the wrong men. Then there was that night I went out with Crewing. That night didn't end for two days." He rose from the chair and crossed to the desk to pour whisky into a well-used glass. "I thought I could earn it all back."

"Oh, Father," Tara said, her stomach sinking.

"I have a bit of blunt. Stephens bought a mare from me. He overpaid, but the mare didn't bring in much." He released his breath as if steadying his nerves before admitting, "And then it becomes worse."

"Worse? I don't think I can properly appreciate worse right now."

"You have to know," he said. His expression had softened into one of deep remorse, and Tara couldn't help but feel a bit sorry for him. Aileen had always been harder on him than Tara was. Aileen didn't trust him.

Tara felt she had to depend upon him, even for all of his notable faults. Beyond everything else, he was her father.

"What is it I must know?" she asked.

"Someone has purchased my paper. He owns it all."

"Your paper?" Tara repeated.

"You can't gamble without money," he said as if

stating the obvious. "I had to reclaim what I'd lost, so I borrowed from moneylenders and a banker here and there. The man who now owns my debts came this afternoon. He expects me to pay. He wants his money now."

"Can you speak to Blake?" she suggested.

Her father's laugh was angry. "No, there will be no money from that quarter. He told me he would no longer cover my debts. He said he'd see that food was on my table, but he'd not cover my losses."

Tara could not blame Blake. She forced herself to take a breath. "What of Annefield?"

His manner lightened. "It's entailed. There is no fear there. It will go to my heirs. I haven't lost that yet."

"But what have you lost?"

"It's what I *could* lose that matters. What I will lose."

"And what is that, Father?"

"My horses. I built my reputation on them. My pride," he added. "It shames a man to know he is that foolish."

"Is there anything else?"

"Aye, the land around Annefield."

"*What?*" Tara came to her feet. "Did you not say it was entailed?"

"The house is entailed, the rest is gone unless I can meet my obligations."

"Then we shall meet them." Here was something she could sink her teeth into. The case of blue devils that had been following her since Aileen and Blake had left was immediately lifted from her shoulders, and in its place stood generations of pride. "We shall not lose the land. It is ours. Tell me all, Father. Between the two of us, we can create a plan. Who is this man who has purchased your paper?"

"Breccan Campbell."

It took a moment for Tara to overcome her shock. "Campbell? He has that much money?"

"He may be a giant oaf of a man, but he has a shrewd mind. He showed me the vouchers. They have my signature."

Tara found her temper. "I have *never* liked that man. I saw him not too long ago, and I thought him a brute. He was so rude."

"Rude?"

"Aye, of the boldest nature. I tell you *I welcome* this fight. So he thinks he can best us. Well, he is wrong."

"You are right, Daughter," the earl said. "Although he did offer me a solution, and one that I have accepted."

"What solution is that, Father?"

The earl sank down on the chair beside hers. "Perhaps. Maybe you made a better impression on him than he did on you." His tone had grown hopeful.

"I don't care what he thinks of me. I don't like him. In fact, I detest him. Yes, that is how I feel. I have no desire to set eyes on him again."

The earl lifted his glass to his lips and poured it down his throat before saying, "That is unfortunate, my girl. Because the terms of receiving all my paper back is that you marry him."

That statement caught her attention. "Marry him? Me? Oh, no, that will not happen—"

"As a matter of fact, it *will* happen, and it will be done in one hour's time. Campbell will be here with Reverend Kinnion and the witnesses. You'd best go dress, girl. You are about to become a bride."

*G*ive in to your Impulses!

**These unforgettable stories only take a second
to buy and give you hours of reading pleasure!**

Go to *w* at we

Av